The Midnight Washerwoman

and Other

Tales of Lower Brittany

ODDLY MODERN FAIRY TALES

Jack Zipes, *Series Editor*

Oddly Modern Fairy Tales is a series dedicated to publishing unusual literary fairy tales produced mainly during the first half of the twentieth century. International in scope, the series includes new translations, surprising and unexpected tales by well-known writers and artists, and uncanny stories by gifted yet neglected authors. Postmodern before their time, the tales in *Oddly Modern Fairy Tales* transformed the genre and still strike a chord.

François-Marie Luzel *The Midnight Washerwoman and Other Tales of Lower Brittany*

Juwen Zhang, editor *The Dragon Daughter, and Other Lin Lan Fairy Tales*

Cristina Mazzoni, editor *The Pomegranates and Other Modern Italian Fairy Tales*

Hermynia zur Mühlen *The Castle of Truth and Other Revolutionary Tales*

Andrei Codrescu, editor *Japanese Tales of Lafcadio Hearn*

Michael Rosen, editor *Workers' Tales: Socialist Fairy Tales, Fables, and Allegories from Great Britain*

Édouard Laboulaye *Smack-Bam, or The Art of Governing Men: Political Fairy Tales of Édouard Laboulaye*

Gretchen Schultz and Lewis Seifert, editors *Fairy Tales for the Disillusioned: Enchanted Stories from the French Decadent Tradition*

Walter de la Mare, with an introduction by Philip Pullman *Told Again: Old Tales Told Again*

Naomi Mitchison, with an introduction by Marina Warner *The Fourth Pig*

Peter Davies, compiler; edited by Maria Tatar *The Fairies Return: Or, New Tales for Old*

Béla Balázs *The Cloak of Dreams: Chinese Fairy Tales*

Kurt Schwitters *Lucky Hans and Other Merz Fairy Tales*

The Midnight Washerwoman

and Other

Tales of Lower Brittany

François-Marie Luzel

Edited, translated, and introduced by Michael Wilson

Illustrated by Caroline Pedler

PRINCETON UNIVERSITY PRESS   *Princeton and Oxford*

Published by Princeton University Press
41 William Street, Princeton, New Jersey 08540
99 Banbury Road, Oxford OX2 6JX

press.princeton.edu

All Rights Reserved

ISBN (pbk.) 9780691252698
ISBN (e-book) 9780691252704

British Library Cataloging-in-Publication Data is available

Editorial: Anne Savarese and James Collier
Production Editorial: Sara Lerner
Text and Cover Design: Pamela L. Schnitter
Production: Erin Suydam
Publicity: Alyssa Sanford and Carmen Jimenez

Cover art by Andrea Dezsö

Image on p. xiv: A veillée in Brittany. Collection of the author

This book has been composed in Adobe Jenson Pro

Printed on acid-free paper. ∞

Printed in the United States of America

10 9 8 7 6 5 4 3 2 1

Contents

■ Acknowledgments

All of this originally emerged from a chance conversation one evening in London with my friend Jack Zipes. Jack was on one of his many visits to the UK and, as I had recently bought an old house on the Cotentin Peninsula in Normandy, the conversation turned to the French folklorists and one in particular: François-Marie Luzel. Luzel's work had been neglected for a long time in France and was largely unknown outside of it. A collection of Luzel's tales, translated for an Anglophone readership, was long overdue, Jack believed, and he encouraged me to take on the project. In the first instance, then, my thanks must go to Jack Zipes for his friendship and sound advice over the years.

I have also been helped by several people along the way and, while they are too numerous to list by name, I would like to extend my thanks to my former colleagues at the University of South Wales and Falmouth University, and my current colleagues at Loughborough University, from whom I have continually drawn collegial and intellectual nourishment, sometimes without their realizing it. In particular, I would like to express my gratitude to Patrick Ryan, who was particularly generous with his time in bringing his long experience as a storyteller and folklorist to bear upon the texts and the possible order in which they might be told in the context of a *veillée*.

Along the way, I have also benefited from the help of two talented research assistants, Madelon Hoedt and Marie Libert, who sifted through a mountain of material. Marie willingly checked my early translations, although the fault for any remaining errors lies entirely with me. My thanks go to both Madelon and Marie.

The illustrations for this volume were drawn by Caroline Pedler, a freelance artist and graduate from the world-renowned MA illustration course at Falmouth. I first met Caroline while conducting another research project in North Cornwall and am very grateful for her dedicated work on the tales.

In January 2019 I also had the good fortune to work with a dedicated and talented group of drama students at Loughborough University, who took some of the tales in this volume and devised a show that toured around a number of community venues in Northern Ireland. Their work on bringing the tales to life provided me with fresh insights. I would like to thank them and storyteller Liz Weir, who hosted us during our visit to the beautiful Glens of Antrim.

I would also like to thank Fred Dalmasso for his help with translation and everyone in the Storytelling Academy at Loughborough University. Our collective efforts in the exploration of storytelling continue to nourish and sustain.

I would also like to extend my gratitude to colleagues at Princeton University Press, whose patience, expertise, and professionalism were invaluable in turning what was an overly long document, strewn with Briticisms, into a book that people might actually want to read. They are Anne Savarese, James Collier, Kim Hastings, Sara Lerner, Susan Clark, and Sydney Bartlett.

Last, but not least, I would like to thank my wife, Jayne, and the rest of my family for their love, support, and tolerance of my disappearing into my study for hours on end instead of doing all the jobs around the house that are still waiting to be done to this day.

PAIGNTON, ENGLAND
December 2022

This is a book about storytelling. That is to say, it is a book about stories, the storytellers who told them, the listeners who heard them, and the events at which they were performed.

They were all collected by the folklorist François-Marie Luzel (1821–1895) in his home region of Lower Brittany, particularly around his hometown of Plouaret and the neighboring villages. His storytellers were often people already known to him and they usually told their stories in the Breton language, which Luzel then translated into French for a wider readership.

Most nineteenth-century folklorists' "entry into oral literature was facilitated by a network of personal contacts—servants, kin and neighbours" (Hopkin 2012, 210), and Luzel was no different in this respect, collecting many of his stories through face-to-face interviews. Either he would seek them out or they would come to visit him with their stories, and he would scribble out their words, as accurately as possible, as they spoke, often asking them to stop and repeat sentences, before making a fair copy.

As befitted a scholar of his time, he engaged in extensive correspondence with other folklorists and intellectuals (see, for example, Luzel 1995g), but unlike some other folktale collectors, he did not rely on a network of far-flung correspondents sending him written versions of stories they had heard. For many of his contemporaries, this was a necessity, as travel to remote areas could be difficult and expensive, or even linguistically impenetrable. Luzel, however, found himself ideally located:

Given the nineteenth-century assumption that their role was to salvage the wreckage of past centuries, folklorists expected to find this best preserved at the fringes of the cultural realm. Brittany as a whole was considered one such "relic region", isolated both by language and a deeply religious culture, which is why the province was so important to the development of folklore studies in France as a whole. (Hopkin 2012, 33)

Luzel and his sister Perrine (1829–1915), his occasional (and sometimes unacknowledged) collaborator, did not have to venture far to collect the material he sought. It also meant that he was in the enviable position of being able to collect stories in their authentic context, that is, not in the study or parlor of the bourgeois scholar, but at the veillées, the social gatherings that took place in the houses and cottages throughout Brittany during the winter months of darkness, where communities of family and neighbors would come together to share news, gossip, stories, and songs.

Luzel had access to these events not only because of geographical proximity, but also because he had been attending veillées since he was a child; many took place in his own home. They were an essential part of his own cultural upbringing and education, and he instinctively understood them as cultural events with their social conventions and dynamics. When he attended veillées, he did so as a member of the community and a participant in the events himself. He had both physical *and* cultural access to these events. This might have been far removed from the notion of the detached observer and his insistence on the application of scientific principles to the study of folklore, but it makes for a fascinating conflict in Luzel's work between his roles as scientist and community member.

Unlike many of his contemporaries, Luzel not only diligently recorded the veillées in which he participated but chose to publish many of the stories he collected within the context and frame of the event at which they took place, giving us access to a kind of ethnography of his own community through the conversations and social activity that took place around their telling. The amount of contextual information that Luzel provides goes far beyond what was common at the time.

It also means that we can fully understand the stories Luzel collected only by considering them in their performative context. The tales published here are not intended as authoritative fixed literary texts, set in stone, but as oral stories should be: as living, fluid, unstable, and unreliable texts that tell us about the daily lives of those who told them, just as if we take them off the page today and refashion them for our own telling, they become stories that form part of our own reality. As Jean Markale remarks in his introduction to *Contes populaires de toutes les Bretagne*, "there is no certainty, only what is probable, and the probable is merely transitory" (2000, 14).

This book is not intended to be primarily a work of comparative folklore, seeking to place these stories within a wider body of French, European, or world folk narrative traditions by identifying common and shared motifs and structures. I have provided some comparative information in the notes to each story at the back of this volume, but I have deliberately restrained myself in this respect. I hope I have provided enough information for the general reader and some starting points for those who wish to pursue this route more seriously.

I invite the reader, therefore, to look at these neglected stories first and foremost as performance texts, or perhaps improvised theatrical texts, to which I have added some information and thoughts about who performed and collected these particular versions, why and where they were performed, and to what purpose. To think of these texts as "theatrical" does not, of course, in itself imply "theatricality" in the way they were performed.[1] Rather, the evidence suggests a more conversational delivery. Nevertheless, as a theater scholar and before that a professional storyteller, I have tried to bring my own way of seeing, reading, and understanding things—the sensibilities of the performer—to this project and I hope that the result will be of interest to a range of readers. More than anything else, though, I hope people will take these stories off the page and tell them again in their own way, to fresh ears, in ways that make Luzel and his storytellers not our predecessors but our contemporaries.

The Midnight Washerwoman

and Other

Tales of Lower Brittany

La Bretagne Pittoresque

3047. - Veillée Bretonne
La Chanson du Barde

■ Introduction: François-Marie Luzel, Folklorist of Lower Brittany

In September 1895, the following obituary appeared in *Folklore*, the journal of the Folklore Society in Britain:

> Breton folklore has sustained an irreparable loss in the death of M. Luzel, on the 26th February last, at the age of seventy-four. It is almost impossible to over-estimate his services in rescuing the folklore of his nation from the bands of romancers and poets. Far be it from us to undervalue poetry and romance. They are frequently among the highest and most valuable efforts of the human intellect; but when they are deliberately palmed off on an unsuspecting public as the genuine products of the popular imagination, of which in reality they are only the bedizened and distorted presentment, it is time for all who have any regard for truth and any feeling for traditional poetry and humour to protect and to show, if they can, a more excellent way. Leaving to others the work of criticism, M. Luzel set an example to collectors of folklore in Brittany; and it is to his example that we owe the admirable work of M. Sébillot, M. Le Braz, and others who are proud to reckon themselves his disciples. His splendid collections of tales and songs from *La Bretagne bretonnante* are prized by all students of the subject, and will long keep his memory green and fresh as the pioneer of the Science of Tradition in Brittany.

While it is in the very nature of obituaries to focus on the positive achievements of an individual, this is a generous testimonial for a folklorist who rarely left his native Brittany and who did not enjoy the privileged upbringing of most of his contemporary folklore scholars. Most remarkable about the obituary is its specific reference to his battles with "the bands of romancers and poets," as he bore the standard of a scientific approach to the study of the Breton folktale. The leading romancer and poet referred to here is Théodore Hersart de La Villemarqué, an aristocrat-born antiquarian who, according to Luzel's biographer Françoise Morvan, had—like many aristocrats who had lost their privileges following the Revolution—reinvented himself as the proud defender of a traditionalist Celtic nation (1999, 15–26). La Villemarqué was everything that Luzel was not, and their long rivalry has come to symbolize much more than positional differences in relation to the collection of folklore, but also the polarities of Breton, and indeed French, nationalist politics. This dispute still rumbles on today between scholars and Breton cultural activists and can in part account for the fact that, despite the volume and importance of Luzel's work, it has often remained out of print in France and has appeared in translation only in modest quantities before.[1] Nevertheless, just as the next generation of folklorists, such as Paul Sébillot (1843–1918), arguably the most important scholar of Breton folklore, and Anatole Le Braz (1859–1926), might have counted themselves among Luzel's supporters, so Luzel's work also ranks in significance alongside that of the generation that followed them: Arnold van Gennep (1873–1957)[2] and Paul Delarue (1889–1956).[3]

There is some confusion around the date on which François-Marie Luzel was born. Archival records give different dates and years, but it seems most likely that he was born on 21 June 1821. More certain is that the event took place in the family home, the manor of Keramborgne (Keramborn in Breton) in the commune of Plouaret.[4] His family were Breton-speaking farmers with Republican leanings (the manor had come to the family as a result of Luzel's grandfather's being a "Capitaine de la Garde Nationale" during the Revolution) and had some education. They were certainly not poor, but nonetheless their existence would have had a degree of precariousness about it. Moreover, it was a life that was inextricably tied to the land and the local community.

An early influence on the young Luzel was no doubt his attendance at the veillées held at the family home in Plouaret, the winter evening gatherings around the fireside with neighbors and visitors when time would be given over to storytelling and singing. In his later years, Luzel wrote about these events and the magical atmosphere that they evoked and he did so not without a little nostalgia.

Of most significance, though, is the influence exerted on the young Luzel by his uncle Julien-Marie Le Huërou, a teacher at the Collège royale de Rennes. In 1835, the young Luzel himself was sent off to the Collège for his secondary education and at first felt completely bewildered and constrained by his new life. However, his uncle was a keen scholar of Breton culture and encouraged Luzel in the same field, introducing him to many of his friends with similar interests. It was a turning point for Luzel and he immersed himself in his academic studies, discovering an aptitude for scholarly activity.

Le Huërou's approach to his research is interesting, because it very much mirrors the philosophical and political positions later adopted by Luzel in his own professional life. Le Huërou sought not to establish Breton as a language and culture with its own purity but to set it in the context of the greater family of European cultures and languages. He also rejected many of the Breton stereotypes, such as the cult of druidism, that were being promoted by many of the early Breton folklorists. Not surprisingly, when La Villemarqué published *Barzaz Breiz*, a collection of traditional Breton songs, in 1839, Le Huërou was highly critical.

Luzel's adult life seems to have been largely dominated by two features: first, a tension between his work as a folklorist and the need to earn money, and second, a difficult relationship with the "establishment." Luzel achieved no university-level qualifications and never held an academic post. He tried his hand at teaching many times but found himself dismissed from numerous positions. There may well be some truth in Morvan's suggestion that he was the victim of an establishment that disapproved of his political and anticlerical opinions, but equally likely Luzel was a less than enthusiastic teacher, primarily focusing his energies on his collecting work.

Although today Luzel's reputation as a folklorist is largely based upon his collections of folktales, his early folklore work had focused on the traditional songs and dramas of the region. It was not until 1870 that he published his first collection of tales, *Contes bretons*, which contained six tales, three of which were published bilingually. Coincidentally, but not insignificantly, 1870 was the year of the disastrous Franco-Prussian War, after which "the French folklore movement suddenly flowered, with the quickening of interest in philology, archaeology and ethnography. These were the years of the founding of journals and societies, of the cultivation of the cultural sciences, of the quest for the Celtic, Romanic, medieval, and peasant contributions to the French soul" (Dorson 1968, vii). Luzel was fortunate enough to be there right at the beginning of this golden age that lasted until the outbreak of the First World War.

It was in Quimper, where Luzel took a position as archivist for the Department of Finistère, that he met and befriended Anatole Le Braz, who became one of the most celebrated of the new generation of Breton translators and folklorists. Le Braz became not only Luzel's disciple, despite his more avowedly nationalist tendencies, but also his literary executor.

A more important ally for Luzel, though, was the writer and philosopher Ernest Renan (1823–1892). Luzel and Renan met at the end of 1857, while Renan was head librarian at the Bibliothèque nationale, and they remained friends until Renan's death thirty-five years later. Renan represented the scholarly establishment. Whereas Luzel was largely self-taught, Renan had a doctorate and led a respectable academic career. Whereas Luzel was anticlerical, Renan had trained to become a priest, although he never took his vows. What brought the two men together, apart from their native Brittany, was an interest in philology (particularly in the relationship of Breton to other languages) and a deep suspicion of the work of the earlier Breton folklorists such as La Villemarqué. In fact, it was with Renan's encouragement that Luzel took on La Villemarqué over the *Barzaz Breiz*. In return, Renan used his influence to help secure funding for Luzel to carry out his collecting expeditions. Luzel's relationship with the establishment had always been problematic, but Renan lent him some respectability and in 1890, two years before Renan's death, Luzel was made a Chevalier of the Légion d'honneur, an occasion made more poignant by the fact that the honor was bestowed by his old rival La Villemarqué. Five years later, both were dead, Luzel in February 1895 and La Villemarqué in December of that same year. Luzel's final collection of stories, *Contes et légendes des bretons armoricains*, a collection of five stories compiled and edited by Le Braz, was published posthumously in 1896.

Luzel the Folklorist

In his essay on Giuseppe Pitrè (Zipes and Russo 2009a), Joseph Russo presents a picture of the nineteenth-century collector of Sicilian folktales as a man ahead of his time. His practice of collecting multiple variants of the same story, of recording often detailed notes about the way individual storytellers *performed* their stories, and of retaining within the texts the "inconsistencies and non sequiturs" (23) that are a common feature of oral storytelling, arguably make Pitrè and Luzel methodological bedfellows. However, to describe Luzel as a man a century ahead of his time may require some qualification. While his working practices, his approach to the study of the folktale, and much of his thinking around its significance were indeed very progressive when compared to those of many of his contemporaries, Luzel was also a man very much *of* his time. He may have had what now seem to us extraordinarily modern insights, but he did so from the point of view of a nineteenth-century scholar.

What makes Luzel stand out from many of his contemporaries is perhaps his willingness to collect and *publish* variants of the same tale. The modern folktale scholar would, of course, do exactly the same, attributing the differences between collected texts to the contextual conditions that governed the performance of the telling. As David Hopkin explains:

> While their nineteenth-century predecessors (under the influence of nineteenth-century textual scholars) attempted to reconstruct ur-texts from the multiple variants at their disposal, twenty-first-century folklorists (like twenty-first-century textual scholars) study the variants themselves. The *mouvance* or *variance* between texts, to borrow terms used by medievalists, is meaningful when related to the specific social contexts in which they were performed. (2012, 26)

Among others, Richard Bauman's seminal text on performative approaches to storytelling analysis, *Verbal Art as Performance* (1984), proposes that a storyteller is engaged in a framed process of communication, that is, "performance," at the moment of telling and that the detail of the performed text (including the words spoken, the manner of speaking—volume, cadence, rhythm, and so on—and any accompanying physical language, such as gesture or facial expression) is entirely determined by the context of that moment. Some elements of that context may be within the storyteller's control; others may not. Thus, *what* is spoken and *how* is determined by *who* speaks it, *to whom*, and *when* and *where*, resulting in a potentially infinite number of story variants of equal value and currency. It is, as Peter Bogatyrëv and Roman Jakobson posited as early as 1929, that "only the language of a specific person at a given time represents reality" (1982, 34).[5] This notion of folklore as process, variance as the norm, and storytelling as performance has been well established in the field of folklore for the best part of fifty years or more and is the fundamental principle that separates most modern folklore scholarship from that which preceded it. In this way, the modern folklore scholar may be thought of as being just as interested in the *difference* between variants of a story as in their similarity, and able to derive meaning from differences and how they arose (see Hopkin 2010, 36). Indeed, variation, not similarity, it could be argued, is the key to unlocking meaning in any given text.[6]

Luzel was interested in variation for quite different reasons. For much of the second half of the nineteenth century, the folklore scholarly world was divided into two rival camps. On one side were the followers of solar or comparative mythology, as first expounded by the German-born Oxford professor Max Müller in 1856 (Dorson 1986, 165). This theory proposed that folktales had their ancient origin in solar mythology. Over the centuries, these myths were thought to have "degenerated" into folktales but the older symbolism was still evident within them. As such, all stories had fixed meanings and fixed symbolism, relating to ancient solar deities, and characters within stories could be classified by type. Furthermore, the key to unlocking meaning lay in the study of language and by making philological connections. By 1873, the theory had already been robustly challenged by Andrew Lang and his followers in the "anthropological" camp, whose counterproposal took Darwin's theory of evolution as its inspiration and created the notion of "cultural evolution." Lang's theory proposed that societies that were at similar stages of cultural evolution could produce similar cultural artifacts without ever having been in contact, thus allowing for variants of the same tale type to be created independently of each other. Aulikki Nahkola summarizes that "while Müller's work represented a degenerative view of human culture, Lang built his theory on a model of evolutionary anthropology" (2001, 123).

In his introduction to *Contes populaires de Basse-Bretagne*, Luzel steers a diplomatic line between the two systems, proposing "mythological eclecticism" over an absolutist adherence to one or the other (1887, vii). For Luzel, the study of folktales had to be founded upon a robust scientific approach.[7] Furthermore, by reducing the texts of the same story down to a set of key shared symbols, a single, authoritative meaning can be determined, allowing for the classification of the story. This might sound like a reductive approach to us these days, but to Luzel and his contemporaries, applying scientific principles to stories, in the way one might to botany, for example, afforded folktales a status they would not otherwise have. At the end of his introduction to the first volume of *Contes populaires*, Luzel makes an impassioned plea to the next generation of folklorists:

> This is, in effect, the literature of the unschooled and the unfortunate, who know how to neither read nor write . . . and . . . we must . . . love it, respect it and hasten to collect it, at the very moment when it is in danger of disappearing forever. (xix–xx)

Luzel was on a mission to do for the Breton folktale what the Brothers Grimm had done for the German folktale (Luzel 1995a, 16) and his deep respect for the storytellers he collected from meant that he published each story as he heard it, in the exact words told to him. However, as Hopkin so rightly reminds us, "for no nineteenth-century folklorist did fidelity mean exactitude" (2012, 41). Luzel did not follow the strict principles of accurate transcription of the modern scholar nor could he, given that he did not have recourse to electronic recording equipment. Neither was he averse to a little editing and correcting here and there to make things more comprehensible to the reader, but his editorial hand was lighter than that of many of his contemporaries and he did not try to tidy up internal narrative contradictions, omissions, or non sequiturs. Luzel did not take multiple variants and reconcile them into a single definitive version of a particular story. For him, the authenticity of the tale lay in the fact that stories changed depending on the teller and the audience and that an eagerness to embellish a tale with episodes from other stories, in order to keep the interest of the listener, is a characteristic of the Breton storyteller (1887, ix).

Collecting multiple variants was also central to Luzel's scientific approach—the analysis of a story to decode its true meaning lay not in the construction of a composite version but in the comparison of different variants of the same story, which would allow the scholar to identify common motifs and episodes. So, whereas the modern folklorist may derive meaning from the *difference* between variants, Luzel derived meaning from *similarity*. Furthermore, while Luzel's attitudes were surprisingly modern in some respects, he did not look for meaning in the moment of performance, in the way we would today. Indeed, he would not have understood the meaning of "performance" in our sense. His understanding of folklore was chronological and archaeological. The folktale existed as an ancient preindustrial relic and the folklorist's duty was to collect and preserve it before it died out—a race against time before it decayed altogether.

Yet even in this respect Luzel's attitude is more complex than might at first seem. For a start, his apparent affinity and empathy with his informants, particularly his two main storytellers, Barba Tassel of Plouaret, who at the age of seventy-two was still delivering on foot telegraphic dispatches and official communications from the local mayor (1887, x), and Marguérite Philippe of Pluzunet, meant that Luzel was fully aware how much the harsh social realities of nineteenth-century peasant life in Brittany were reflected in the tales. These were stories of social struggle and survival, where the poor pitted their wits against the wealthy and the powerful, and usually came out on top.[8] They often reflected a thinly disguised hatred of the seigneurial system and displayed a natural sympathy, Luzel felt, with the poor and downtrodden, reflecting a world where the underdogs were the natural heroes, overcoming all kinds of trials and battles with the forces of evil and stupidity (1995a, 13). Ancient tales whose origins lay in the mists of time, these were stories that had been updated to reflect the daily struggles of the people who told them. Luzel was critical of earlier studies that simply reflected vague memories of traditions, written as if they were genuine but failing to capture the authentic popular voice (10).

Nineteenth-century folklorists also commonly believed that the further back a story or song could be traced, the more "authentic" it was. This drove Luzel's keen interest in the folktale as a form, which he believed to be much older (and therefore more authentically Celtic) than forms such as the folksong or poem. Folklorists often sought out storytellers in the farthest reaches of Europe, far from the centers of civilization, untouched by the industrial revolution, where agrarian communities and ways of life persisted. If folktales were vestiges of earlier civilizations, then it stood to reason that the best and most authentic storytellers would be found in those parts of the world that remained untouched by the civilizing hand of Western thought, the Enlightenment, industrialization, and capitalism. This might seem questionable today, but it led folklore collectors in Britain, for example, to venture out to the west of Ireland and the Highlands of Scotland, leaving the cities of London and Manchester to the social observers and political philosophers. The more remote—the more "savage"—the better.

In his "Deuxième rapport" (1995a, 125–31), Luzel recounts his journey into the remote inland area of Cornouaille, around the mountains of Avez. In contrast to the areas nearer to the coast that had benefited from contact with other cultures through trade and the fishing industry, isolated communities existed here. Luzel may have set out on his mission with the hope and expectation of a fruitful journey, but he had a pretty miserable time of it. Not only did he have to tolerate the discomforts and indignities of traveling everywhere on foot, but he considered the material he collected inferior to what he had collected in the coastal towns and villages. It may not be surprising, on reflection, that Luzel had greater success in collecting stories from within his own and neighboring communities, where he was known, than in remote areas where the villages and their inhabitants were unfamiliar to him, and vice versa. Luzel, however, came to a different conclusion. Contrary to popular opinion at the time, he determined that, far from diluting the purity of traditions, contact with other cultures strengthened and enriched folk traditions with new ideas, thoughts, and stories.

The *Barzaz Breiz* Controversy

If Luzel's career as a folklorist is remembered for one thing, it is for the controversy around La Villemarqué's *Barzaz Breiz*, which was the cause of a deep disagreement and an ideological split that rumbled on for many years. On the surface, Luzel and La Villemarqué make perfect rivals, one the precocious and affluent son of aristocratic stock, the other from a modest Republican background, impecunious for all his professional life. Their quarrel came to symbolize the animosity between two different positions within the complex and fraught world of Breton nationalist cultural politics and still divides the community, with *Barzaz Breiz* continuing to be celebrated by Breton cultural nationalists through the twentieth century (Gemie 2007, 47).

The relationships between Brittany and the rest of France, and its associated politics, are both complex and ever-changing.[9] While contemporary Breton nationalism is more closely associated with the politics of the progressive Left—according to Gemie, "Bretons are more likely to adopt pro-European union attitudes than other French people, and significantly less likely to vote for the far-right *Front National*" (9)—the predominant leaning has previously been toward conservatism, and the nationalist movement is still partially tainted by its attitude toward the Vichy Government during the years of occupation.[10] In the nineteenth century, the relationship was equally complex and, at times, contradictory.

The renaissance of interest in Celticism at the beginning of the nineteenth century was in response to both the rise of romanticism and the postrevolutionary nation-building agenda in what was a country widely fragmented by language and cultural traditions.[11] The "othering" of Brittany as a place of refuge and remoteness, representing the relics of France's Celtic past, sought to legitimize it as a distinctive part of the wider nation, but as an alternative to the centralizing, post-Enlightenment, and anticlerical tendencies of the Revolution and "an instrument for the conservative right to use against the revolutionary legacy" (Gemie 2007, 43).

Théodore Hersart de La Villemarqué was born in 1815 into a pro-Royalist family with aristocratic connections and, although he became disillusioned with the restored monarchy, his instincts remained deeply conservative and pro-church, in contrast to Luzel's strong anticlerical roots. La Villemarqué was certainly no separatist, though. His belief was that Breton culture reflected the true character of the French nation and he proposed a "reorientation of French culture . . . with Brittany to be the focus for the new order" (Gemie 2007, 48), drawing inspiration from Breton culture for a simpler, more spiritual way of life. *Barzaz Breiz* was intended as a tool in this campaign, linking Celticism to Christianity, that expressed "codes of morality and spirituality which would inspire the French people to return to a Celtic and religious mode of being" (Gemie 2007, 48) and it secured La Villemarqué's reputation as one of the most important antiquarian scholars of his generation.

Luzel first raised his suspicions around the authenticity of the songs contained within the volume in 1868, but it was four years later, in 1872, that the row burst into the open, after Luzel spoke at the Congress of the Breton Association in Saint-Brieuc, condemning *Barzaz Breiz* as a fake and accusing La Villemarqué of manufacturing the songs contained within the book. Luzel's suspicions were at least in part owing to La Villemarqué's use of unified Breton, a form of the language that was free of the influence of other languages, whereas the Breton used by Luzel's singers and storytellers inevitably bore the hallmarks of other linguistic influences, especially French. Others, including Renan, shared his concerns and Luzel came under pressure to publish his own collection of Breton songs, *Gwerziou*, that when placed alongside *Barzaz Breiz* would expose the earlier work as fraudulent. The plan was to publish *Gwerziou* in two volumes, the first covering epic verse, the second containing sentimental and romantic poetry, thus mimicking the structure of *Barzaz Breiz*. The first volume, published in 1868, sold only twenty subscriptions (Morvan 1999, 179) and the second volume did not appear until 1874.

Recent works by scholars such as Donatien Laurent (1989), Nelly Blanchard (2006), and Ellen Badone (2017) suggest that while the songs in *Barzaz Breiz* were very heavily edited, even rewritten into composite versions, by La Villemarqué, he was nonetheless familiar with the range of Breton dialects and worked with texts that he had genuinely collected. On this basis, it is difficult to condemn La Villemarqué. The Brothers Grimm, who inspired the work of early folklorists from the first half of the nineteenth century, were themselves heavy editors of the stories they collected and created composite versions from multiple variants. In Luzel's opinion, the quarrel was a disagreement between two methods, with the exponents of the new scientific method eager to discredit those who hung onto old practices. We should be careful not to denounce La Villemarqué from the position of the twenty-first-century folklorist, who would operate with quite different principles.

Luzel and Breton Culture

Sharif Gemie (2007) asserts that prior to the Romantic period the distinctiveness of Brittany, including its language, was thought of as being no more or less significant than any other region of France, but the idea of Breton nationalism emerged from the rise of Celticism in the early 1800s. By the time Luzel had grown up, a movement to preserve, protect, and promote Breton culture was already established, even though it was still in its relative infancy. In other words, Luzel was entering a world where a sense of distinct Breton identity was gathering pace and yet there were still opportunities for people like him to make a definite contribution to the formation of that identity and how it might relate to the wider French and other regional identities.

There can be no doubt that Luzel was fully committed to this project for all of his life. In addition to his folklore work, he published poems and other literary works in Breton under various pseudonyms, and lobbied for schools to teach the Breton language, as the principal defining characteristic of the region.

The central problem for Bretonists was that there was very little written historic record, so folklore (and particularly the folktale) was seen as serving an important function in providing an alternative historical record of the Breton people. In fact, the situation was not unlike that faced by Jacob and Wilhelm Grimm when they began collecting folktales in Germany. In his book *Nations, Identity, Power: The New Politics of Europe*, George Schöpflin recognizes "the potential importance of memory to forms of nationhood" (2000, 74) and a written historical record and a literature are critical elements in the memory-making process. When the short-lived Académie Celtique was founded in 1804 (see Senn 1981), it naturally turned to folklore as a way of finding a route back to the region's Celtic heritage in the face of a distinct lack of written artifacts (Gemie 2007, 42). Emile Souvestre was in a nostalgic mood when he wrote in 1849:

it is above all in the countryside that we have tried to rediscover the popular tradition. There, among isolated families with fixed lives, away from the great events which disrupt their conduct, without books, the traditions of storytelling has (sic) been preserved. (quoted in Gemie 2007, 42)

It is not surprising, then, that when Luzel published *Contes bretons* in 1870, his first volume of folktales, he felt that this was the most important phase of his work.

The scene takes place in an old Breton manor house, in the middle of the woods, half-way along the road between the town of Plounévez-Moëdec and the town of Plouaret, the manor of Keramborgne, where I spent my childhood. It is the twenty-fourth day of December, Christmas Eve. The weather is cold and snow covers the ground. The Christmas veillée begins. With the evening meal finished, after the life of the day's saint has been read in Breton and the communal prayers recited, the whole household—masters, servants, children and day laborers—come together in a circle around the Yule log, an enormous oak trunk that burns in the vast kitchen fireplace. A wandering bard and beggarman, old Iouenn Garandel, has arrived at nightfall looking for hospitality, his bag thoroughly decorated with newly printed ballad-sheets and poems on loose-leaf paper ... and he has been received with joy and happiness, especially by the children, and he has been shown to the storyteller's stool, at the corner of the hearth, with a full bowl of golden cider on hand. He begins by recounting the latest news from the parishes that he's passed through since his last visit: deaths, births, engagements, accidents, and adventures of all sorts. Then he sings the old ballad of *Lezobré* and the whole audience hangs on to the old man's every word, whose memory is inexhaustible when it comes to talking about the old days. (Luzel 1995b, 169–70)

As Françoise Morvan says, the cultural event of the veillée "occupies a very particular place in the work of Luzel" (Luzel 1995b, 7), as the "mise-en-scène" of storytelling. It was, for Luzel, at the very heart of the storytelling experience, because, as Morvan explains, "it reminds us that the tale is also the location of the tale, that it is nothing without the authenticity of the moment in which it is written down" (16). This awareness of the importance of the storytelling *event* as the context that gave meaning to the stories made Luzel stand out from many of his contemporaries. The scientific approach, championed by Luzel and others, demanded an emotional detachment from the stories being collected, so that "on the page they appear depersonalized, disconnected to experienced reality" (Hopkin 2012, 29), yet Luzel found himself completely drawn into and enchanted by the event of the veillée. This scientific approach did not sit easily with Luzel's interest in the performance event, as it is "suspect as regards the scientific objectivity required" (Morvan in Luzel 1995b, 14). This is a tension that remains at the heart of Luzel's work (Morvan in Luzel 1995a, 175).

Luzel and his sister Perrine provided us with numerous accounts of veillées and while the one quoted above, first published in the *Revue de Bretagne et d'Anjou* in January 1888, specifically recounts the events of a Christmas veillée, the descriptions of other veillées reveal some common features.

First, however, it is important to try to understand the veillée, given that so many of the stories Luzel published, including those in *Contes bretons* (1995a) and *Contes du boulanger* (1995c), were collected at such events. He attached great importance to the veillée as a cultural occurrence. The verb *veiller*, from which *veillée* is derived, means "to stay awake or keep vigil" and also relates to the practice of sitting up with a patient or a corpse. *Veillée*, then, might, on the one hand, be translated as a "wake," in the Irish sense of the word, whereby company gathers to drink, eat, tell stories, and generally celebrate the life of the deceased. The veillée was not an event reserved for such occasions, however, but a more common occurrence, predominantly during the winter months, when family, friends, servants, and visitors would gather in a house, around the fireplace, to share and discuss news, stories, and songs. As Pierre-Jakez Hélias says, "The month of November was the month for tales" (1978, 57). Darnton identifies the veillée as "an important French institution" (1984, 17), indicating that the first account of such an event was written in the mid-sixteenth century by the Breton writer Noel du Fail (1520?–1591). The veillées that Luzel describes took place mainly either at the family manor house at Keramborgne or at Coat-Tugdual, the manor house in which his sister Catherine lived at Plouguernevel. These affairs were largely attended by members of Luzel's family, the workers at the manor (servants or agricultural day-laborers), as well as visiting friends and traveling beggars seeking shelter. And, of course, all their children. Everybody was involved, it seems, regardless of age, gender, or social position:

> The only time of the year when stories are habitually told is the winter, during the long evenings. Every fireplace, whether it is a manor house, a rich farm, or a humble cottage, has its singers and storytellers; everybody is there together. (Luzel 1995a, 112–13)

At one veillée held at Coat-Tugdual (Luzel 1995b, 85–127), the priest from Ploëzal was also in attendance and even contributed two ghost stories himself to the proceedings. The veillée, it seems, was largely a place where social divisions were left behind and a sense of community was built.

Particular excitement was reserved for those times when a traveling tailor or a wandering beggar would be attending. These people were regular visitors to the larger houses, where the hospitality would be plentiful. They were renowned for their storytelling abilities and were always made welcome, not only for their skills as storytellers and singers, but also because they brought the news from neighboring, and not-so neighboring, parishes.[12] Luzel describes them as the community's "living newspapers" (1995b, 25). These included Iann Gourlaouën, Robart Menguy, Iouenn Gorvel, Iann Kergolor, and, most frequently, Garandel,[13] the blind beggarman, whom Luzel called "a true Homer in clogs" (2002, 130).[14] Others, such as Pierre-Jakez Hélias's grandfather, a clogmaker, known locally as "Jean the Wonder-Man" (1978, 68), were valued in their community for their skills in storytelling: "Indeed, his reputation for knowing so many tales was such that at the end of harvest-time, he was sought out . . . in order that he might transform a gathering of peasants in a farmhouse" (73–74). Hopkin reminds us that in such communities "narrative talent (was seen) as a form of cultural capital" (2012, 64).

By contrast, the veillée attended by Perrine in 1890 in Morlaix would have attracted neither these traveling virtuosos at one end of the social scale, nor the landowners or clergy at the other end, so had a narrower social range in its audience. The focus is once again on conviviality, social cohesion, and community-building:

> During the winter of 1888–9, there met in the town of Morlaix a group of popular singers and storytellers, made up of Breton laborers and artisans. The singing and storytelling were only in Breton. They gathered every evening during the long winter evenings in a bakehouse and, as the oven was stoked for baking the bread, a double benefit could be enjoyed of passing an evening among friends in a well-heated space and listening to beautiful Breton songs and all kinds of marvelous stories . . . (Luzel 1995c, 7)

At these particular events, each person paid an entrance fee of one sou for cider that would "liven up the singers and the storytellers and . . . help keep the interest of the audience" (7). In describing the veillées that he himself attended, as a child and as an adult, Luzel does not mention money changing hands, but there is plenty of cider and he does tell of an almost ritualistic event with distinct phases.

The evening would begin with the laying and lighting of the fire, followed by the arrival of the guests and the setting-up of spinning wheels at the back of the room—where the women would continue to work throughout the entertainment—and the seats for others (a large bench or two, sometimes a more comfortable chair for the head of the household, and the storyteller's stool, next to which rested a full bowl of cider). Once everyone was gathered, there would be communal prayers and a reading from the life of the saint whose feast day it happened to be. Next came conversations about the day's work and the swapping of local news. If a traveling storyteller was present, there would also be news from elsewhere. During this time, the women at their spinning wheels might have been quietly singing to themselves as they spun, perhaps occasionally being asked to sing louder for the benefit of the whole room. Then, with the children becoming restless, the storytelling would begin.

Besides the longer folktales that clearly played a significant role at these gatherings, along with singing and more general conversation and discussion, ghost stories took up a substantial part of the evening. Very often these were short and told as true, either in the first person or as having happened to a relative, an acquaintance, or a "friend of a friend." Luzel considered these stories to be of only minor significance, in comparison to the longer tales, but he did acknowledge their crucial role in creating an atmosphere of mystery, excitement, and anticipation, which was a central feature of the veillée. The audience, it seemed, enjoyed the thrill of a scary story just as much as we do today.

The number of stories told on any given evening depended on several factors, including when the veillée started and finished, the amount of news and gossip to be shared, and the length of the stories themselves, as well as how much discussion each telling generated. In the five veillées described by Luzel in *Veillées bretonnes* (2002), the evenings consisted of between two and ten stories along with one or two songs. The evenings concluded at around ten o'clock, often with a song or two to counteract the tales of the supernatural that had gone before and to send the company on their way with smiles on their faces.

Darnton proposes that reading formed an integral and regular part of the veillée:

> Perrault's version of the tales reentered the stream of popular culture through the *Bibliothèque bleue*, the primitive paperbacks that were read aloud at *veillées* in villages where someone was capable of reading. These little blue books featured Sleeping Beauty and Little Red Riding Hood as well as Gargantua, Fortunatus, Robert le Diable, Jean de Calais, les Quatre Fils Aymon, Maugis l'Enchanteur, and many other characters from the oral tradition that Perrault never picked up. (1984, 63)

Although Luzel makes no reference to such activity at a veillée, Darnton's mention of Perrault is significant. France, of course, enjoyed a particularly rich fairy-tale tradition, begun by Charles Perrault (1628–1703), Mme d'Aulnoy (1650/1–1705), Marie-Jeanne L'Héritier (1664–1734), and others in the seventeenth-century salons,[15] and it would be a mistake to assume that the influence of oral culture on literary forms was all one-way traffic. Almost certainly the widespread availability and circulation of literary fairy tales in chapbook form meant that they found their way into popular culture, either through the kinds of readings Darnton describes or by the storytellers' hearing these stories and then reinterpreting and remaking them as oral stories that were *told* at the veillées. Indeed, Catherine Velay-Vallantin argues for a far more complex set of relationships between oral and written versions of stories and even questions the convenient distinction between the two in a society where oral and printed variants would circulate freely in different forms, constantly being reworked by the communities that told them. As she says: "there is not a tale that escapes the multiplicity and diversity of treatments" (1992, 39). Furthermore, she suggests that the *Bibliothèque bleue* did not merely reprint the tales of Perrault, but often reworked them, sometimes restoring elements from the earlier oral tales that had been expunged by Perrault for the courtly audiences (46–49).

The relationship between oral and printed forms, however, goes beyond the French literary tales of the seventeenth and eighteenth centuries. Writing in September 1872, Luzel himself declared, "I have recently read *The Facetious Nights of Straparola* and I was astonished to find just how the stories in this very interesting collection, which are truly popular and ancient, are all to be found in our Breton cottages, and often barely modified" (1995a, 153–54).[16] There is no evidence to suggest that Luzel's storytellers made distinctions between different genres and forms and several of the stories collected by Luzel are redolent of literary fairy tales, such as Perrault's "Le Petit Poucet" and "Goulaffre the Giant." As Darnton rightly asserts, "Cultural currents intermingled, moving up as well as down, while passing through different media and connecting groups as far apart as peasants and salon sophisticates" (1984, 63).[17]

What Luzel captures most admirably in his descriptions are the conversations that took place in between the more structured moments of storytelling. Here are discussions evaluating the merits and veracity of each story and about the nature of supernatural belief. On occasion, a narrative summary or fragment is offered in response to a story. Most importantly, though, it is through these internarrative conversations that the next storyteller and story are negotiated and determined, sometimes by somebody volunteering (or being volunteered) to tell a story that the previous story has reminded them of, sometimes by a request for a particular storyteller to tell a contrasting narrative (either to lighten or darken the mood), or at other times simply because one person's voice has not been heard for a while (that is, it is simply their turn to contribute).

It is clear from these discussions that most of the stories were already familiar to many in the room, but that did not seem to diminish their enjoyment of them at all, supporting Marina Warner's statement that the "stories' interest isn't exhausted by repetition, reformulation or retelling, but their pleasure gains from the endless permutations performed on the nucleus of the tale" (2014, 45). As the evening drew toward its end, there were often requests to keep the stories short, so that everyone could head off to bed, or to save the ghost stories for the next evening, lest the children be unable to sleep. As Bogatyrëv and Jakobson posit, "the milieu trims the work to suit its needs" (1982, 36).[18]

What may appear to us to be everyday and familiar conversations are, in fact, critical in determining the shape and form of the performance event and, therefore, its meaning and the meaning of the stories themselves. Furthermore, the transitions between conversation and narrative performance are relatively seamless. There is no sudden major shift in register once a story begins or ends, no grand introduction of the storyteller to the audience at its start and no applause offered at its conclusion, but the stories seem to flow out of the previous conversation so that the performance remains low in intensity[19] and the language used in the storytelling remains "closely related to the language of everyday communication" (Hopkin 2012, 14). It is part of the performance of everyday discourse and in this way, it also becomes a space in which the clear distinctions between performer and audience identities can be challenged and become blurred.

It is Luzel's recording of the whole veillée in this manner, therefore, that allows us to understand storytelling as a social and historical act, "as part of a conversation between members of one family, or one neighbourhood" (Hopkin 2012, 29). And, while this may not have been Luzel's intention, it is only by considering the stories in this context that we are able to understand them not as relics or survivals of a past agrarian culture, nor as "a bourgeois version of the countryside and its residents" (Hopkin 2012, 16), but as contemporary statements that reflect the concerns, fears, hopes, and social realities of the communities that told them. In so doing, these stories enhance our understanding of those communities, as more a matter of historical record than fantastical whimsy.

Luzel as Collector, Translator, and Editor

According to Luzel's biographer Françoise Morvan, it was almost by accident that Luzel began his work on collecting folktales (Luzel 1995a, 166). Prior to 1868, Luzel's collecting had concentrated on theater texts, songs, and poetry, but the folktale was a new, unexplored area for research and he came to realize its significance to a broader understanding of Breton culture. He began collecting large amounts of material, especially around his home of Plouaret and the neighboring villages. His first collection of tales, *Contes bretons*, published in 1870, contained just six stories and provides us with a fascinating insight into his working methods.

It was not unusual at the time for folklorists to rely heavily on trusted correspondents to provide material for their collections and it was not always possible to fully verify the stories that were submitted. Luzel, in contrast, collected all the stories himself, wherever possible. He did to some degree rely on his sisters (especially Perrine, who not only collected tales on his behalf but also brokered introductions with women storytellers, in particular) and friends, such as Jean-Marie Le Jean, although this was not publicly acknowledged for fear of casting doubt on the authenticity of Luzel's work, especially in the wake of the *Barzaz Breiz* controversy. It was only much later, after the remarkable collection of the stories of François Thépault at Morlaix, published as *Contes du boulanger* (Luzel 1995c), that Luzel fully acknowledged his sister's contribution to the greater project.

In the preface to *Contes bretons*, Luzel gives us a somewhat contradictory set of statements about his approach to the texts he was collecting. He describes how he would occasionally interrupt storytellers and ask them to repeat certain phrases to make sure he had written them down accurately (although it is not easy to understand how he did this within the context of a veillée without destroying the atmosphere of the occasion). At the same time, when discussing the issue of translation (1995a, 8–9), he introduces two schools of thought. The first allows a relatively free hand in the translation process, especially as the stories are not specifically Breton but variants of tales found in the wider European (and especially French) corpus. The second proposes a much more "rigorously faithful and literal" text (8). Luzel comes down clearly on the side of the former approach. Since these stories are from oral tradition, he argues, the importance of the exact words spoken should not be exaggerated, as these are fluid and ever-changing. Instead, one should show "an absolute respect" (9) for the fable, that is, the structure and the content.

Luzel was intent on collecting and recording the oral traditions of Brittany in a way that reflected the reality of a region where many dialects of Breton were spoken and whose oral culture did not exist in a kind of splendid isolation. Nevertheless, we should be wary of attaching to Luzel the sensibilities of the modern folklorist regarding accuracy, verbatim transcription, and editorial intervention. Luzel was not about to abandon his editorial responsibilities.

As Luzel set out on his project of folktale-collecting, he seemed to be almost at a loss as to how to negotiate the thorny issue of transcription and translation. For the six stories contained with *Contes bretons*, therefore, he adopts three different approaches and asks his readers to provide him with feedback and suggestions. The first three stories ("Goulaffre the Giant," "The Man with the Two Dogs," and "The Godson of the Holy Virgin") are presented in relatively free translations from Breton into French. The fourth and fifth ("Jesus Christ in Lower Brittany" and "The Fisherman's Two Sons") appear in Breton alongside a fairly close French translation. The final story ("The Miller and His Seigneur") also appears bilingually, but this time the translation is a literal one.

The central problem that Luzel was dealing with was the very nature of the Breton language itself, which existed in multiple dialects (not all of which were comprehensible to each other) and also as a purely oral form (unlike the literary invention of unified Breton). As he transcribed the stories (and later prepared them for publication), Luzel was therefore having to invent a spelling and a grammar, while at the same time using a mixture of three different Breton dialects— which would retain the oral nature of the tales as told and be more comprehensible for a broader Breton-speaking readership—without having to resort to the artifice that was unified Breton.

Morvan explains the editorial process that Luzel eventually adopted (Luzel 1995a, 180–81). Working from his Breton text, as compiled from his fieldwork notes, Luzel would first create a literal French translation. He would then "rewrite" this French version with the purpose of improving its style, rendering a more readable text, clarifying and correcting where necessary, but avoiding unnecessary elaborations. Finally, he would return to the Breton text and, with reference to his French translation, modify the Breton text into something suitable for publication. So although Luzel's editorial hand remained relatively light compared to many of his contemporaries, he did alter the texts through quite a complex process as he prepared them for publication.

Luzel was, after all, trying to balance several conflicting demands. He was engaged in a project that sought to expose Breton folktales to the scrutiny of modern scientific approaches. At the same time, he needed to sell books to a wider public and his editorial work was aimed at preparing texts that would make a good read.

While Luzel concentrated his collecting in Lower Brittany (the northwestern Breton-speaking part of the region), the prolific Paul Sébillot was similarly, and significantly, occupied in Upper Brittany.[20] Nevertheless, Luzel's collecting was not evenly distributed across Lower Brittany and the vast majority took place in his home area of Trégor. This may, of course, have partly been pragmatism. Traveling in remote parts of Brittany was no easy task in the nineteenth century and Luzel's own accounts of the discomforts he endured while conducting fieldwork across Léon and Cornouaille suggest that he was not the happiest of travelers. In a report dated 2 August 1870, he tells of how he arrived in the village of Kymerc'h at eleven o'clock in the evening, after a long day traveling alone and on foot, and was unable to persuade anybody to provide him with lodgings:

> I have for a long time been familiar with Cornouaille and I was under no illusion as to the wide range of challenges that awaited me: long walks beneath a burning sun, on uneven roads and across a treeless landscape; the dreary comforts of the hostelries of our small Breton towns, beds with heavy hemp blankets, where one is eaten alive by enraged and starving fleas. I was counting on all of this. But what I didn't expect, in spite of everything, was to have to sleep outdoors. Even so, that is what happened to me. (1995a, 125)

Luzel was well connected, as one might expect, in the villages around Plouaret, and was able to recruit storytellers and gain admittance to veillées without much difficulty. By contrast, he appears to have encountered much less cooperation during his travels throughout Léon and Cornouaille. Once outside his own community, Luzel found it much more difficult to relate to his storytellers. Morvan observes that "as soon as he left Trégor, he saw people and things as would a stranger, a romantic traveler, a tourist" (Luzel 1995a, 192). Furthermore, much to his surprise, although he was able to collect material from places as remote as Ushant, he found the storytelling traditions there much poorer than he had expected.[21] In the summer of 1870, for example, he ventured into the Monts d'Arrés, a range of granite hills that traditionally separated Léon and Cornouaille:

> I had always thought that Braspartz, situated in the middle of the mountains, not far from Mont Saint-Michel,[22] the highest point in the Arez chain, would be an excellent base for a collector of old popular traditions. But how very wrong I was. (1995a, 126)

From his travels that summer, however, Luzel drew an important conclusion. The most vibrant traditions were to be found in the towns and villages closer to the coast, enriched by contact with other cultures through fishing and trading, and not in isolated communities that had no external influences to nourish them (1995a, 126). This was a radical idea that suggests Luzel was, in many ways, ahead of his time; it was further supported by his experiences in Léon that same autumn.

Luzel's Storytellers and Their Audiences

Luzel was blessed with having access to prolific storytellers within a few miles of his home. In total, Luzel collected from seventy different informants and most are recorded by name, profession, and the village or town they came from (see Luzel 1995a, 213–15). The storytellers' professions varied, but the men tended to be servants, laborers, and artisan craftsmen (including itinerants), rather than shopkeepers or small business owners, and the women mainly in service or beggars (a general term for anybody without regular work and living off the charity of others), although he also collected from housewives, farmers' wives, spinners, and a dressmaker. Many of the women were engaged in multiple activities. Catherine Doz from Plouaret, for example, was variously a beggarwoman and a builder's wife (Luzel 1995a, 213–14). Although forty-two of his storytellers were men, representing 60 percent of the total, most of the stories Luzel collected were, in fact, from women.[23] He relied particularly on two women for his material: Marguérite Philippe (Marc'harid Fulup) from Pluzunet, who made her living from both spinning and as a "pilgrim-by-proxy,"—that is, traveling to holy shrines on behalf of other people to seek the intervention of a saint on her client's behalf—and Barba Tassel, a beggarwoman from Plouaret, who was charged with delivering the mail to Plouaret.

Marguérite and Barba were the only two storytellers from whom Luzel collected stories throughout the whole period of his folktale research. Of the two, Barba appears to have originally been the more prolific storyteller. Marguérite, in contrast, was principally known for her singing. According to Luzel, she sang "constantly . . . as she turned her spinning wheel" and was "much sought after at the country farms to enliven the long hours of the winter evenings" (1995a, 89). However, it is Marguérite for whom Luzel reserves the highest praise; he claims she knows 60 stories in addition to her reputed repertoire of 150 songs.[24] What seems to have impressed him most was her "prodigious memory" (1995a, 89), which enabled her to recite her material to Luzel with a precision and confidence that must have made the job of collecting and transcribing that much easier. Contrary to the popular image of the aged storyteller, she was, in fact, a relatively young woman in her early thirties when Luzel began collecting stories from her (she was sixteen years his junior and lived until 1909, although a picture taken of her in 1906 shows a woman seemingly much older than her sixty-nine years).

Over the years, Luzel came to rely increasingly on these two women. As he himself became more selective about the stories he would collect, he seemed confident about the quality of material that he would get from them. It is not clear whether he resorted to directly paying them for reciting the stories to him. It is quite possible, although Charles Le Goffic's reported conversation with Marguérite Philippe throws some light on the arrangements. Rather than paying her for each individual song, it seems that he gave her an annual "Christmas box" of ten francs and would feed her, give her the occasional coin, and put her up at his house, whenever she needed it.

From our twenty-first-century standpoint, Luzel, along with other folklorists of his generation, appears to have been strikingly naïve in terms of his inability to recognize the impact his collecting techniques may have had on the stories and the storytelling performances themselves, be it his interruption of storytellers at veillées so that he could (ironically) more accurately note down the words spoken, or the nature of his relationship with his informants, especially if there was some kind of economic or other benefit for the storyteller. As Hopkin reminds us:

> narrators might, either out of an eagerness to please or in the hope of a reward, concoct the kinds of stories they know the folklorist wants. After all, it is part of the art of storytelling to please one's audience. (2012, 39)

Clearly, both Marguérite Philippe and Barba Tassel were remarkable women.[25] Marguérite, in particular, took great care to continually develop her repertoire, picking up songs and stories on her travels. In her work as a professional pilgrim, she also appears to have commanded the confidence and respect of community members across the social spectrum and was as comfortable exchanging stories with beggars on the road as with educated scholars like Luzel and his friends. Between them, the two women provided Luzel with enough material to allow him to make comparisons between the corpus of Breton tales that he had collected and other great collections of European folktales.

Luzel also noted that his storytellers would personalize the stories, collectively claiming ownership of them and authenticating them on behalf of their audiences, by locating them in their own villages or changing the names of the protagonists to people they knew, or simply claiming to have been present themselves when the stories took place. For example, Guillaume Garandel, the itinerant tailor, was particularly well known for introducing long digressions into his stories to include local references and even introducing people in the audience into the stories (Luzel 1995f, 15–22). This technique was also employed by Pierre-Jakez Hélias's grandfather, the storyteller-clogmaker:

> Over and again he would invent anecdotes out of whole cloth, which he'd then expand to include memorable events, and he did it in the very presence of the characters he was portraying. In fact, he was so precise about place, time and personalities that the heroes, in spite of themselves, ended up believing that it had all really happened to them. (Hélias 1978, 74)

Populating the stories in this way with real and known individuals may well have been a trait of Breton storytelling at this time. Besides bringing a certain playfulness into the storytelling performance, it invites us to understand these stories as having a rootedness in the here and now. Whether the story is true or not becomes irrelevant, but it insists that the struggles and challenges depicted are also those of the gathered community, building a sense of solidarity, constancy, and survival.

Even where stories were not personalized in this way, they can be understood as social and historical texts and the characters within them as responding to a particular set of social conditions. Indeed, to understand this better, we might adopt the language of the theater, as did Vladimir Propp in his seminal 1928 work *Morphology of the Folktale*, where he refers to the "characters" of the folktale as the "dramatis personae." In using this term, Propp acknowledges that these persons exist in relation to the story. They are *of* the drama and do not exist independently of it. This is different from the idea of the "character" associated with psychology that suggests someone who is self-determining and made up of complex mental and emotional capabilities, closely related to notions of "personality" (see Thomson 2000, 3–15). He also acknowledges them as *persons*; that is to say, they are not things or props but have a purpose, a role, or a function in progressing the narrative, rather than simply appearing in it. So, we might usefully consider the dramatis personae of the folktales as roles, purposeful persons who do things in the service of the story. In this sense, "Cadiou the Tailor," for example, is not a story about Cadiou the tailor, but a story in which Cadiou the tailor plays an important part. It is the story that is the prime unit of currency, not the persons within it.

This helps us to understand the stories as vehicles of social meaning, reflecting the daily struggles and aspirations of the people who told them. If we accept that the dramatis personae of the stories are playing roles within them, then we become less interested in them as individuals. Instead, they are seen as persons who operate within the social milieu of the story and their actions draw attention to it. If we take the side of the miller in the story "The Miller and His Seigneur" (which we inevitably must), it is not because we like him as a person. In fact, we know nothing about either the miller or the seigneur as individuals. We know the miller only in his role of exposing the injustices of the seigneurial system and getting the better of the seigneur who represents it. As Darnton says more generally of French folktales:

> By showing how life was lived, *terre à terre*, in the village and on the road, the tales helped orient the peasants. They mapped the ways of the world and demonstrated the folly of expecting anything more than cruelty from a cruel social order. (1984, 38)

Or, as Zipes says:

> He who has power can exercise his will, right wrongs, become
> ennobled, amass money and land, win women as prizes. This
> is why the people (*das Volk*) were the carriers of the tales: the
> *Märchen* catered for their aspirations and allowed them to
> believe that anyone could become a knight in shining armour
> or a lovely princess, and they also presented the stark realities
> of power politics without disguising the violence and brutal-
> ity of everyday life. (1992, 29)

Luzel himself also identified characteristic themes within the
stories he was collecting. He acknowledged the emancipatory
potential of the tales, placing "marvels and adventures" at the
heart of Breton traditions, which expressed "the desire to explore
the unknown and test the boundaries of terrestrial horizons"
(1995a, 11). This desire is expressed in the numerous supernatural
tales that Luzel collected, such as the tales of midnight washerwomen. He also drew attention to the role of animals within the
corpus of tales. These are often "transformed by the imagination
into intelligent beings" (11) and are nearly always benevolent to
human beings.

Perhaps most importantly, Luzel declared that Breton folktales
expressed "a tender compassion for the weak and wretched" (13).
This natural sympathy with the underdog was expressed by the
heroes of these stories, invariably the ordinary people of the
Breton villages, undergoing various trials and tribulations, living
by their wits and abilities to overcome all manner of evil and stupidity. However fantastical these stories may appear, they had their
place and purpose within the everyday world, articulating strategies
for daily survival in a world of few comforts.

Ultimately, these stories reflect communities that appreciate the narrative skills of individuals, that value charity as a Christian virtue, that are deeply religious but also antiestablishment and anticlerical, that have a strong relationship with nature and the environment, and that accept the supernatural as an everyday reality. A strong work ethic also runs through the stories: although work may be seen as a burden, there is a certain nobility attached to it. People are recognized for their hard work and skill, and work confers an identity and status on an individual. Those who stay out late, carousing and neglecting their duty to be up early for work in the morning, are punished. These communities lay great store by social justice, often a justice unattainable on earth.

Living as they did in circumstances where hunger was an everyday hazard, many storytellers, as Luzel noted, finished their stories with magnificent descriptions of extravagant banquets and feasting. Doing so drew attention to the social deprivations they suffered, as well as serving as an act of defiance, a rebellious cry of "We will survive!"

In this same spirit, the final word then should go to Barba Tassel, the beggarwoman, who undoubtedly experienced more deprivations firsthand than most. She concludes her telling of "The Cooking-Pot Man" with a great sense of playfulness and humor, drawing attention to the inequalities that exist within society and, no doubt, between herself and Luzel:[26]

> And there was a banquet so beautiful you could hardly believe it! If I could have gotten there myself, I think I would have dined better than I do at home, where I usually feast on fried spuds with potatoes.

■ The Tales

What follows are twenty-nine tales, representing a range of the types of story that Luzel collected from his informants in the latter half of the nineteenth century. In *Contes populaires de Basse-Bretagne* (1887), Luzel organized the stories according to mythological and other themes, although in other publications they are ordered in no discernible fashion. In *Veillées bretonnes* (2002) and *Nouvelles veillées bretonnes* (1995b), the stories are, naturally enough, presented in the order in which they were performed within the context of a specific performance event.

Much careful thought has been given to the order of the tales presented here. I considered following, to the extent possible, the chronological order in which they were collected. This seemed to be as logical a system as any but led to a rather disjointed reading experience. Another option would have been to group the stories by tale type or by common motif, placing stories next to others that bore similarities or were easily comparable. That would undoubtedly have been the correct system were this a work of comparative folklore. However, this is a book with performance at its core, so the stories have been arranged in a *possible* performative order, according to a performative logic.

In *Veillées bretonnes*, Luzel describes in some detail the storytelling, singing, and conversations that took place during five separate veillées. Each event is distinctive, evolving its shape as the evening unfolded, as one story is told in response to another or a request. In total, across the five evenings, Luzel records twenty-five stories, two resumées, and eight songs. In addition, there are internarrative conversations and discussions. Bearing in mind that this book contains no songs or resumées, but that the reader may engage in some reflection after each story (even if it is only reading the brief commentary),

I felt that the twenty-nine tales here are roughly equivalent, in terms of length, to the material contained in *Veillées bretonnes*. The tales in this volume, therefore, have been organized into five imagined veillées of approximately equal length and placed in an order in which they *could* be told, were they being performed in the context of such an event.

This has largely been a creative exercise and, as with all creative exercises, other equally legitimate choices could have been made. Yet, this collection is not entirely without its own system. Careful thought has been given as to which stories might work well to open or close an evening, which stories might naturally lead from one to another ("that reminds me of another story . . ."), which stories might make for a balanced program in terms of content, length, rhythm, and so on.

With the help of Patrick Ryan,[1] folklorist and professional storyteller, I have tried to bring a performer's perspective to the tales and, although some may disagree with my choices, there are few enough stories here for readers to be able to reorder them in any way they like. In any case, you may wish to read these stories sitting by the fire, with the storyteller's voice filling your head, and a full bowl of cider within arm's reach.

A Note on the Translations

The translator of any text faces challenges and the translator of folktales contends with yet others that are specific to the task in hand.[2] There is the task of rendering words from one language into another, although this is a gross simplification of what a translator does. Ideas, concepts, and ideologies are all embodied in language, so a translator is also translating from one culture to another, expressing one set of commonly accepted truths into a context where such truths may not be considered self-evident at all.

The translator of historical texts must also deal with a temporal shift. Darnton warns us that

> nothing is easier than to slip into the comfortable assumption that Europeans thought and felt two centuries ago just as we do today—allowing for the wigs and wooden shoes. We constantly need to be shaken out of a false sense of familiarity with the past, to be administered doses of cultural shock. (1984, 4)

For the folktale translator, the question of translating across historical periods is even more complicated. In this book, I have been working with texts that were written down and published by Luzel up to 150 years ago. However, even when Luzel was collecting those stories, they were already historical texts in themselves. While it is true that the tales reflect many of the social and economic realities facing the rural poor in Brittany in the second half of the nineteenth century, they are nevertheless set in a historical past. It is sometimes said that folktales take place in a timeless setting, but this is not true. They may take place in an undetermined historical period, but that is a different matter. Luzel's stories take place in a world familiar to his storytellers and their listeners, but it is also a "previous" world. There is little sense of the growing influence of the centralized French state, or of industrialization, or the mechanization of agriculture, which were already beginning to change things forever at the end of the nineteenth century. Instead, this is a world familiar enough (some of Luzel's storytellers say that the story took place one or two generations ago, or even within living memory), but it is also inhabited by local kings, princes, and princesses and displays elements of feudalism. This seems less an expression of misty-eyed nostalgia for a previous age than a means of relating the present to the past. As Joseph Russo says of the tales of Giuseppe Pitrè, "Life is seen as a continuing struggle to survive and get ahead, while at the same time it is a theater of extraordinary fantasies and amusing incidents, as well as a repository of traditional wisdom" (Zipes and Russo 2009a, 31). Something very similar could be said of the tales of François-Marie Luzel.

So, it may be more useful to talk about translation between contexts, rather than across historical periods and cultures. The translator is faced with a series of choices that allow for negotiation between these contexts. For example, in these tales I have decided against "anglicizing" the texts by translating names or specific cultural references. The title of "seigneur," which relates to the much-hated seigneurial system, a form of feudalism prevalent in prerevolutionary rural France, is so culturally specific that I have chosen not to translate it when it is used to describe somebody's social position—"*le* seigneur." When the term is used as a form of direct address, however, ("*mon* seigneur" or simply "seigneur"), I have chosen to variously translate this as "sire" or "my lord," unless the specific context seems to warrant the use of the French term.

The translator of folktales must inevitably navigate through a series of opposing positions, or at least a set of tensions: past and present; the agrarian and the postindustrial; change and constancy; the written and the spoken (and also what is read and what is heard); the schooled bourgeois and the skilled peasant; fantasy and (social and economic) reality; the respectable and the lewd; the printed and the performed; text and context. At the heart of this is the question of the status of the text and an understanding of it in terms of its relation to a performative mode of communication. In his preface to *Contes bretons*, Luzel provides us with some insight into his methods of collection and his emphasis on the importance of the accuracy of transcription:

I collect *everything in Breton*,[*] often interrupting the storyteller and making them repeat certain passages in order to reproduce the movement, the nuances, even the physiognomy of their narratives, with as rigorous a fidelity as possible. (1995a, 16)

As admirable as this may be, any claim that the published texts are faithful replications of the stories as told to Luzel starts to unravel fairly quickly. In the first instance, the stories were told in Breton. That Luzel chose to publish the stories he collected sometimes in Breton, sometimes in Breton and French side by side, and most often in French is important to bear in mind. Publishing in French was for Luzel a crucial part of his mission to get Breton culture more widely recognized and accepted, both within France and within the world of folklore scholarship. By publishing in French, Luzel could reach a much wider readership, beyond the confines of the Breton-speaking areas, and this would enable the tales to stand alongside the growing number of other significant folktale collections from around Europe. These stories, as published by Luzel, are therefore *already* translations and, moreover, they are translations of transcriptions. The original texts were spoken, performed in the instance and then gone forever, as ephemeral as any moment of performance.

The texts that appear in this volume are translations of translations of transcriptions of oral texts, following a five-step process of transmission from the nineteenth-century Breton storyteller to the twenty-first-century English-language reader:

Text 1: the story, spoken/performed to Luzel
Text 2: Luzel's transcription of the story into his notebook

[*] Luzel's italics.

Text 3: Luzel's creation of a "fair copy" of the transcription, correcting errors and making amendments to clarify the narrative

Text 4: Luzel's translation into French

Text 5: My translation into English

If one were to adopt a notion of authenticity that is essentially chronological and bestows greater status on the idea of an urtext—that is, an "original," authoritative text from which all future variants emanate—then we would be facing a pretty depressing state of affairs and all folktale translators would be facing an impossible task. We would then only be contributing toward the terminal decline and dilution of the texts we were working on.

However, if we are to take a performative approach, rather than a literary approach, to storytelling texts, where fluidity of text is the norm and where the retelling of stories, including in different languages and across various media, is the usual process of dissemination, then we can have more confidence in the "authenticity" of both Luzel's texts and these translations. "A fairy tale," as Marina Warner asserts, "keeps on the move between written and spoken versions and back again, between print and performance and, since the coming of mass media, between page and screen; this peripatetic character confirms the sense that the fairy tale genre . . . is as fluid as a conversation taking place over the centuries" (2014, 44). In this sense, no singular telling is more authentic than another, as each telling is a response to a particular moment. The process of transmission as described above mimics the process of one storyteller passing on the story to another, an attempt to remain as faithful as possible to the previously heard version while also reinventing the story for a particular audience and set of circumstances. The "fidelity," therefore, is not so much to the notion of a fixed text, frozen in time, but to a living tradition of storytelling performance.

My aim has been to render texts that are both readable and performable, in an idiom that is familiar to the modern reader but does not wear that idiom so heavily that the style of the original teller is obscured. The texts are intended to be easily taken off the page and back into oral performance.

The Notes about the Tales

Each story is accompanied by a brief commentary to provide additional context to its collection and performance, and to offer an occasional observation on the text, intended to enhance reading of the stories. I have also provided a reference to the tale type to which each story conforms, where appropriate, for those readers interested in making further comparative study. For this, I have relied greatly on Hans-Jörg Uther's impressive three-volume updating of the Aarne-Thompson typology, *The Types of International Folktales: A Classification and Bibliography* (2011). Deriving as it does from the Finnish School of collection, classification, and comparison, the compendium sits uneasily within a study that argues for the treatment of folktales as performance texts, defying easy and stable classification. Nevertheless, it remains for me an invaluable reference work for textual comparison, and readers who long for a fuller list of comparative texts would be well advised to consult it. For those interested in comparisons between the tales collected by Luzel and the wider corpus of French folktales, I have referred to Paul Delarue and Marie-Louise Tenèze's multivolume *Le conte populaire français*, whose work Josiane Bru has extended over a number of years, including the recent addition of a supplement (2017). Where particular tale types have been subject to more extensive analysis, I have also provided some references to this effect.

First Veillée

■ 1. Cadiou the Tailor

Told by Barba Tassel, Plouaret, December 1868

Cadiou, known as Cadiou c'hoéon, was (with all due respect) a tailor by trade. He lived in the village of Parc-ann-Itron, in Plouaret, about one kilometer from the town. Each morning, he went out working around the farms and the big country houses and, as he was unmarried, he made a good living from his needle.

One day, he took it into his head to go to the September fair on the hillside at Bré, one of the best fairs in the country. He changed into his Sunday best and cheerfully set off.

After he had been all through the fair, having seen the bulls, the horses, the cows, the pigs, and having gone and prayed to Monseigneur Saint-Hervé in his church on the top of the hill, he also wanted to play the young man about town a little bit, even though he was already in his forties. He loved women from the bottom of his heart.

In the field where the dances were taking place, he noticed a beautiful young woman with cheeks as red as little apples, black hair, and bright eyes. "She's the one for me," he said to himself right away. "I shall ask her if she would like to have a look around the fair with me."

Nothing could have pleased the young woman more. After they had explored all corners and danced many different dances, Cadiou said to his partner, "Now, my pretty thing, I would like to buy you a little something from the fair to thank you for your company." And Cadiou bought her a sou's worth of almonds.

The young woman, a little put out by her gentleman's generosity, thought to herself, "I will return you the favor in due course."

So, they walked around the church two or three times, holding each other by their little fingers, in the way courting couples do,

after which Cadiou said, "The sun is starting to go down and my
house is a long way from here."

"Then come along and I will buy you a little something from the
fair," the young woman said to him. And she led him to the stall of
a traveling haberdasher.

"Choose whatever you like," she added, "as long as it costs no more than one sou."

Cadiou chose a large needle and then, tipping his hat to the young woman, said, "And now I bid you farewell, my dear pretty thing, as the sun is setting and I live far away."

"I too shall go home," she replied, "and as you are from Plouaret and I am from Louargat, we will be taking the same road for a while and you will even pass by the door of my father's house, which is at the foot of the hill."

They went down the hill together. The young woman, having reached her father's house, an old tumbledown manor house, said to her companion, "This is my father's house. Come in for a while, light your pipe and have a taste of our cider."

Several compliments later, Cadiou went into the house. There he saw a large old man sitting in a large armchair next to the fire with his legs stretched out over the fireplace. And his legs were so long that they reached the other side of the fireplace, which was itself enormous. At first, he stood still in astonishment. Never before had he seen anything quite like it.

"Is that you coming home, my darling daughter?" said the old man when he heard the door opening.

"Yes, Father, I'm not too late, am I?"

"And as usual you have not come back alone. What a good girl you are. We shall eat well tonight, it seems."

"No, dear father, this is not for this evening but for tomorrow morning."

"Very well, for tomorrow morning then, as you wish, my daughter, but go and fetch me my scythe so that I can slaughter him right away in case he escapes during the night."

"I'll go and get it for you, Father."

Cadiou, on hearing this conversation, stood still as a stone pillar, but as the young woman opened the door, he hurled himself outside and ran.

"Release the dogs!" cried the old man. And the young woman released the dogs, enormous bulldogs that started barking like raging demons.

Fortunately, Cadiou had a good head start and he ran across the fields toward the river Léguer, thinking he would be safe if he put the river between himself and the dogs. Just as he entered the water, one of the dogs grabbed hold of one of his trouser legs and it was then left dangling in its mouth. But Cadiou was now safe because the old man's territory stopped at the river.

The poor tailor was overcome with tiredness and fear. So, as he emerged from the water, he stretched himself out on the grass and immediately fell asleep.

When he woke up, it was the middle of the night and he noticed there were haystacks all around him, so he burrowed himself down into one of them to wait for the morning without getting cold.

A little while later, he was astonished to hear the following words being spoken just by the haystack in which he was hiding.

"This is the best haystack. Let's take this one."

They were hay thieves and they started to lift the haystack up with iron forks in order to carry it away. Poor Cadiou was completely of two minds. "If I stay here," he said to himself, "they are going to injure me with their forks, but if I try to run away, they're sure to catch me and perhaps kill me to stop me from turning them in. Oh God, what am I to do?"

At that moment, he felt the cold iron of one of the forks scrape against his right thigh and he left his hiding place and started to run. But, alas, he was quickly caught.

"Well, well," said the robbers, recognizing him. "If it isn't Cadiou the tailor. What are we going to do with him?"

"Let's kill him right away so that he can't turn us in," said one of them.

"No," said another. "We can easily get rid of him without troubling our consciences with such a great crime."

"How?"

"Like this. We'll stretch him out on his back, secure him by his arms and legs to the ground with wooden stakes, and leave him for the wolves to come and eat him up. For sure they'll be along in no time and they'll soon deal with him."

"That's right. Let's do that," said the others.

Poor Cadiou wept and pleaded, gave his word that he would never tell anybody what he had witnessed that night, but they wouldn't listen to him. The thieves tied him to the ground, as they said they would, and then they left, taking the haystack with them.

Soon afterward, a she-wolf appeared in the meadow. She came up to Cadiou, sniffed him, sat down on his chest, and started to howl, to call her young ones.

"Oh God, this is the end for me," thought Cadiou. He could feel the wolf's tail on his face, so he bit into it. The she-wolf let out a cry and tried to run away, but Cadiou bit down with all his might and wouldn't let go until the animal, in her efforts to get away, managed to pull the stakes that held the tailor down out of the earth. And then he let go and the she-wolf went away without harming him.

Cadiou, too, couldn't get away from the place quickly enough and he didn't stop until he came to a little thatched house made of cob. He knocked at the door but nobody answered, so he gave a push on the wicker gate that blocked the entrance to the house. It easily gave way and he saw at the back of the house a little old woman with a beard and long black teeth, busily making crêpes.

"Good evening, grandmother," he said to her.

"What do you want, my boy?" replied the old woman.

"Some shelter until morning, if you would be so kind."

"Christians are never welcome here, my child. I have three sons who are giants who will soon arrive home starving to death, and if they find you in the house, they're sure to eat you up."

"You're frightening me, grandmother. But still, where could I rest until morning? If only you knew everything that has happened to me since sunset!"

And he told her of his adventures.

"I feel sorry for you, my child. Very well, stay. I know how to make sure that they won't do you any harm. I shall tell them that you are my nephew and their cousin, one of my brother's sons. Now, eat some crêpes while we're waiting." And Cadiou set about eating the crêpes. But soon he heard a great noise in the chimney, like that of an owl: "Hoo! Hoo! Hoo!"

"What's that, grandmother?" he asked, shaking with fear.

"It is my son, January, coming for his supper."

And immediately from out of the chimney and into the cottage appeared an old man with a long white beard, blowing on his hands and crying, "Hoo! Hoo! Hoo! I'm starving to death, Mother. Give me something to eat. Quickly now, hurry up!"

"Yes, my boy, here are some lovely crêpes. Eat as many as you like."

And he started to eat. Great piles of crêpes disappeared into his belly, as if it were a bottomless pit. Once the edge had been taken off his hunger, he looked up, sniffed the air, and cried out, "I smell a Christian and I want to eat him up!"

"Calm down, my son, calm down, and eat your dinner quietly," the old woman said to him. "You know full well that Christians never come here."

January gobbled up several more dozen crêpes and then said once more, "I smell a Christian, Mother, and I'm going to have to eat him up!"

And he got up from the table to search the house. Cadiou had hidden himself under the table and wished he were far away.

"Sit down by the fire, my son, and behave yourself. My brother's son, your cousin, has come to see me and I won't have you frightening him like that or talking about eating him up. He is hiding under the table and daren't come out after hearing you behaving like a savage. I'm going to introduce you to each other, but don't do him any harm because, and I repeat, he is my nephew and your cousin."

The old woman then took Cadiou by the hand and led him out of his hiding place, saying to him, "Come on, my child, come and meet your cousin January and don't be afraid of him, he's not as bad as he looks."

"If this is my uncle's son and my cousin," said January, "I certainly won't harm him. Why didn't you tell me this before?" And Cadiou and January became friends, just as cousins should be.

A little while later, the old woman's other two sons, February and March, arrived, one after the other, both of them as starving as January and both wanting to eat up Cadiou.

Their mother calmed them both down and fooled them in the same way as January and all four became great friends and sat chatting quietly by the fire, waiting for daybreak. Meanwhile, Cadiou was still nervous in the company of cousins such as these and he was just waiting for the opportunity to get rid of them and leave.

"If you wish, cousins," he said to them, "we could have a game of something to pass the time."

"Yes, cousin, let's have a game of something to pass the time."

"Would you like me to teach you 'Past and Future'?"

"Yes, cousin, teach us 'Past and Future.'"

Cadiou took two clubs and placed them on the floor in the shape of a cross and said, "Cousins, each of you sit down on the end of one of the sticks and my aunt should sit down on one end too in the same way, as we need four people to play the game." The mother and her three sons sat down on the four ends of the sticks.

"That's good," said Cadiou. "Now, I'm going outside for a bit to look at the stars and when I come back, I'll teach you how to tell the past and the future. But don't move and stay like that."

Cadiou left and started running in the direction of Plouaret! As he wasn't coming back, the old woman and her sons began to get bored with sitting in this position.

"January, go and tell him to get a move on," the old woman said to her eldest son. "I can't stay like this for much longer."

January got up and went out, but although he searched high and low and called out Cadiou's name, he couldn't see his cousin anywhere. And he went back inside and said, "We've been had! The rascal has cleared off! But let's run after him and if we catch him, we'll teach him not to make fools of us."

So, off they went, like three mad devils, roaring and tearing down any trees and upturning any houses that got in their way. Cadiou heard them coming and, seized with fear, said to himself, "They're coming! Where can I hide?"

Then he noticed some beehives in the garden of a house, the largest of which was empty and lying on its side, so he climbed inside it and hid there. The old woman's sons evidently loved honey because when they saw the hives, they cried out, "Oh, look at those beautiful beehives." And they gave up their pursuit. "Let's take them away," they added.

And each of them took three hives. March took the one that Cadiou was curled up inside. "I've got a real heavy one here, lads," he said to his brothers. "There must be plenty of honey inside it!"

Meanwhile, Cadiou took out of its cover the long needle that the giant's daughter had bought for him at the fair and he stabbed March in the back.

"Ouch!" he cried. "These bees ain't half stinging!"

Cadiou carried on using his needle to taunt March until he couldn't hold onto the hive any longer and threw it into a pond by the side of the road. Cadiou very nearly drowned inside the hive as it sank into the mud, but he managed to wriggle out of it. He was in such a state that he had to take off all his clothes, even his shirt, so that he could wash his clothes. He hung them out to dry on a bush and then went into the water to do the same thing to himself. The local miller, who had risen early to fetch the water, happened to pass by at this very moment and, seeing clothes apparently abandoned there, carried them away.

When Cadiou climbed out of the water, he went to the bush where he had hung out his clothes to dry, but they were nowhere to be found. He was quite astonished and couldn't understand who might have taken them. He was so embarrassed to find himself like this, completely naked—all the more so because it was now quite light. He started to run, hoping to reach home before he could be recognized by any of the artisans and journeymen who were on their way to work.

He had to cross the town square and, just as he was passing, an old woman by the name of Guyona Ar Soaz opened her door and came out. Cadiou quickly jumped over the wall into the yard of Iouenn Thépaut the carpenter and hid himself among the planks and other timber that were in one corner.

Now, the church in Plouaret was in need of a new statue of Saint Crépin, as the old one was full of woodworm and crumbling to dust. The day before, Iouenn Thépaut had been to Kerminic'hi with the priest to pick up a statue of Saint Isidore, which had been sitting in an attic ever since the chapel there had fallen into ruins. The poor saint had only lost his nose and a few fingers and Iouenn Thépaut had been charged by the priest with replacing them and restoring old Saint Isidore with a new coat of paint in such a way that he would make an excellent Saint Crépin. That morning, he rose early and went out into the yard to look for some wood to repair the saint's missing bits.

Imagine his astonishment when he found a man, totally naked, among his wood. At first, he was frightened, but then he pulled himself together. "What are you doing there?" No answer. Cadiou stood there as if he were made of wood.

"Jesus!" said Thépaut, who was a simple man. "Perhaps this is a statue of Saint Crépin, sent by God to replace the old one!"

And he went to find the priest and said to him, "It's a miracle, Father! God has sent us a new Saint Crépin! Come quickly and see for yourself!" And the priest followed the carpenter.

He greeted the saint and asked him where he had come from. No answer. He touched his hand. It was cold, just like a wooden saint! "There is no doubt," he said, "that this is certainly a miracle." He ordered the bells to be rung to summon the parishioners so that the new saint could be carried to the church with due solemnity.

And when the bells were pealing out with full force, the parishioners came running from all corners and Cadiou was triumphantly carried to the church and placed in the recess reserved for Saint Crépin. The news spread quickly throughout the parish and the parishioners flocked to see the saint.

"Oh, what a beautiful saint!" everybody cried. "What clear eyes he has, as if he were alive!"

A woman came along with a lighted candle and, as there was no candle holder, she placed the candle between the toes of the new saint. When the candle was almost completely burned through, Cadiou felt his foot burning, jumped down from his alcove, and, to the great astonishment of those present, ran out of the church. He ran through the town, as fast as lightning, and nobody knew what became of him.

Some said he had returned to Heaven. Others said he was a devil, not a saint at all. He quite simply returned home without meeting a soul and went straight to bed.

All this is true because my grandmother knew Cadiou, known as Cadiou c'hoéon, and I learned the story from her.

■ 2. The Priest of Saint Gily

Told in Breton by Catherine Stéphan, dressmaker, Plouaret,
1 March 1892

Long ago, before the great Revolution, there was a priest who ministered at the chapel of Saint Gily.*

Iouenn Loho, a poor horse dealer who traveled to all the country markets and never made a fortune, lived in the village of Kerouez, close to the chapel. One day his wife, Godic Ann Thao, said to him, "The priest has a lovely, young, nicely fattened cow that would make an excellent beef broth. Soon there'll be nothing left in the pantry—no lard, no salt beef. Just think about it, Iouenn."

Iouenn Loho did not reply for the time being, but all night long he thought about what his wife had said. On the third night, he got up about one or two o'clock in the morning and stole the priest's cow from its stable. He slaughtered it right away, skinned it, cut it up, salted it down, and put it in the storehouse. This was all done in the greatest secrecy without the priest or the neighbors knowing anything about it.

The swindled priest complained about it in his sermon the following Sunday and invited the guilty party to return his cow at night, so as not to be seen, and he promised forgiveness and

* Luzel's note: The chapel of Saint Gily, which is the place in question here, is to be found in the commune of Plouaret in the village of Kerouez.

anonymity. But it was in vain. The cow did not return and Iouenn and Godic now dined on fine soup and good salt meat every day and grew fatter and thrived.

Iouenn always had some worn-out old nag or some half-starved old cow to take to market and which his son, Laouic, a child of seven or eight years, would take out to graze along the roads and across the barren fields. Laouic was so happy with the food that his mother was serving them up these days that he sang away at the top of his voice as he watched over the half-starved cow along the roads around Kerouez:

> Father stole the priest's cow
> And I have meat and fine soup now
> Red meat! Red meat!

One day, he was singing this as he leaned against an embankment in the shade of a flowering gorse bush, when the priest came passing by and stopped, astonished to hear him. Then he went up to him and said, "You are a good singer, my child. Who taught you such a pretty song?"

"Nobody. I made it up myself," replied Laouic.

"Sing it again."

And Laouic repeated:

> Father stole the priest's cow
> And I have meat and fine soup now
> Red meat! Red meat!

"Very good, my child! Look, here are ten sous for having taught me the song and if you will come to mass tomorrow morning (it was a Saturday) and climb up into the pulpit and sing your song, exactly as you have sung it just now, I will give you another ten sous. Then I will give you a dinner at the clergy house and I will even give you coffee and some lovely apples to fill your pockets." The child promised and the priest went on his way.

As the sun went down, Laouic arrived home with his cow and gave the ten sous to his mother.

"Where did you get this money from?" Godic asked him, astonished.

"The priest gave it to me because I sang him a song that I made up."

"And what song was this? Come on, sing it for me as well."

And Laouic sang once more:

> Father stole the priest's cow
> And I have meat and fine soup now
> Red meat! Red meat!

"What? You sang *that* to the priest?"

"Yes. Have I done something wrong?"

"Something wrong? You imbecile! That would be enough to send your father to prison. Just wait until your father gets home! He'll box your ears and thrash you with his stick . . . and what did the priest say to you?"

"He seemed very happy and gave me ten sous and promised me ten more and a good dinner at the clergy house if I would sing my song tomorrow in church from the pulpit at morning mass."

"And you agreed?"

"Of course."

Godic was quite distraught and chided her son and was weeping and wailing when Iouenn arrived home. "What is the matter," he asked her in astonishment, "and why are you crying like that?"

"Why? I have good reason. To think that this idiot of a child has been passing the time by singing this around the streets:

> Father stole the priest's cow
> And I have meat and fine soup now
> Red meat! Red meat!

And then along came the priest, who stopped to listen."

"Really? And what did the priest say?"

"He gave the child ten sous and said that if he would sing the song again tomorrow in the church at mass from the pulpit, he would give him another ten sous and a good dinner at the clergy house."

"And Laouic promised?"

"Yes, he promised."

"He has done well. Now, calm down and don't worry. I know how to get out of this one. He who laughs last, laughs longest." And he turned to his son. "I am going to teach you another song, my child, for you to sing tomorrow in the church instead of the one the priest asked you to sing. Now, listen carefully:

> When my father goes away
> The priest comes round ours to stay.

Have you got that? Repeat it back to me."

And the child sang back:

> When my father goes away
> The priest comes round ours to stay.

"That's it! Very good! So, that is what you must sing from the pulpit, when the priest asks you to sing, and not the other song. And be careful not to forget or to sing the wrong song."

"Oh, I won't forget and I won't sing the wrong song."

The following morning, Iouenn made Laouic repeat the song again and they all went off to mass. Laouic went straight to the clergy house and his father met up with a group of other folks who were passing the time.

The priest was waiting for the child. He made him sing his song, just to be sure that he hadn't forgotten it, then he gave him ten sous, as promised, and a cup of milky coffee and then they went off to the church together.

The time arrived and the congregation filled the church. The priest approached the altar and began the mass as usual. The moment of the sermon arrived and he approached the pulpit, accompanied by Iouenn Loho's son, which amazed everyone.

What did this mean?

Everyone waited with bated breath.

And so, the priest began: "My dear brothers and sisters, you are all surprised to see this child with me in the pulpit. I have brought him here because he has something true to tell you. Listen well and believe what he is going to tell you, because, as I have said often enough, only the truth is spoken from this pulpit."

And then, turning to the child, he said, "Go on then, my child. Sing them your little song." And Laouic sang, without hesitation:

When my father goes away
The priest comes round ours to stay.

The astonishment of the congregation was something to behold, as was that of the priest, who, confused, said to the child, "But what is that you are singing, my child? That's not right. Sing what you sang to me yesterday. Have you forgotten? Listen ... Father st—"

"No, no," Laouic quickly interrupted. And he repeated:

> When my father goes away
> The priest comes round ours to stay.

"Do not believe a word that this single-minded child says, my dear brethren ..."

But Laouic carried on singing the verse at the top of his voice, without a care for the priest's denials and desperate gestures, as he shouted at him, "You're lying! You're lying! Who paid you to lie like this? Don't listen to what he says, my dear brethren, don't believe a word of it; he's out of his mind!"

The congregation, initially struck dumb with shock, were soon laughing with their mouths wide open and somebody raised his voice and said, "But Father, you started by assuring us that everything the child was going to say was true and that nothing but the truth was ever spoken from the pulpit of truth!"

The poor priest, quite bewildered and losing his mind, came down from the pulpit to the jeers of those assembled and ran away to hide in the clergy house without concluding the mass.

Iouenn Loho followed him and addressed him angrily, "Father, you know full well the seriousness of the scandal you have just unleashed. I must be compensated, otherwise I will lodge a complaint with the judge."

"But the child was fibbing," replied the priest, "and somebody has put him up to it."

"First of all," replied Iouenn, "you told us that everything that was going to be said was absolutely true and that nothing but the truth was spoken from your pulpit."

"Very well! Keep your voice down! I'll give you dinner, a large glass of brandy, and six livres to settle the matter."

"No, I'm not satisfied with that deal."

"What do you want then?"

"I want one hundred silver crowns and not a penny less."

"One hundred crowns! But where am I supposed to get that kind of money? I don't even earn that much in a whole year! I'll give you fifty crowns. That's all the money I have and that's all there is to it!"

"No, I want one hundred crowns or I will go to the judge and you know that I have no shortage of witnesses."

The poor priest, who was afraid of appearing before the judge more than anything else, finally handed over the one hundred crowns.

Iouenn treated all his friends to unlimited cider and mead all evening and the next day too, as the taverns were filled with their singing and their laughter. He also bought a fine cow that he showed off at the fairs, which he continued to visit.

■ 3. The Purveyor of Paradise

Told by Barba Tassel, Plouaret, n.d.

Once upon a time there lived a countrywoman who was comfortably off and whose husband had died about a month before. She had a son who was a priest and he would often visit her and he stabled his horse at her place.

One Wednesday afternoon, she was alone in the house eating hot pancakes with milk and she said, "Oh, my poor husband, where are you now? Only a month ago you were sitting opposite me eating hot pancakes—how you loved hot pancakes! I think you must

be in Heaven because you were a God-fearing and God-loving
Christian. Still, I would pay a tidy sum to be sure that you were happy."

And the poor woman wept and her tears fell into the bowl of
milk that was in front of her. A rogue, who was passing by, was listen-

ing behind the door and as he heard these words, an idea came to him for playing a trick on the poor widow. He opened the door, quickly stepped into the house, pretended to be out of breath—as if he had been running a long way—and said, "Good day, my dear lady."

"Good day, dear sir. What can I do for you?"

"I am the purveyor of Paradise and I have come to find you on behalf of your husband."

"On behalf of my husband, my God! I never stop thinking of him, day or night. Tell me about him. He has a good place in Heaven, doesn't he?"

"He is not yet in Heaven, my dear lady. But let me reassure you because he is well on the way and not very far from there."

"But what does the dear man need to get in?"

"Not very much at all—three hundred silver crowns, half a dozen fine linen shirts, and a bottle of vintage wine."

"Really?! Three hundred crowns is a lot of money, but there is nothing in this house that I would not give to help my dear husband reach Heaven!" And the widow went to the cupboard and counted out three hundred crowns, put them into a purse, and gave them to the purveyor of Paradise. Then she also gave him six fine linen shirts and a bottle of vintage wine, saying, "Take these, my good man, and deliver them as quickly as possible to my poor husband and tell him that it will not be long before I join him."

The purveyor of Paradise took the money, the shirts, and the wine and said, "Many thanks on behalf of your husband, my dear woman. Now he is certain to go to Heaven right away."

And he was just heading toward the door when the widow called after him and said, "Wait! Wait a moment and I'll give you some hot pancakes as well. How my husband loves hot pancakes!" And she gave him half a dozen pancakes, wrapped up in a white cloth. Then, seeing as he was a little loaded down with everything and that it would slow him on his journey, she said, "So that you can travel more quickly and not keep my dear husband waiting, take his horse from the stable, climb onto his back, and go quickly."

"My word, what a good idea!" said the rogue. And he took the horse out of the stable, saddled it up, climbed onto its back, and galloped away.

So, the widow was filled with happiness and joy, thinking that her husband would be entering Heaven at any moment. And when her son, the priest, arrived at the house a little later, he was astonished to hear her singing, "Tra la la! Tra la la!"

"What on earth has happened, Mother, to make you so happy?" he asked her.

"Haven't you heard the news? Rejoice and sing along with me for your father has gone to Heaven!"

"Well, I hope so, Mother, because my father was an honest and God-fearing man."

"Yes, but in spite of all that he would still be waiting to get in, if I hadn't given the necessary three hundred crowns, half a dozen fine linen shirts, and a bottle of vintage wine."

"What? What? What are you talking about, Mother?"

And she told him the whole story.

"Alas, my poor mother, you have been taken in by some trickster! Which way did he go?"

"He went off to the right. In the direction of Heaven."

The young priest ran to the stable and climbed onto his horse, which was much quicker than his father's and set off at full gallop. It wasn't long before he spied the purveyor of Paradise on the road ahead of him. But the rogue, hearing a horse galloping up behind him, turned his head and, upon seeing the priest, said to himself, "I'll be caught if I stay on the road because the priest's horse is much faster than mine."

So, he got down off the horse and went into a field of broom by the side of the road. The priest ran after him, leaving his horse by the side of the road. But since the broom had grown tall and thick, he couldn't see the man he was after and, as he searched, the man came back out onto the road, climbed onto the priest's horse, and set off, leaving him the other horse.

When the priest had been all over the field without finding anyone, he also went back to the road. But when he saw his father's old horse there all by itself, while the other was gone, he said to himself, "The rascal has tricked me as well! It's no use, my chasing after him now on this old nag." And so, he climbed up onto his father's old horse and slowly returned to the house. When his mother saw him returning, she said, "Well, my son?"

"Ah well, Mother. I caught up with him easily enough and I gave him my horse instead so that he could travel more quickly and Father would not be kept waiting too long." He did not want to admit that he had also been fooled, like his mother.

"You have done well, my son. Your father is surely now with God in Heaven!"

And she started to sing once more, "Tra la la! Tra la la!"

But her son was not so happy.

■ 4. The Just Man

Told by J. or P. Corvez (Luzel is unsure about the first name of the teller, but elsewhere refers to him as "Pierre") at Plourin, near Morlaix, 1876

There was once a poor man whose wife had recently given birth to a son. He wanted his son to have a godfather who was a just man and so he set off to look for one. As he was walking along, his stick in hand, he soon met a stranger who had a very honest look and who asked him, "Where are you going, my good man?"

"I am looking for a godfather for my newborn son."

"I see! Well, will I do? I would be happy to oblige, if you like."

"But I am looking for a just man."

"Ah, well then, you could not choose better. I am your man!"

"But who are you?"

"I am God."

"You? God? Just? No, no! Everywhere I go, all over, I hear people complaining about you."

"Really? Why is that? Do tell me. Please."

"Why? For thousands upon thousands of different reasons. For a start, there are some people you made weak, deformed, or sickly, while there are some who are strong and healthy but no more worthy than the others. And then there are those honest folk—I know many—who though they work like dogs, remain poor and wretched, while their neighbors, the idlers and the loafers, the good-for-nothings. . . . No, look here, you're not going to be godfather to my son. Goodbye!" And our fellow went on his way, muttering to himself.

A little farther on, he met an old man with a long white beard.

"Where are you going, my good man?" the old man asked him.

"To find a godfather for my newborn son."

"I would happily be his godfather, if you like. How does that sound?"

"Well, I have to tell you first of all that I want my son's godfather to be a just man."

"A just man? Well, I think I am the one!"

"Who are you, then?"

"Saint Peter."

"The gatekeeper of Heaven? The one who has the keys?"

"Yes, the very same."

"I see. But you are not just! Not at all!"

"Me? Not just?" replied Saint Peter, slightly annoyed. "And why not, if you please, my good man?"

"Why not? I'll be happy to tell you. For any trifling weakness, despite poverty and suffering, I am told that you refuse entry to honest folk, long-suffering men, like me. And why? Because after working hard all week long, they might drink one bottle of cider too many on a Sunday. And shall I tell you something else? You are the Prince of the Apostles, the Head of the Church, are you not?"

Saint Peter nodded his head in agreement.

"Well then. In your church, it is the same as everywhere else. Money counts for everything and the rich man comes before the poor man. No, you will not be my son's godfather either. Goodbye!" And he continued on his way, all the while muttering to himself.

Then he met a shifty-looking character who carried a large scythe over his shoulder, like a farmhand on his way to work.

"Where are you going, my good man?" he too asked.

"To look for a godfather for my newborn son."

"Would you like me to be the godfather?"

"First of all, I must tell you that I am looking for a just man."

"A just man! You won't find anyone more honest than me."

"That's what they all say! Who are you, then?"

"I am Death!"

"Ah yes indeed, you are truly just. You show no favoritism to anyone and you carry out your work properly. Rich and poor, noble and serf, king and subject, young and old, weak and strong . . . you come calling for them all when their time has come, without being persuaded or distracted by their tears, menaces, prayers, or gold. Yes, you are truly just and you will be my son's godfather. Come with me!" And so, the man returned to his cottage, accompanied by the godfather he had chosen for his son.

Death held the child at the baptism ceremony and afterward there was a modest meal at the poor man's cottage, where, as a special treat, there was cider and white bread. Before he went on his way, the godfather said to his friend, "You and your wife are good, decent people. But you are very poor. Since you have chosen me to be godfather to your son, I want to show you my gratitude by letting you in on a secret that will make you a lot of money. You, my friend, will become a doctor and this is what you must do. When you are called upon to visit sick people, if you see me standing at the head of the bed, then you can declare that you will save them and you can give them whatever medicine you want, even just water, if you wish, and they will always recover. On the other hand, if you see me with my scythe at the foot of the bed, then there is nothing to be done and the patients will certainly die, no matter what you do to try to save them."

And so, our man pretended to be a doctor, putting into practice his friend Death's system and he was always able to predict with absolute certainty whether his patients would live or die. Because he was never wrong and his medicines were inexpensive—he only ever gave his patients water, whatever their ailment—he was in great demand and gradually became rich. Meanwhile, whenever Death happened to be passing by from time to time, he always called in to see his godson and to have a chat with his friend.

The child grew into a fine young man whereas the doctor grew older and weaker with each day.

One day, Death said to him, "I always come and see you, whenever I'm passing by, yet you have never once visited me. You must come and see me so that I can repay your hospitality and you can see where I live."

"That would always be too soon, my friend," replied the doctor, "since I know that if ever anyone pays you a visit, it's rather difficult for them to come back."

"You don't need to worry about that, because I will never take you away before your time. You know that I am a most just man."

And so, one night the doctor left to pay his friend a visit. For a long time they traveled together, up hill and down dale, crossing arid plains, through forests, across rivers, and through countryside that was quite unfamiliar to the doctor. At last, Death stopped in front of an old castle, surrounded by high walls, in the middle of a dark forest and said to his friend, "Here we are."

They went in. At first, the lord of this dismal castle treated his guest magnificently and then, after they had left the table, he led him into an enormous hall where millions of candles of all shapes and sizes—long, medium, and short—were burning. Some had a long time to burn, others less so; some burned brightly, some burned dimly. At first, our man stood before this sight completely astonished, dazzled and unable to speak. Then, when he could speak, he asked, "My friend, what are all these lights?"

"They are the lights of life, my friend."

"The lights of life? What are they?"

"Each human being currently alive on the earth has a candle here, to which their life is attached."

"But some are long, some medium-sized, some short, some burning brightly, some beginning to fade, and some almost gone out. Why is that?"

"It is just like the lives of human beings. Some have only just begun to burn. Others are at full strength and shining at their strongest. Others are weak and flickering. Others have nearly gone out at last."

"There is one that is long and tall!"

"That belongs to a child who has just been born."

"And this one is burning brightly and beautifully."

"That belongs to a man in the prime of his life!"

"And this one is about to go out—there's little left of it."

"That is an old man who is dying."

"And mine? Where is that one? I would like to see it."

"It is right there, next to you."

"This one? Ah, my God, it is almost completely finished! It is about to go out!"

"Yes, you have only three more days to live!"

"What did you say? Only three more days? But you are my friend and you're in charge here. Couldn't you make my candle burn a bit longer? You could perhaps take a bit of wax from the one next to it, as it's really quite long, and just add it to mine?"

"The long one next to yours belongs to your son and if I did what you ask, I would no longer be the just man you were looking for."

"You're right," replied the doctor, resigning himself to his fate and heaving a great sigh. And he returned home, put his affairs in order, sent for the parish priest, and died three days later, just as his friend Death had predicted.

■ 5. The Light-Fingered Cow

Told by J.-M. Le Jean, 1865

An old judge had a wife who was both young and rather pretty. He also had a maid by the name of Jeanne and a manservant. The manservant was a handsome lad and was popular with the two women. He was called Alanic.

One day, the judge had to go away on a rather long journey.

When the evening came and it was time to go to bed, his wife said to the maid, "I am not used to sleeping alone and I am frightened. Come and sleep with me while my husband is away."

"Gladly," replied the maid.

So, the two women were in the same bed. But they had no sooner put out the candle when they heard a noise in the attic above them. No doubt it was the cats and the rats waging war—or it might equally have been Alanic, who was cooking up a scheme of his own.

The two women were frightened and they cuddled up to each other. But rather than calming down, the noise just got louder and the judge's wife, seized with fear, said to the maid, "Good Lord Jesus! I'm going to die of fright if this carries on. What shall we do?"

"Should we ask Alanic to come?" asked the servant.

"Do you think that's a good idea? What if he doesn't behave himself?"

"Oh, the two of us will get the better of him, if he doesn't show us due respect."

"Very well, go and tell him to come."

And the maid went to fetch Alanic, who was sleeping in the stable. He came quickly.

"Jesus, Alanic," the judge's wife said to him, "there are definitely ghosts in the house tonight and we'll die of fright if we have to stay here alone."

"I shall stay with you," replied Alanic, "and you will be safe while I'm here with you. I'm not afraid of any ghosts."

"Very well, Alanic, as it's cold, you can come into bed between us. But you'll have to behave, do you hear?"

"I will give you the respect due to you, madam."

"Yes, and just to be absolutely sure, you must let us tie up your old nag with a ribbon."

"He's not at all naughty, I assure you."

"Oh, we don't want to take any chances."

"Very well, tie it up, if you wish, madam. He'll let you do it if I tell him to."

Once Alanic had been sorted out in the way just described, he lay down in between the two women and as there were no more noises to be heard from the attic, he pretended to be asleep and started to snore.

Meanwhile, the two women were not asleep either and just tossed and turned in bed.

"Jeanne," said the mistress to the maid. "Have a look and see if his old nag is still tied up." And the maid explored the area with her hand and said, "The old nag is still tied up, madam."

"Very well. Untie it and let's see what happens." The servant did as she was told.

But the old nag, as soon as it was untied and free, started fooling around, plundering to the left and to the right, and the two women, who at first offered a token resistance, gave in easily. This went on for three or four days, after which the judge returned from his journey and everything returned to normal.

Meanwhile, after a few months, the maid and the mistress both started to display a suspicious stoutness that grew with each day. At last, it came to a point when the judge could no longer harbor any doubts. He flew into a great rage and said to the two women, "Who is to blame here, so that I can have them strung up?"

"It was Alanic," they replied, sobbing. "He took advantage of us while you were away."

"Alanic!" he shouted out the window to his manservant, who was busy in the yard. "Come here, quickly!"

Alanic went up to see his master, who said to him furiously, "You wretch! How dare you?! I'm going to string you up right here and now!"

Without a flicker of emotion, Alanic replied, "Master, you are a judge of integrity and fairness. Everybody in the whole country knows that and you would not condemn any man before you had heard them out. So, listen to this little story and then pass judgment in your wisdom."

"Speak then and hurry up."

"There was once a man who had a cow. He led it to graze in a field where there was wheat on one side and oats on the other side. The middle of the field, which belonged to the owner of the cow, was left to pasture, but the grazing was poor. He took his cow there and tied her up in a way that she could reach neither the wheat to the right, nor the oats to the left. But the wife and the maid of the owner of the wheat and the oats came and untied the cow and, naturally enough, she set about plundering to left and right, munching away at the wheat and oats without anyone trying to stop her. The owner of the wheat and the oats took the owner of the cow to court. Tell me, you are a fair judge—who would you condemn?"

The judge understood the story and sent Alanic away, absolved. As for the two women? I have no idea.

Second Veillée

■ 6. Goazic Who Went to the Land of Earthly Delights and Tricked Death for Five Hundred Years

Told in Breton by Anne Trutto, Pédernec,
16 September 1888

> Listen all, if you so wish
> And you will hear a pretty little tale
> That contains no word of a lie
> Or perhaps a word or two.

There was a young man called Goazic. He disliked living with his father, who owned a small farm in Brittany and made Goazic work alongside him in the fields. So, he wanted to go off in search of the beautiful princesses who lived in the Land of Earthly Delights and about whom he had heard many stories by the fireside on winter evenings.

And so, one fine morning he set off with an empty purse but full of hope about the future.

After many days walking without anything remarkable happening, as he was passing through a large wood he met an old woman, bent with age and with teeth as long as my fingers. She was spinning flax. "Good morning, grandmother," he said to her as he approached.

"Good day, my child," she replied, "and where are you going?"

"I am off to find the beautiful princesses who live in the Land of Earthly Delights, grandmother."

"It is a long way from here, my child, but do you know which road to take?"

"No, grandmother. Might you be able to show me the way?"

"Yes, I know the way that leads to the Land of Earthly Delights and, as you are a polite young man, I will help you, for otherwise you will never get there. Now, listen. Take this white staff, which will lead you to my sister's house. She is older and wiser than I and lives in a house made of clay and sticks in another forest a hundred leagues from here. When she sees my white staff, she will know that I have sent you and will tell you how to get to the Land of Earthly Delights and what you must do to see the princesses."

Goazic took the white staff that the old woman held out to him and went on his way, led by the staff, which ran on ahead.

After a long, hard walk, he came to the house of the second old woman. She too was sitting at her spinning wheel by the door of her cottage, which was as dingy as her sister's and was by an old hollow oak tree. Goazic approached her, having removed his hat, and greeted her respectfully.

"Good day, grandmother."

"Good day, my child," she replied. "I can see by your white staff that you have been sent by my younger sister. Tell me what I can do for you."

"I would like to go to the Land of Earthly Delights, grand-mother, to see the king's daughters, the four princesses, who live there. Back home I heard so much about them, but I do not know the way and your sister told me that you could help me and show me the way."

"Yes, my child, I can tell you where to go to see the princesses and what you must do to be able to go with them to the Land of Earthly Delights. In the wood, there is a lake where they come every day at midday to bathe. Tomorrow, a little beforehand, you should go down to the edge of the lake and hide behind the laurel bush that you'll see there. At exactly midday, the four princesses will fly down from the sky with their white wings. As soon as they land, they will take off their wings and their clothes and enter the water completely naked. You must then come out of your hiding place and very quickly take the wings and the clothes of the youngest. She will be the last one to enter the water. All four of them are very beautiful, but she is even more so, as you will see for yourself. Take care not to give yourself away by crying out before they are all in the water, because they will immediately fly away and you will never see them again. As soon as they notice you, they will come out of the water, crying out in alarm, and gather up their wings and clothes and fly off. But the youngest will not find her wings or clothes and will cry out to the others for help. They will already be in the air. They will come back down to earth, crying, pleading with you, threatening you, to give back their sister's wings and clothes. But do not listen to their pleading or their threats and return nothing until they have promised to carry you back on the wings of the youngest and she will take you to the Land of Earthly Delights. If you follow my instructions to the letter, you will succeed. But if you fail to do so in any way whatsoever, you will never reach the end of your journey."

Goazic once again thanked the old woman and promised that he would follow her instructions to the letter.

The following day, he went down to the edge of the lake a little before midday and hid behind the laurel bush, just as the old woman had told him. At midday, the sky suddenly became dark. He looked up and saw four enormous birds swooping down to the edge of the lake close by him. But as soon as they landed, out of each bird skin stepped a naked woman of dazzling beauty and they left their plumage on the riverbank. They immediately dived into the water and began to swim and frolic. Then Goazic quickly came out of his hiding place and seized the plumage of the youngest. He had managed not to betray himself by crying out when he saw her, on account of her beauty. When they saw him, the princesses came out of the water and ran for their plumages. Only the youngest was unable to find hers in the place where she had left it. When she saw Goazic holding it, she cried out to her sisters to come and help her, and all four of them gathered around the young man, pleading with him, pressing him, and threatening him. But he held firm and handed back the feathered garment only once the princesses had solemnly promised to carry him on their wings to the Land of Earthly Delights. He climbed on the back of the youngest and the two of them flew up into the air.

Goazic had a fine time with the four princesses in the Land of Earthly Delights. He had such a fine time that when five hundred years had passed, it seemed to him that he had been there for only five years.

Even so, eventually he wanted to return home to see his mother and father again, who must have been worried about him and no doubt believed that he was dead, as he had been unable to send them any news since he had left home. The princesses brought him back to our world after they had made him promise to return to them without delay.

When he arrived home, he was astonished to find that things had changed. He didn't recognize anybody and nobody recognized him. No one had even heard of him, nor of his father, nor of his mother. In the place where their house had been, there was now a large oak tree that was over four hundred years old. When he saw this, he thought that the best thing to do would be to return to the Land of Earthly Delights. So, he set off back toward the lake where the princesses always went to bathe.

Meanwhile, because his hour had come a long time ago, Death had been searching for Goazic everywhere and since he had been unable to find him, he was not pleased. He had to account to his master for everyone who lived on the earth to deliver their souls to him at the appointed hour.

One evening, as Goazic approached the forest where the princesses' lake was, he had a nasty mishap. He came upon a wagon that had become stuck in a rut. The driver, an old man with a white beard and a scythe, was trying in vain to get it out. He called over to Goazic to help, as he passed by. Goazic rushed over and they managed to get the wagon out of the rut. It was loaded with the bodies of people of all ages and of all kinds. They were the mortal remains of all those whom Death (because the old man *was* Death) had cut down that day from all over the place and it had been a plentiful harvest.

"So, what is your name?" the old man asked Goazic suspiciously.

"Goazic is my name, grandfather. At your service!"

"Goazic! Well, I never . . . my friend! I have been looking for you for the best part of five hundred years!"

Five hundred years! With these words, Goazic saw clearly who it was he was dealing with and he pleaded with Death to spare him on account of the help he had given him.

"You have long passed your allotted time," replied the resolute old man. "I am swayed by neither pleading nor threats and I strike down everyone the same, the rich and the powerful as much as the poor and the wretched, when their time has come. I am a just man above all else."

And with one swing of his great scythe, he cut off Goazic's head, threw his body onto the wagon with all the others, and continued on his never-ending journey across the world, spreading grief and desolation wherever he went—but nevertheless, always without prejudice.

■ 7. The Two Friends (A Ghost Story)

Told in Breton by François Thépault, Plouaret, February 1890

There were two young men, Primel and Ewen, who were such good friends that there were no secrets between them and they were inseparable, sharing all their troubles and joys. Primel was the son of a well-to-do farmer and Ewen was one of his laborers. For fifteen years, they had lived together as very good friends without a single word of anger passing between them. Only Death would separate them and they made a pact that whoever died first would return, if God allowed it, to tell his friend what awaited in the afterlife.

Primel was the first to die, when he was still young. Ewen didn't leave his side for a single moment until his body had been laid to rest. The night after the funeral, he was unable to sleep. He thought about his friend, wondered where he was at that moment, and waited for him to return.

Around midnight, he heard the sound of footsteps, which he recognized as belonging to his friend, outside in the courtyard. They both used to sleep in the stable, together.

"Here he comes now," Ewen said to himself and, although he was expecting Primel to come and wanted him to come, he felt a shiver spread through his body. Three gentle knocks came on the door and a voice that he recognized asked, "Are you asleep, my friend?"

"No, Primel, I am not asleep. I was waiting for you."

"That's good! Get up and come here."

Ewen got up, opened the door, and was astonished to see Primel standing there, wrapped in his shroud.

"This is all I own now," he said.

"My poor friend! But tell me, where are you now and what is it like? Are you suffering or are you happy?"

"Follow me and you will have your answer."

And they made their way, sadly and silently, toward the local mill pond. Once they were by the edge of the pond, the dead man said to the other, "Take off your clothes so that you are completely naked."

"Why are you telling me to take off my clothes so that I am completely naked?" asked Ewen, astonished.

"So that you can come into the pond with me."

"But, my friend, it will be very cold and, besides, I don't know how to swim."

"Fear not, you are not going to drown."

"I have promised to follow you and I will follow you wherever you will lead me." And they both threw themselves into the water and went to the bottom of the pond.

"Do I have to stay here long?" asked Ewen.

"As long as I myself am going to stay," replied Primel.

"But I'm cold and I'm suffering greatly."

"I too am cold and I am suffering three times as much as you. You are free to go, if you wish, but if you stay you will reduce my suffering and the length of my ordeal."

"I will not abandon you, but for how long do I have to stay like this? I am in terrible pain."

"Until we hear the morning Angelus bell."

When the Angelus bell rang out, the dead man led his friend out of the water and returned him safe and sound to the edge of the pond and said to him, "Get dressed and go home immediately. This evening I will come back at the same time for you and, if you are as true a friend as I believe you to be, you will come and spend another night with me in the pond."

"I shall not abandon you, my friend, and I will follow you wherever you will lead me."

Then the dead man returned to the water and Ewen returned home, both sad and worried. The other laborers had already had breakfast by the time he arrived and were getting ready to go off to the fields with their tools. He quickly breakfasted and went to join them. The farmer said nothing, although he was aware that Ewen had not spent the night in his own bed.

Out in the field, Ewen appeared to be tired. He was sad and did not join in the conversations with his friends, who put his silence and sadness down to his grief over the loss of his friend. That evening, he returned from the fields with the other workers, but he could not eat anything and he went to bed early. Around midnight, he once again heard Primel's footsteps in the farmyard, followed by knocking on the stable door.

"Are you asleep, Ewen?"

"No, Primel, I am not asleep."

"Very good. Now get up and follow me."

So, he got up and they went back to the pond, sadly and silently. Ewen didn't dare ask his friend what happens after death and Primel said nothing more to him. When they came to the edge of the pond, the one removed his shroud and the other his clothes and once more they jumped into the water.

As with the night before, they stayed there until the ringing of the Angelus bell. When the Angelus bell rang out at daybreak, Primel took his friend back to the water's edge, shivering and dying of cold, and said to him, "My friend, do you feel brave enough to endure the ordeal for a third time? My deliverance depends on it."

"I am suffering more than I can say, but I will remain faithful to you until death."

"This evening then, I will return again for you, for the last time."

Primel returned to the water and Ewen returned to the house, as sad as could be. Once again he spent the day working in the fields but he was a sorry sight to behold.

On the third night, the farmer got up around midnight to check on his cattle in the stable. There was a full moon and he could clearly see his son Primel and Ewen leaving the farmyard together. For a moment, he stood stock-still in astonishment. Then he followed them at a distance, without losing sight of them. They led him as far as the edge of the pond, where they stopped. He hid behind a bush so that he could watch them and to his amazement he saw one remove his shroud and the other his clothes, then throw themselves into the water. He approached the water's edge where they had been standing and listened to them speaking from the bottom of the pond.

"Oh, how cold I am and how I am suffering!" said Ewen.

"Be brave, my friend," replied Primel, "this is our final test."

"How long must we stay here suffering like this?"

"Until the Angelus bell rings, just like the other nights."

"But I can't hold out until then!"

"Be brave, my friend. Just a little more suffering and you will have opened the gates of Heaven for me, where you will join me in due course."

Primel's father spent the rest of the night in the same place and, when the Angelus bell rang at daybreak, he saw an angel, bathed in light, come down from the sky and into the pond. In each hand he carried a crown of gold and he heard the angel speaking to Primel at the bottom of the pond.

"Oh blessed one, your ordeal is now over and God has sent me to give you the crown of the blessed and to tell you that the gates of Heaven are now open to you."

And then he turned to Ewen: "And you, who have helped bring your friend to salvation by sharing his ordeal and staying forever faithful to him, you will not be separated from him after death. Furthermore, God will reward your faithfulness and your devotion. You will return home and, when you arrive there, you will go to bed and die immediately, without pain, and you will join your friend in Heaven." And the angel rose into the sky, leading Primel after him.

Ewen returned to the farm, his crown glowing on his head, went to bed and immediately died. His soul flew straight to Heaven in the form of a white dove.

And so, the two friends were united in death, as they were in life.

■ 8. The White Lady (A Ghost Story)

Told in Breton by François Thépault, baker's boy, Plouaret,
17 February 1890

In the old castle of Kerloster, in the commune of Lannéanou, it is said, a white lady would appear, probably a former resident of the castle. She was seen every evening between the hours of eleven and midnight. She would slowly walk down an old stone staircase that led from a derelict bedroom, cross the enclosed courtyard, and head out the other side to the long avenue of ancient oak trees that led to the town of Lannéanou. In the castle lived two farming families, one at each end of the main house, and they had all seen the ghost many times, with the exception of the eldest son of the youngest farmer, who was called Raoul. He didn't believe in the ghost and made fun of those who talked about it, treating them as deluded and cowardly. What's more, Raoul's general behavior was poor, as

he headed off to a neighboring village every evening after supper, where the young people from thereabouts would meet to drink and play cards, and he would not return until between eleven o'clock and midnight, often even later.

At the back of the courtyard there was an old outbuilding, consisting of a ground-floor room and an upstairs bedroom, which was used as a washhouse for both households. Downstairs there were also some gardening tools such as pick-axes, hoes, spades, and forks; in the bedroom there were spinning wheels, reels, skeins of yarn, bobbins, and tow. Every Sunday after church on fine days, games of boules were played on the avenue and, when the games were over, the boules were stored in a corner of this outbuilding until the next Sunday. There were also two beds in the building, one downstairs and one upstairs, although nobody wanted to sleep there for any length of time, because although the place was peaceful during the daytime, it was haunted at nighttime and one hell of a racket could be heard. Boules was played in the bedroom, the spinning wheels and reels would turn with the speed and the roar of farm machinery, and men in clogs could be heard walking and running noisily across the floor.

Raoul grinned and found it amusing when people would tell him such things and one day, when he was challenged to spend a night in the outbuilding, he said, "Very well, I will do it and woe betide anyone who tries to frighten me, even if it is the Devil himself." And so off he went, armed with nothing more than a large cudgel.

Around midnight, the racket began. The boules rolled from one end of the room to the other and the spinning wheels and reels also started to turn. It surprised Raoul a little, but he wasn't frightened for all that and shouted, "What devil is making all this din? Woe betide anyone up there, be they man or devil, be they alive or dead, if they don't pack it in and let me sleep in peace."

But the noise continued even more loudly. So, he got up, picked up his cudgel, and went upstairs to the bedroom. To his great astonishment, everything was still. He saw nothing out of the ordinary; everything was in its rightful place and there was complete silence.

"I don't understand it," he said. And he went downstairs and back to bed. But no sooner had he laid down when the racket started up again. He got up once more, furious, and went back up to the bedroom, cursing and saying that he would give a thrashing to anyone he found up there and then throw them out of the window, no matter who they were!

But again he saw nothing out of the ordinary, although the moon was shining brightly. Everything was still in its rightful place and there was complete silence. He went back downstairs, went back to bed, and decided not to get up again until daylight, but he was starting to get frightened.

Then he heard somebody coming down the stairs, slowly and noisily, in big clogs. They came to the foot of the bed and, taking hold of a pickaxe, violently hit the frame of the bed. Then they opened the door and left.

Raoul, the fearless Raoul, was no longer feeling quite so brave. He hid his head under the bedsheets and made not a sound. When, finally, he dared to get up at cockcrow, he found everything in its rightful place, as if nothing had been moved. The following night, or ever again, he wouldn't sleep in the outbuilding and he started to think that those who believed in ghosts weren't quite so wrong after all.

Nevertheless, he still went off gallivanting and drinking with his friends every night. One night, returning home late, as usual, with his pipe in his mouth and his tobacco pouch in his right hand, just as he came into the courtyard, he saw the white lady as she came down the staircase of the derelict building. She went right up to him. He took his pipe out of his mouth and, gripped with fear and not knowing what to say, he automatically asked, "Do you have the time, please, madam?"

"It is time," the phantom replied, "that all honest folk should be in bed." And she took him by the left hand and said, "Follow me."

Raoul wanted to resist and break free, but he couldn't. The woman's hand gripped his own like an iron clamp. And it seemed to him that she was leading him down a long avenue of ancient oak trees in the middle of a forest and he heard the crying, wailing, and howling of all kinds of wild animals, which made his hair stand on end.

"She must be taking me to Hell," he thought.

And she led him like this for a long time. At last, he heard the cock crow and the church bells at Lannéanou ring out five o'clock. Immediately, the white lady let him go and vanished and he recognized where he was and saw that he was only a few paces away from the graveyard at Lannéanou. If the white lady had managed to take him all the way to the graveyard before the cock had crowed, then he would never have returned.

His tobacco pouch and his pipe were found by the road the following day by a rag-and-bone man.

From that day on, Raoul settled down. He no longer stayed out all night, nor did he make fun anymore of the ghost stories that he heard at winter gatherings.

■ 9. The Midnight Washerwoman (Plougonven)

No record of either the storyteller or the date

Three young men were returning home together after having spent most of the evening playing cards at a farm in the parish of Plougonven. It was about two or three o'clock in the morning.

It was in the month of December. It was cold, the moon was full, and they talked about their various fortunes at the game, as they smoked their pipes. As they came to a stream with a wooden footbridge across it, one of them, Iannic Meudec, said, "They say that the midnight washerwoman appears over there. If we see her, let's throw her straight into the pond headfirst!"

The pond was in a field by the side of a road, alongside which ran an embankment. Iannic climbed the embankment and said to his two friends, Ervoan Madec and Pipi Al Laouenan, "There she is, the midnight washerwoman! Come to the top of the embankment and you'll see her."

They climbed the embankment and saw with astonishment a strange woman who was dunking linen into the pond, then taking it out, rubbing it, and hitting it with a large paddle, the noise of which echoed down the valley. Thunderstruck, they stayed watching her silently for a while, but they had drunk a fair bit of brandy and were boasting to each other that they weren't frightened. One of them, Pipi Al Laouenan, cried out, "Would you like us to help you wring out your linen, washerwoman?"

The washerwoman did not reply, but she put her paddle down on the stone by the laundry, got up, and looked in the direction where the voice had come from.

Suddenly the three friends, seized with panic, leaped down from the embankment and made a mad dash for it, as if the Devil were at their heels. Iannic Meudec fell over, grazing his nose and his forehead. Then he got up again and set off once more, leaving behind his clogs and his hat.

The other two also threw away their clogs on the road and luckily soon found a safe place to hide, in the thatched cottage of Ervoan Madec, which was just by the side of the road. The washerwoman was hot on their heels, her paddle raised in the air, and, had she caught them, she would have battered them over the head.

She could not get into the house, but she threw her paddle against the door with such force that she broke it. And before she left, she shouted at them, "You can count yourselves lucky, because if I had caught you, I would have taught you to go spending the night playing cards and being out on the road so late without good reason!"

The three friends breathed not a word, scared to death, and they dared not leave until it was daylight. They then went to look for their clogs and their hats in the place where they had abandoned them, but they found them broken and torn into a thousand pieces on the stone by the pond where the midnight washerwoman had been washing her linen.

■ 10. The Devil's Horse

No record of either the storyteller or the date

Jeanette Ar Beuz was a widow with three sons. The eldest was Ervoan, the middle one was Alain, and the youngest was Fanch. They were handsome young men with their feet planted firmly on the ground and, what's more, they weren't at the back of the queue when brains were handed out. The other young men from around there were a little jealous because at all the *pardons*[*] and the *aires neuves*[†] Ervoan, Alain, and Fanch had their choice of the pretty girls and the widow's sons were called goldfinches,[‡] dandies, and high-spirited lads.

---

[*] A traditional Breton religious festival and penitential ceremony, typically involving a procession and followed by a social event, such as a community picnic or fair.

[†] In French, "aires neuves." The aire neuve is a traditional Breton dance that takes place in summer outside a peasant's house in order to flatten the ground and thus prepare and renew the threshing floor. As Segalen notes, "Here work and pleasure were wholly fused into one; they were two facets of a single activity. For it was through dancing on it that the new threshing-floor was flattened and smoothed" (1991, 221). For a full description of the aire neuve, see Guilcher 1960.

[‡] According to Luzel, this was a term used for handsome young men because the goldfinch is the most beautiful bird.

Actually, old men called them high-spirited and mothers called them smooth-tongued. During the summer, they were seen everywhere at the pardons, at the aires neuves, and at the fairs.

During the winter, they were regulars at the houses where you could play cards and have fun in the evenings and they never returned home before two or three in the morning. They would leave home together as soon as they had eaten, but they rarely came home together, because each of them would go wherever pleasure or passion would lead him. More than once, their mother would receive complaints about wronged or mistreated young girls, but she would merely reply, "What do you want me to do? I can only give you some advice: gather up your hens when my cocks are about!"

One January night, the three brothers had gone together to Kerminic'hi, where a sausage festival was taking place. After the food, there was dancing and card-playing. Ervoan and Alain, whose girlfriends were there, left to walk the lovely girls home between ten and eleven o'clock.

Fanch stayed behind playing cards. An argument broke out over some cheating and the hotheads started shouting, hurling accusations around, cursing, and it all came to blows. Fanch was one of those who made the most trouble. The party finally broke up around one o'clock in the morning and everyone set off home in different directions. Fanch was alone and in a bad mood because he had lost the game. The moon shone brightly.

He had to go by the sunken lane at Melchonnec, which was reputed to be haunted by evil spirits and even by the Devil himself and nobody would normally go that way after nightfall. He summoned up all his courage. The road there is enclosed on both sides by high banks that rise steeply and the branches of the trees on either side overhang the road and are entwined together to form a

thickly tangled archway that blocks out all light, even on the sun-
niest of summer's days. And what's more, it is so narrow that two
people would have difficulty walking side by side. Halfway along,
where it is at its narrowest, Fanch noticed something black blocking the road.

"What the Devil is that?" he said to himself.

He was not easily scared, especially when he had had one too
many, and he stepped forward and soon realized that it was a horse,
a beautiful, black horse. He stopped for a moment to admire it and
could not resist shouting out, "What a beautiful horse! I've never
seen anything like it before. But whose is it and what is it doing
here on the road all alone? It's certainly not from around here, so
must belong to some stranger who no doubt has had an accident.
It is bridled and saddled."

Fanch wanted to go past it, but the horse continued to obstruct
the road and would not let him through. Brave Fanch felt a slight
shiver of fear run down his spine and decided wisely to retrace
his steps without trying to force his way through. When he got
to the spot where the bank was at its lowest, he climbed up onto
it and walked parallel to the road. But before long, he had to climb
back down again and the horse was once more standing in front of
him, with a stirrup in reach of his foot, as if inviting him to climb
onto its back.

Fanch climbed up the bank again and tried to come down at a
different spot. But the horse was still there. And he climbed back
up the bank so that he could go farther along. More than ten times
he tried the same ploy but each time the horse was there in front
of him blocking the way. Eventually, he heard the church bells in
Plouaret strike three o'clock. He made the sign of the cross and the
horse disappeared at a triple gallop with fire coming from its hooves
and nostrils.

Fanch could now go home and when he got there he was out of his wits and shaking with a fever, so that he was confined to his bed all day.

And from that day on, he changed his behavior, settled down, and stopped running around at night.

This was told to me by the very person it happened to and he thought that the horse was the Devil's horse. Old Guyona was sure that it was the Devil's horse and if Fanch had climbed onto its back, it would have thrown him over some cliff or other, or even have taken him alive, straight to Hell.

■ 11. The Little Ant Going to Jerusalem and the Snow

Told by G. de La Landelle, 1876

Once upon a time there was a little ant who was going to Jerusalem. On the way, she met the snow, which caused the little ant who was going to Jerusalem to break a leg.

"Oh snow, you are so strong that you have broken the leg of the little ant who is going to Jerusalem!"

And the snow replied, "The sun that melts me is stronger."

"Oh sun, you are so strong that you melt the snow that broke the leg of the little ant who is going to Jerusalem!"

And the sun replied, "The cloud that blocks me out is stronger."

"Oh cloud, you are so strong that you block out the sun that melts the snow that broke the leg of the little ant who is going to Jerusalem!"

And the cloud replied, "The wind that blows me away is stronger."

"Oh wind, you are so strong that you blow away the cloud that blocks out the sun that melts the snow that broke the leg of the little ant who is going to Jerusalem!"

And the wind replied, "The mountain that stops me is stronger."

"Oh mountain, you are so strong that you stop the wind that blows away the cloud that blocks out the sun that melts the snow that broke the leg of the little ant who is going to Jerusalem!"

And the mountain replied, "The mouse that burrows into me is stronger."

"Oh mouse, you are so strong that you burrow into the mountain that stops the wind that blows away the cloud that blocks out the sun that melts the snow that broke the leg of the little ant who is going to Jerusalem!"

And the mouse replied, "The cat that eats me is stronger."

"Oh cat, you are so strong that you eat the mouse that burrows into the mountain that stops the wind that blows away the cloud that blocks out the sun that melts the snow that broke the leg of the little ant who is going to Jerusalem!"

And the cat replied, "The dog that chases me is stronger."

"Oh dog, you are so strong that you chase the cat that eats the mouse that burrows into the mountain that stops the wind that blows away the cloud that blocks out the sun that melts the snow that broke the leg of the little ant who is going to Jerusalem!"

And the dog replied, "The stick that beats me is stronger."

"Oh stick, you are so strong that you beat the dog that chases the cat that eats the mouse that burrows into the mountain that stops the wind that blows away the cloud that blocks out the sun that melts the snow that broke the leg of the little ant who is going to Jerusalem!"

And the stick replied, "The fire that burns me is stronger."

"Oh fire, you are so strong that you burn the stick that beats the dog that chases the cat that eats the mouse that burrows into the mountain that stops the wind that blows away the cloud that blocks out the sun that melts the snow that broke the leg of the little ant who is going to Jerusalem!"

And the fire replied, "The water that quenches me is stronger."

"Oh water, you are so strong that you quench the fire that burns the stick that beats the dog that chases the cat that eats the mouse that burrows into the mountain that stops the wind that blows away the cloud that blocks out the sun that melts the snow that broke the leg of the little ant who is going to Jerusalem!"

And the water replied, "The cow that drinks me is stronger."

"Oh cow, you are so strong that you drink the water that quenches the fire that burns the stick that beats the dog that chases the cat that eats the mouse that burrows into the mountain that stops the wind that blows away the cloud that blocks out the sun that melts the snow that broke the leg of the little ant who is going to Jerusalem!"

And the cow replied, "The man who slaughters me is stronger."

"Oh man, you are so strong that you slaughter the cow that drinks the water that quenches the fire that burns the stick that beats the dog that chases the cat that eats the mouse that burrows into the mountain that stops the wind that blows away the cloud that blocks out the sun that melts the snow that broke the leg of the little ant who is going to Jerusalem!"

And the man replied, "God (or the Devil) who carries off the man who slaughters the cow that drinks the water that quenches the fire that burns the stick that beats the dog that chases the cat that eats the mouse that burrows into the mountain that stops the wind that blows away the cloud that blocks out the sun that melts the snow that broke the leg of the little ant who is going to Jerusalem is stronger!"

Third Veillée

■ 12. The Three Hairs from the Devil's Golden Beard

Told by Barba Tassel, Plouaret, 1870

This all took place in the days
When hens had teeth.*

His name was Malo and he was the king's gardener. As he was already quite old, he no longer worked himself but supervised the other gardeners at the court. The king, who liked to pass the time talking to him whenever he went for a walk in the garden, said to him one day, "So, Malo, I see your wife is pregnant again?"

"Yes, sire, I'm soon to be a father for the sixth time—as you know, I already have five children. But what is bothering me most is how to find a godfather for the sixth."

"Ah, don't you worry about that. Come and see me when your child is born and I will find him a godfather."

Eight days later, Malo went out to find the king and said to him, "My sixth son has been born, sire."

"Very well," replied the king, "I will be his godfather."

The baptism was solemnly celebrated and the child was christened Charles. Then there was a great banquet in the king's palace. Toward the end of the meal, the old gardener, who had drunk a little more than usual, was rather merry and, raising a full glass, said, "To your health, sire, and may God grant that one day my new-born son will be united with your daughter, the princess." Only a few days earlier, a daughter had been born to the king.

The king was not pleased with the gardener's toast and he fired him. Malo went to work at the house of a fine lord. Before long,

* Ceci se passait du temps / Où les poules avaient des dents (Kement-man oa d'ann amzer / Ma ho devoa dent ar ier)

though, the king missed his old gardener and asked him to return to court as before. Malo, who missed the beautiful garden, where he had spent all his life, as well as the pleasant conversation with the king, went back willingly. The king wanted to take care of Charles's education and Malo gladly gave his consent.

The old king had not forgotten the gardener's ill-advised words at the baptism dinner and he wanted to take early measures to prevent the toast from coming true. So, Charles was set out to sea in a glass crib to float away and was abandoned to the mercy of God.

The king was expecting his wine merchant from Bordeaux, who was supposed to be bringing him some wine. While at sea, the merchant from Bordeaux came across the crib with Charles in it. He gathered up the child, marveled at his beauty, and resolved to take him back to his wife so they could adopt him. In his joy and his eagerness to show him to his wife, he turned the boat around and returned home to Bordeaux without delay.

His wife was happy with the present that her husband brought her, as they had no children of their own, despite being married for a long time. From that moment on, Charles was brought up and educated as if he were the merchant's own son. He was baptized all over again, just in case he hadn't already been so, and by sheer chance he was once again given the name Charles. He was taught all kinds of things and he called the merchant and his wife father and mother, as they never told him the truth about his early life.

Many years later, the king made a trip to Bordeaux. When he saw Charles, he admired his fine appearance and asked the merchant if the boy was his son. The merchant told him the story of how he found him afloat on the sea in a glass crib, rescued him, and adopted him as his son. Then the king realized that this was his gardener's child, the same one he had wanted to be rid of, and so he asked the merchant to hand him over to him so that he could take him on as his private secretary. The merchant handed the child over to the king, but with sadness.

The king did not have to return to Paris immediately, so sent Charles ahead and gave him a letter to give to the queen, in which it was written that the bearer should be put to death immediately on arrival. He added that he would be returning without delay and that his order of execution should be carried out before he got back.

Charles set off with the letter without suspecting that it contained his death warrant. On the way, he stayed overnight in a village and there he dined with three strangers—tax collectors.

After eating, they played cards and Charles lost all of his money and even his watch. Then he went to bed. The three tax collectors all shared the same bedroom and Charles was in a small room next door. The only thing that separated them was a partition made of planking and he could hear their conversation.

"That poor boy!" said one of them. "He has lost all his money. How is he going to pay his bill and get home now? I feel sorry for him. What if we were to give him his money back?"

"Yes," the other two replied, "let's give him his money back."

And one of the three went into his room to return the money. Charles was sleeping soundly as his journey had tired him out. The tax collector noticed a sealed envelope on the bedside table—it was the letter the king had given Charles to deliver to the queen. Curiosity getting the better of him, the tax collector broke the seal, read the letter, and was astonished by what it contained.

"The poor boy," he thought. "He is carrying his own death warrant and he doesn't even know it." He showed the letter to his companions and they substituted it with another letter, which informed the queen that the bearer should be received and treated well.

The following morning when Charles got up, the tax collectors had already left. In his pockets he found his money and his watch, and his letter too was on the bedside table where he had left it. He paid his bill and set off on his way without an inkling that the letter had been substituted.

He walked and walked and finally he arrived in Paris. He went straight to the royal palace and delivered the letter to the queen. She could not have treated Charles any better. He was invited to eat with her and he accompanied her and her daughter, the princess, as they went walking or visited people.

The king returned at the end of the month and to his great astonishment and equally great anger, he found Charles enjoying the company of his wife and his daughter.

"What is going on?" he said to the queen. "Why haven't you done what I asked in my letter?"

"But I have," she replied. "Here is your letter. Read it." The king read the letter that the queen handed to him and he realized that he had been tricked, but he didn't know by whom.

So, Charles was sent off to the army as a common soldier. And he was a model soldier. He quickly became an officer and, as he acted so courageously in all his battles and contributed more than anyone else to victory, he quickly progressed through the ranks and was the talk of both the army and civilian life. The princess fell in love with him and asked her father to let him marry her.

"Never!" replied the king.

A great war broke out and the king of France was on the verge of losing a decisive battle when Charles arrived with his soldiers. Immediately, the course of events changed and the French grasped a great victory from the jaws of the desperate defeat that had threatened. Once again, the princess asked her father for permission to marry the young hero.

"This time I will agree," he replied, "but on the condition that he will bring me three hairs from the Devil's golden beard."*

"And where am I going to find the Devil?" asked Charles.

"In Hell, of course!" the princess told him.

"That's easy enough for you to say, but how am I going to get to Hell?" All the same, he set off on his way, at the mercy of God.

After walking for a long time and passing through many lands, he arrived at the foot of a tall mountain, where he saw an old woman who had just drawn water from the well with a battered barrel that she carried on her head.

"And where are you going, young man?" the old woman asked him." No living person ever comes this way. I am the Devil's mother."

"Well, then it's your son that I'm looking for. Take me to him, please."

"But my poor child, he will kill you or swallow you up alive, if he sees you."

"Perhaps. Do as I ask and then we'll see what happens."

"You don't appear to be at all frightened. But tell me, what is it that you want with my son?"

"The king of France has promised to give me his daughter's hand if I bring him three hairs from the Devil's golden beard, and I'm sure, grandmother, that you wouldn't want to deny me such a wonderful marriage for the sake of three beard hairs?"

"Very well, follow me and we shall see. I like the look of you." And Charles followed the old woman, who led him to an old, dilapidated castle that was completely dark. As soon as they arrived, she set about making pancakes for her son in a frying pan that was bigger than a millstone. Before long, a terrible racket could be heard.

---

* Luzel's note: Up until this point, our tale belongs to a different type from "Journey toward the Sun" and this subtle change of direction is due to my storyteller.

"Here comes my son," said the old woman. "Quickly, hide yourself under my bed!" Charles hid under the bed and the old woman's son entered, shouting, "I am starving, Mother, I am starving!"[*]

"Very well then. Eat, my son. Here are some lovely pancakes." And he started to eat the pancakes, which disappeared as if into a chasm. When he had gobbled up a few dozen of them, he paused for a moment and said, "I smell the scent of a Christian here and I'll have to eat him up."

"You're wrong, my son," said the old woman. "Eat your pancakes and don't worry about any Christians. You know full well that none of those ever come here." And he gobbled up another few dozen pancakes, then sniffed the air and repeated, "I smell the scent of a Christian here and I'll have to eat him up."

"Give it a rest with these Christians," the old woman said to him, "and eat up your pancakes or go to bed if your belly is full."

"Yes, Mother," he said, calming down. "I'm tired and I am going to bed."

He went to bed and a moment later he was snoring. The old woman approached him and plucked a single hair from his golden beard. He scratched his chin, but he didn't wake up. A moment later, the old woman plucked a second hair and then a third. Finally, he woke up and leaped out of his bed, saying, "I can't sleep in this bed, Mother, there are too many fleas. I am going to sleep in the stable."

"Go to the stable, if you want, my son. Tomorrow I will change the sheets." And he went out to the stable.

"Come here, quickly, now!" said the old woman to Charles. And she gave him the three hairs that she had just plucked from her son's chin.

---

[*] Luzel's note: In all popular tales where Von represents the Sun returning from his day's journey, he begins by asking for food. Clearly the Devil has been substituted here for the Sun.

"Here are three hairs from the Devil's golden beard. Take them quickly and go and marry the king of France's daughter." Charles took the three hairs, thanked her, and quickly left.

When he arrived back at the king of France's palace, the queen and her daughter were out walking in the garden. He went to find them and as soon as she saw him, the princess asked, "Have you got the three golden hairs from the Devil's beard?"

"Here they are," he replied, showing them to her. The princess ran to tell her father. When the old king saw the three hairs, he was taken by such a fury that he plunged his dagger into his own heart and died immediately.

"Go to the Devil!" said Charles when he saw what had happened. There was now nothing to stop the marriage between Charles and the princess. He wrote to the merchant in Bordeaux and asked him to come to Paris without delay. The merchant came and told the whole story and so they learned that Charles was the son of the old palace gardener and the godson of the king.

And it did not go unnoticed that the toast that the old gardener had made to the king's health at the baptism dinner had also come to pass. "To your health, sire, and may God grant that one day your daughter and my son will be united."

The marriage was celebrated and it was a beautiful wedding with feasting, dancing, and games of all kinds that went on for fifteen days.

> I was the cook.
> I had a crumb to eat and a drop to drink,
> A spoonful from the pot into my mouth
> And since then I have never gone back.
> But for five crowns and a blue horse

I will go there again.
For five crowns and a brown horse
I will go there a week tomorrow.[*]

■ 13. The Three Promises or The Devil Outwitted

No record of either the storyteller or the date

Three young men were traveling together, their pockets empty but their hearts full of hope. One of them said to the others, "If I could only find someone to lend me one hundred sovereigns, I would agree to anything."

"Me too," said each of the others.

No sooner had they said these words when alongside them appeared a stranger on a black horse, which sent out flames from its feet, eyes, nostrils, and ears.

"Where are you young gentlemen off to in such a manner?" the stranger asked them.

"To seek our fortune," they replied.

"And with empty pockets, no doubt?"

"Alas, yes!"

"Well then. If you like, I will give each of you one hundred sovereigns."

"That would do fine! But where's the catch?"

"Oh, merely a little thing—on the condition that each of you speaks no more than two words, just two words, for a year and a day, and if you fail to keep your word, you will be mine and I will return to do with you as I wish."

---

[*] Luzel's note: In Breton the final formula rhymes.

"Let's shake on it! It's a deal!" replied the three companions. And they shook hands to seal the deal and the stranger gave them each one hundred sovereigns in shiny new gold coins. Then he disappeared on his horse at a gallop.

"Well," said the first of the three, "he didn't tell us where we would find him again in a year and a day's time."

"Don't worry, he'll know where to find us, wherever we may be," said the second, suspecting that they had made a pact with the Devil.

"In the meantime, we each have one hundred sovereigns and we can have a rare old time while they last," said the third. And they hurried off to the nearest village, where they went to the best hotel and made merry all night long.

The following morning, the landlord, anxious at having seen them going at it so ferociously, always ordering the most expensive dishes and wine, without ever asking the price, asked them to settle their account before ordering anything else.

"All three?" asked the first.

"To pay?" asked the second.

"Fair enough!" said the third.

And so, they paid and the landlord, seeing that they had money, continued to serve them whatever they asked for. But they had each spoken their two words and they could only repeat the same ones, or else be silent.

The following night, a rich merchant arrived at the same hotel with a bag full of gold. The landlord and his wife killed the merchant and relieved him of his gold, then accused the three companions of the murder and the theft. They were brought before the court.

"You lot killed this merchant and then you robbed him," the judge said to them.

"All three?" said the first of the companions.

"Probably," replied the judge.

"To pay?" said the second companion.

"Yes, to pay your bill, no doubt," replied the judge.

"Fair enough!" said the third.

"There you are! They've admitted it!" said the judge. And they were condemned to death by hanging. A priest was sent for, to be with them in their final moments.

"Repent!" he said to them. "You are about to stand before your supreme judge . . ."

"All three?" said the first.

"Yes, all three of you," the priest replied.

"To pay?" said the second.

"Yes, everyone must pay, if not in this world, then in the next."

"Fair enough!" said the third.

"Let's go then, they are resigned to their fate," said the priest.

And they climbed the ladder, sad and silent.

As they stepped onto the third rung, a stranger was seen arriving on a black horse, riding at full speed.

"Stop!" cried the stranger. "Set these men free, as they are not guilty! It was the landlord and his wife who murdered the merchant!" And he went and untied the three companions himself and nobody dared stop him.

"Off you go!" he said to them. "You are relieved of your promises and you may now speak as you wish."

As for the landlord and his wife, they were arrested there and then, judged, condemned, and hanged.

■ 14. Goulaffre the Giant

Told by Barba Tassel, Plouaret, 1869

Once upon a time there was a poor widow who lived with her son. Every day the mother and her son would go begging from door to door at the farms and manor houses, receiving a slice of barley loaf here, a buckwheat pancake there, a few potatoes elsewhere. And so they lived off the charity of kindly souls. The child was called Allanic and the mother Godic or Marguérite. When Allanic reached the age of fourteen or fifteen, he was strong and healthy, but still he continued to go begging with his mother and often the countryfolk would say to them, "It is high time, Marguérite, that the young lad went out to work to earn his bread. You've fed him for long enough without his doing anything. Now it's his turn to help you. Look how strong and healthy he is. Have you no shame, you good-for-nothing, to sponge off your old mother like this?"

Every day he was harangued in the same way and every day they went home in the evening with their basket a little lighter. Noticing this, Allanic said to his mother, "I would like to go to France, Mother, to try to earn my living and take my turn in helping you." Godic was sad to hear this but she knew she couldn't hold on to him forever and she didn't stand in the way of his decision to leave.

So, Allanic set out one beautiful spring morning, taking with him, on the end of a stick, a rye loaf and six crêpes, and he was rather proud of the six *réals** in his pocket that his mother had given him. He wandered randomly, wherever the road took him. Around midday, he noticed that by the side of the road that he was following there was a freshwater spring, clear and in the shade of a clump of

---

* The equivalent of 1 franc 50 centimes.

trees. He stopped to rest for a while and to eat a slice of bread and a crêpe before continuing on his way. As he sat in the shade and ate his meager meal, another traveler, who looked no better off than himself, approached the spring to quench his thirst. Allanic offered him a crêpe and they started to chat and soon became friends.

"So, where are you going, my friend?" Allanic asked him.

"Well, I'm just walking forward, that's all I know. And you?"

"I'm going to France to try to earn my living."

"Well, we can travel together, if you like."

"That would be ideal. What do you do for a living?"

"I am a dancer and my name is Fistilou."

"That is wonderful, because I'm a musician and I'm called Allanic."

"Well, what instrument do you play? I don't see you carrying one."

"Oh, getting an instrument is no problem. I can always find one when I need one. Look, there's a field full of them. Every one of those reeds is an instrument."

"What do you mean? Surely you're joking?"

"I'm not joking and I'll prove it to you." And jumping over the fence into a field of rye, he took his knife, cut himself a stalk of rye, and in next to no time he had fashioned a whistle, similar to those that you see the young shepherds with in springtime, and he started to play it with a rare skill and artistry. When Fistilou heard it, he began to dance and jig and throw his hat into the air, shouting, "Iou! Iou! Hou! Hou!" as they do in Cornouaille. And so, they became the best friends in the world and carried on their way, chatting, laughing, and dreaming of making their fortunes.

Around evening, they arrived in a town whose name I forget. They soon found themselves in a square with houses on all sides and full of people walking about. Allanic started to play his reed whistle, Fistilou started to dance and jig about and throw his hat in the air, shouting, "Iou! Iou! Hou! Hou!" and people came running from all sides, forming a crowd and pushing each other aside so as to get a view of them. Never before had the townsfolk heard such music or seen such dancing.

The two friends were showered with coins and soon there was a magnificent pile, five or six crowns at least. The next day, they did the same thing again and they had excellent takings once more. They were overcome with joy.

But then Fistilou came up with a bad idea. He thought that since they had earned so much money with a simple reed whistle, they would earn ten times as much if they had a violin. So, they bought a violin and Allanic started scratching away on it in a manner that would grate on even the least delicate ears.

No matter! They thought it rather charming and convinced themselves of the success that lay ahead. So, they went to another town to try out their new scheme and soon they started to play and dance in the public square. But they were surprised to see that these townsfolk, instead of hurrying toward them, were running away with their fingers in their ears. And instead of the loose change, this time all they received were curses and stones, so that they had to leave town as quickly as possible.

"Obviously these people don't appreciate beautiful music!" they said to themselves, once they had taken shelter from the stones. "We'll have to go back to the whistle."

Allanic cut a stalk from the first rye field they came across, and they continued on their way, but less joyfully than before because they were now penniless.

Before long, they found themselves in front of a castle surrounded by high walls. "We must try out our music and dancing here," they said. But they didn't know how to get in. They could see a door with a knocker, but the knocker was so high up they couldn't reach it.

"If you stand up against the door," said Fistilou to Allanic, "I'll climb on your shoulders so that I can reach the knocker."

So, that's what they did. The door opened immediately and they went into a garden where two beautiful girls were taking a walk. These were the daughters of Goulaffre the giant, who lived in the castle. Allanic started to play his reed whistle, Fistilou started to dance and jig about, and the girls ran out to watch them. They never used to leave their garden and so they had never seen anything like this and they thoroughly enjoyed the music and the dancing and the shouting. Their mother, a ten-foot-tall giant, then arrived as well and they pleaded with her to keep the two men in the castle to entertain them, as they never went out.

"But my children, what about your father?"

"They are so funny and lovely that our father will like them as much as we do and will let them live."

"I am not at all sure about that, but they can stay anyway, since you like them."

So, the two young giantesses were very happy. When it was dinnertime, a bell was rung and the giant came in. The two friends were hiding in a large chest, but when the giant came into the dining room, he immediately shouted, "I smell a Christian and I want to eat him!"

"Well, I'd like to see that!" replied his wife. "What, you'd eat my two nephews who have come to see me, two boys who are so charming and whom your daughters are so fond of, because they are so clever? And you'll like them too!"

"Let your nephews come here then, woman, so I can see them."

The two companions were brought out of the chest, trembling with fright.

"Your nephews are very small, woman! What can they do then?"

"They dance and make music to die for!"

"Very well, but let's eat first because I'm starving and then we'll see."

And they sat down at the table. First they had soup in a broken barrel. Then a roasted Christian was brought in on a platter. Goulaffre the giant carved it up, kept the largest portion for himself, and then his wife shared out what was left between herself and her two daughters. She also gave a foot to each of the two strangers. Sadly, they stared at each other and ate nothing.

"What, aren't you eating anything, boys?" the giant said to them.

"We're not hungry, sir."

"But it's good stuff!" And taking the two feet from their plates, he swallowed them whole.

When the meal was over, he said, "Now, let's see what you're made of, boys, and see if you can entertain me a bit." And Allanic began to play his reed whistle and Fistilou began to dance, to jig about and throw his hat in the air, shouting out, "Iou! Iou! Hou! Hou!" The giant burst out laughing and enjoyed it immensely, as did his wife and two daughters.

After an hour of this, Goulaffre said to them, "I'm satisfied with you, so now go to sleep with my daughters and tomorrow I'll decide what to do with you." Then the giant's wife took them up to bed, gave Allanic and Fistilou red nightcaps to put on their heads and white nightcaps to her daughters, and then she went away.

It wasn't long before the two young giantesses had fallen asleep and were snoring so that the windowpanes shook in their frames. But Allanic and Fistilou didn't sleep. They soon heard a noise in the room below. The giant and his wife were quarreling. Allanic leaped out of bed, pressed his ear to the floor, and this is what he heard.

"I'm telling you, woman, I'm going to eat them tomorrow morning for breakfast."

"At least wait a few days. You'll enjoy their music and dancing. And what about our daughters? The poor children never have anything to do and you've seen how jolly and happy they are. Spare them, for their sake."

"There's nothing more to be said on the matter. I'm going to eat them tomorrow morning. Where's my cutlass?"

And a moment later, they heard the giant's footsteps on the stairs. Allanic ran back to his bed, swapped his red cap for the white cap of one of the young giantesses, who was still asleep, told Fistilou to do the same, and then they turned to face the wall and pretended to be fast asleep. Right away Goulaffre entered the room, holding a lantern in one hand and a large cutlass in the other. He approached the first bed and, with a single blow, cut off the head that was wearing the red cap. Then he went over to the second bed and did likewise, letting the heads roll across the floor. He went downstairs, carrying the bodies of his two daughters under his arm, and threw them onto the kitchen table without looking at them.

When he returned to his bedroom, he said to his wife, "Job done! What an excellent breakfast we'll have in the morning!"

"As long as you haven't made a mistake in your haste," the giantess said to him.

"How could I have made a mistake? I do know the difference between a red cap and a white cap, you know!" Then they peacefully fell asleep.

As for Allanic and Fistilou, as soon as the giant had left their bedroom, they went down into the garden, using their bedsheets, and were away!

The next morning, Goulaffre woke his wife up early so that she could get his breakfast ready. But when she went into the kitchen and recognized her daughters, she started to cry out so that the castle shook.

Goulaffre came running when he heard her and he then added his own cries and wailing to those of his wife. He ran to his daughters' bedroom, thinking he would find his guests there, but all he found was a piece of paper on which was written (Fistilou knew how to read and write a little): "Fistilou and his friend Allanic thank Goulaffre the giant for the hospitality he has shown them and they promise to come back and see him."

The giant, roaring with anger, put on his seven-league boots and set off in pursuit of the fugitives. They were already a long way from the castle but Goulaffre soon caught up with them. Seeing a large leg with enormous boots passing over their heads, they said to themselves, "Here comes the giant!" and they hid beneath a large stone nearby so that Goulaffre passed by without seeing them. When they thought he was long gone, they came out of their hiding place and continued on their way.

Toward sunset, they came to a great moorland plain that was scattered with enormous blocks of granite, either on their own or piled on top of each other, and among them they saw two large boots. Then, a little farther on, in the back of a dark cave, they saw something red and shiny, like a bull's eye. They approached on tiptoe and realized that it was Goulaffre, who, tired out from the chase (because seven-league boots are very tiring), had stopped for a little rest. The shiny red object that they saw at the back of the cave was his only eye. He was fast asleep.

They stayed where they were for a few minutes, watching the giant, and then Allanic said, "If we could take off his seven-league boots, we could make fun of him."

"Yes, but what if he wakes up?" replied Fistilou.

"He's sleeping too heavily for that. Listen to him snoring! Let's have a go and see what happens."

They removed one of his boots without his budging, but when they were pulling on the second one with all their might, the giant moved and they thought they were done for. Luckily, he didn't wake up and they were able to remove that one as well. Allanic then put on the two boots and he was about to leave when his companion said to him, "What about me? Are you just going to leave me here?"

"Climb on my back—quickly!"

And off they went, one carrying the other. When Goulaffre woke up and saw that he no longer had his boots, he roared so loudly as to frighten the animals for three leagues thereabouts. He had to go back to his castle without his boots and when he got there, his feet were covered in blood.

Meanwhile, Allanic and Fistilou had arrived in Paris. They went and knocked on the door of the king's palace to ask for work and they were taken on as stable boys.

The king's son loved hunting, but with him it was not a happy passion, because at the end of the day his bag usually remained empty, so that one day Fistilou said to his friends, "My friend Allanic could catch as much game in a single day as the young prince could catch in a whole year."

The boast came to the ears of the prince, who sent for Allanic and took him hunting the very next day. Allanic did not forget to put his seven-league boots in his bag (since they were magic boots, they grew bigger and smaller, as he wished). He was given a good gun, the first he had ever held in his hands, and the prince and he went off into a large forest where there was plentiful game of all sorts. On the pretext of giving due respect to his companion,

Allanic let the prince shoot at everything—hares, deer, foxes—and as he was spectacularly clumsy, he missed the lot.

Around midday, they sat down on the moss at the foot of an oak tree to eat a slice of pâté and drink a glass of wine. Then Allanic said to the prince, "Have a little rest, sire, while I go off a little way in this direction. I'll be back with you within the hour at the outside."

"Off you go," the prince said to him, "and I hope you have more luck than I did."

After a few paces, Allanic put on his seven-league boots and in less than an hour he had caught so much game, of all sorts, that he had to ask for a cart from a nearby farm so that he could carry it all back to the palace.

"And how did you manage to kill so much in so little time?" the prince said to him, when he saw him coming back with his fully laden cart.

"It was just luck, sire, and a little skill too. But you know there are days when you feel cursed with bad luck, and it looks like you are having one of those days." The prince seemed happy with this explanation and they returned to the palace, where everyone was astonished to see them coming back with so much game.

From that day on, Allanic was made welcome by the king and especially the prince, who took him out hunting nearly every day. Fistilou, jealous of his favoritism, tried to stir things up for his old friend. He told the stable boys, and others besides, about their visit to the castle of Goulaffre the giant and how they had managed to get away without coming to any harm. He also talked about the giant's seven-league boots and how Allanic was able to be such a superb hunter. The rumor soon came to the king's ears, Allanic was sent for, and the king said to him, "They say that you have been to the castle of Goulaffre the giant and that you came away unharmed?"

"Nothing is more true, sire."

"Ah, this Goulaffre is such a thief and a monster! And the harm he has done to me! He stole my crescent moon from me, a wonderful thing beyond compare, and my golden cage, which was my pride and joy. Ah, if only I could get revenge on him and get back my crescent moon and my golden cage! But as you've already been to his castle and you returned unharmed, you could easily go back again!"

"Ah, sire! If only you knew what a terrible monster this giant is. He would certainly eat me alive if I went back."

"You have already been there and you have his seven-league boots. You must go back and bring me my crescent moon or you'll be burned alive."

"It makes little difference to me if I'm burned alive or eaten by Goulaffre, so as that's the way it is, I'll take the challenge!"

So, Allanic set off and, as he knew the way and had the seven-league boots, he soon arrived at the giant's castle. Workmen were repairing the roof, so he hid in the forest and waited until night. About ten o'clock, as it had gone very dark, the crescent moon was hung from the highest tower. It lit up everything for miles around. The workmen had gone home at the end of the day and had left their ladders against the castle walls. Around midnight, Allanic came out of the forest and, with the help of the ladders, climbed to the top of the tower, took down the crescent moon, put it in a bag he had brought with him, and left without wasting any time.

As it had become dark all of a sudden, the giant came out to see what was the matter. He saw Allanic as he was leaving with the crescent moon on his back. He shouted out and roared like a wild animal. He wanted to give chase to the thief but, alas, he no longer had his seven-league boots.

When Allanic arrived in Paris with the crescent moon, he immediately hung it from the highest tower of the king's palace and the whole town was one minute in complete darkness and the next suddenly lit up as if it were the middle of the day. The townsfolk got up and ran to the palace, where the light was coming from, and, seeing that their king had got back his crescent moon, they were all happy. The king himself could not contain his joy. He ordered that there be a great celebration to which the princes, princesses, generals, and all the bigwigs in the kingdom were invited, and he introduced Allanic to them as the conquering hero of the crescent moon and asked them to treat him as they would his best friend. The feasting and partying lasted for fifteen whole days throughout the whole of the town.

After he had been admiring his crescent moon for three months, the old king started to miss his golden cage as never before and each day he became less and less happy and more and more sad. Allanic noticed it, as did everybody else, and he said to himself, "This is not good. The king will never come to terms with the loss of his golden cage and I'm afraid that one of these days he will tell me to go and fetch it for him."

And sure enough, a little while later the king called him to his room and said, "Allanic, you see how I'm wallowing in sadness and pity and all because of the loss of my golden cage and if I don't have it back in my palace, I'll surely die. You took Goulaffre's seven-league boots from him and you also got back my crescent moon. Now you must go and fetch me my golden cage."

"Ah, sire, there's not a man in the world who could do what you ask. Just imagine, this cage is hung above the giant's bed by four chains. How am I supposed to break into his bedroom and cut the four chains without waking him up? It's impossible!"

"You managed to bring back my crescent moon and now you must bring me back my golden cage, or it's death that awaits you!"

"You are sending me to certain death, but it makes little difference to me if I die here or I die there, so I'd rather take up the challenge. Have made for me a pair of scissors capable of cutting through the golden chains as if they were threads of cotton or hemp and then I'll be on my way."

A craftsman was found who was skilled enough to make the scissors required and Allanic went on his way. When he arrived close by the castle, he was delighted to see that the roofers had not finished their work and their ladders were still leaning up against the wall.

Around midnight, he broke into Goulaffre's bedroom by smashing a window. The giant was sleeping so deeply that he didn't hear a thing. The room was lit up. Allanic saw the golden cage above Goulaffre's forehead. He put one foot on the edge of the bed and the other against the wall and, with one snip of the scissors, he cut the first golden chain. Clink!

The giant didn't budge. Then he cut the second chain. Clink!

The giant made a slight movement. Then the third. Clink!

The giant turned over in his bed but didn't wake up. Finally, the fourth chain was cut. Clink!

But alas! The cage fell onto Goulaffre's face and woke him up. He grabbed Allanic by the waist, recognized him, and cried out, "Ah, so it's you, you little monster! I see what you're up to, but this time you won't get away. I shall eat you for breakfast this very morning."

"Alas! I see that it is hopeless and that the game is up. It's only what I deserve after all the harm I've done you. But, tell me please, what sauce do you plan to eat me with?"

"I'll roast you alive on a spit above the fire."

"Then I can see that you don't know the first thing about good cooking. Do as I tell you and you'll have the most delicious meal that you've ever eaten."

"Well, go on then."

"Put me in a sack, then go into the forest, pull up a medium-sized tree, and come back and beat me to a pulp with the tree trunk. Then put it all into your large pot with a little butter, some salt and pepper, and light a good fire underneath. I'll tell you again that you'll have a meal that will have you licking your fingers for the next twenty-four hours."

"That sounds like a good idea. That would be very tasty, so I'll do as you say."

Then the giant put Allanic in a sack and went to the forest to pull up a beech tree to beat him with. No sooner had he gone outside than Allanic started to cry out for help at the top of his voice. The giant's wife came running.

"Who's there? Who's doing all the shouting?"

"Alas, my good woman, it's a poor man who has never harmed a soul."

"And who put you in the sack?"

"Your husband."

"Why?"

"Because I took a few pieces of dry wood from the forest."

"So, why did you steal wood from us?"

"So I could cook potatoes for my wife and my children's dinner. I am so poor. And I have six children and I have nothing but my work and the charity of generous souls to support us. Have pity on me and my poor wife and poor children, who are at home, dying of hunger. Help me to get away from here. Your husband will think that I managed to escape by myself."

The giant's wife was moved and she untied the rope around the sack. Allanic leaped out and bundled her in, in his place. Then he ran to the giant's room, took the golden cage, and left.

Goulaffre soon arrived back with an uprooted tree and he started to beat the sack.

"Stop, you fool, I'm your wife!" cried out the giantess from inside the sack. But Goulaffre wouldn't listen to her and he carried on hitting, as if he were deaf. After half an hour, when he could no longer hear anything, he opened the sack.

"My wife!" he cried out, recognizing her clothes. And he began to tear out his hair and howl like a wild animal. Meanwhile, Allanic had arrived back in Paris with the golden cage. The old king, who had been so sad and miserable before, was now happy and full of joy again upon seeing his cage once more, and he spent whole days just looking at the wondrous thing. But after a few months, his happiness started to vanish again, little by little.

"What's he going to ask me to do now?" Allanic said to himself anxiously.

Eventually the king said to him one day, "I shall never be happy until you have brought Goulaffre the giant himself here to me in my palace."

"Ah, sire! You're asking the impossible! And after all I have done for you, won't you give me a moment of peace?"

"I'm telling you, you must bring me Goulaffre the giant, or death alone awaits you!"

"Well, I can see now that you want me to die. But at least give me everything I ask for in order to attempt this impossible task."

"Ask for anything you want and I will deny you nothing."

"Very well, have built for me a carriage made of pure gold, decorated on the inside with sharp spikes and with a single door that will close by itself on anybody who gets into the carriage, so that they will be unable to open it, no matter how hard they try. And I will also need twenty-four strong horses to pull it."

"You shall have it all," replied the king.

Blacksmiths and locksmiths of great skill were found and in no time at all the carriage had been built according to the desired specifications. Twenty-four magnificent horses were hitched to it and Allanic climbed onto the seat, dressed as a coachman. And off he went.

When he arrived in the forest that surrounded the castle, he saw the giant walking about. He was weeping and wailing and moaning wildly. Allanic went toward him and politely asked him, "Sire, what is the cause of such great sadness?"

"Oh, I am the most wretched of all giants. A little runt by the name of Allanic made me kill my two daughters and my wife and, what's more, he stole my seven-league boots, my crescent moon, and my golden cage. Oh, if only I could get my hands on him. But I don't know where to find him or where he even lives."

"Allanic! But I know him very well and I also have a bone to pick with him and I would like to take my revenge on him for all the trouble he has caused me. Climb aboard my carriage, sire, and I'll take you to him without delay."

Goulaffre, who didn't recognize Allanic disguised as the coachman of a grand house, climbed into the carriage without hesitation and immediately the door closed itself on him with a bang and the coachman whipped the horses, which set off at a great gallop. The poor giant, buffeted about inside his prison, torn by the spikes that pierced his body from all sides, let out terrifying screams and tried as hard as he could to open the door and smash up the carriage. But it was all to no avail. His screams of rage terrified man and beast as he passed by.

They arrived in Paris, but once the giant had been led into the palace courtyard, they didn't know what to do with him. Everybody trembled when they heard him yelling and roaring from inside his prison.

The Council was summoned to deliberate on what should be done. Nobody was able to give any sensible advice. Everybody was overcome with fear. Then Allanic said, "I will drive the carriage to the middle of a great plain. Arrange for fifty wagonloads of oak to be stacked around it, along with the same number of wagonloads of kindling. There we will set fire to it and Goulaffre will be burned alive and reduced to cinders in the middle of the inferno and won't be able to harm a soul."

They followed his advice and so they rid themselves of the terrible giant Goulaffre. Then Allanic married the king's daughter and, as he was good at heart, he appointed Fistilou as commander-in-chief of the army, even though Fistilou had tried to cause a lot of trouble for him.

For a whole month there were public celebrations and endless feasting. I was young then and was taken on in the palace kitchen to turn the spit and that's how I came to learn the story of Allanic and Goulaffre the giant and am able to tell you everything just as it happened.

■ 15. The Miller and His Seigneur

Told by Barba Tassel, Plouaret, December 1868

It had been four years since he had paid any rent to the seigneur. That's how poor he was! One day, the seigneur was on his way home from hunting and was in a bad mood because he hadn't caught a single thing and so, finding the miller's cow blocking the road, he shot and killed it. The miller's wife saw what happened and she ran up to the house, crying in dismay, "Alas! Alas! Now we are really done for! Our cow has been killed by the seigneur!"

The miller said nothing, but he was furious nonetheless. During the night, he skinned the cow and he set off to sell the hide at Guingamp. Because it was a long way away and he wanted to reach the town by the early morning, he left the house around midnight. As he walked through the wood, where according to rumor there lived a band of fearsome robbers, he became frightened and he climbed up a tree and waited for the morning.

Soon a band of robbers arrived at the tree to divide up their money. And there was so much squabbling and noise, they just couldn't agree on anything.

"Jesus, if only I could have that money!" said the miller to himself. And the idea came to him to throw the cow's hide down into the middle of them to scare them. On seeing the horns and the black skin (the cow was black, you see), they thought it was the Devil himself who had come looking for them. And so, they fled in all directions, leaving all their money behind.

"Well, my trick seems to have worked!" said the miller. And he got down out of the tree, gathered up all the money in the cowskin, and ran back to the house! He and his wife spent until morning counting the money, but even then they were unable to come to a final figure, as there was too much money!

The following morning, the miller told his wife to go to the seigneur's house and ask to borrow the large scales so they could weigh the money. His wife went off and asked for the scales.

"What do you need the scales for?" the seigneur asked her.

"To weigh all our money, sir."

"To weigh all your money?! I think you're pulling my leg."

"Oh, my lord, no sir. I'm telling you the truth. Come with me and I'll show you."

The seigneur went with her. When he saw the miller's table covered in gold coins, he was astounded and said to him, "Where did you get that money from?"

"I got it from the sale of my cowskin in Guingamp, sir."

"From your cowskin?! Cowskins must be fetching a good price then!"

"Yes, sir, they certainly are, and you did me a great favor by killing my cow."

And the seigneur ran straight back home and had all of his cows killed and skinned. The following morning, he sent his servant into town with the skins (there were so many of them, he needed a horse to carry them) and told him to ask for a pile of money for each one. The servant went off to town with the skins.

"How much for each skin?" a tanner asked him.

"A pile of money!"

"Come on! Don't mess around with me, how much for each skin?"

"I've told you, a pile of money."

And when he gave the same answer to everyone, the tanners became angry and gave him a thrashing, knocked him to the ground, and even stole the skins from him. When he arrived back at the house, the seigneur asked him, "Where is the money?"

"Ah, the money! To tell the truth, all I got was a good kicking and a beating and my poor body is black and blue."

"The miller has tricked me!" the seigneur cried out in a rage. "But not to worry, I'll get my own back!"

The miller laid out a small feast with the cow that had been killed and he told his wife to go and invite the seigneur as well. The miller's wife went off and delivered the invitation.

"How dare you come to make fun of me again and in my own house?!"

"Jesus! Me, sir, make fun of you? Neither I nor my husband would ever dare to do a thing like that."

"Well then, I'll come anyway and I'll speak to the miller. Perhaps he thinks that he's cleverer than me?"

The seigneur went to eat at the mill. There was loads of grub—pork fat, a spit roast, cider and wine too! Toward the end of the meal, when things had gotten properly warmed up, the miller said to the seigneur, "Everybody, sir, knows that you are very clever, but all the same I would like to wager that you cannot do what I can do."

"And what is that then?"

"Kill my wife in front of everybody and then bring her back to life by playing this violin here."

"I'll bet twenty crowns that you can't do that."

"Twenty crowns that I can!"

"Come on then, let's see!" everyone shouted, seeing that the seigneur had accepted the bet.

And the miller took his knife, jumped on his wife, and pretended to cut her throat. But he was only cutting a blood-filled bladder that he had placed around her neck. The seigneur, who was unaware of the trick, like everyone else, was horrified to see the blood flowing. The woman fell to the ground as if she were quite dead. The miller then took his violin and started to play. And right away his wife began to get up and dance, like a madwoman. The seigneur could only stand there and watch her, his mouth open.

"Give me your violin," he said to the miller, "and I'll let you have the mill rent-free for two years."

The deal was done and the seigneur ran back to the house, carrying his violin and very happy. "My wife is getting a little old," he said to himself as he went along. "If only I could make her young again!"

When he got home, he found his wife in bed, fast asleep. "That's good," he said. "This way she won't know a thing."

He took a knife from the kitchen and cut his wife's throat. And then he started to play his violin! But however much he played, the poor woman neither danced nor budged an inch. She was as dead as could be!

"What a fool that miller is!" he said to himself. "I killed my wife and I played the violin beautifully, but still she's not restored to life! He must have forgotten to tell me something. I'll go and see him quickly."

He ran to the mill. When he got there, he saw the miller in his shirt sleeves, holding a whip and whipping a large cooking pot that stood in the middle of the yard and inside which the water was boiling. (He had just that minute cleared away the fire from underneath.) He stood watching the miller, his mouth open, and he forgot all about his wife.

"What is that you're doing, miller?"

"I'm boiling the stock, sir. Quickly, come and have a look at it bubbling away." The seigneur stepped forward to look inside the pot and said, "Why, so it is. And you're using your whip to make it boil like that?"

"Of course, sir. Wood is very expensive and it would be too pricey for me."

"That's true enough. Give me your whip and I'll let you have the mill rent-free for another two years."

"Seeing as it's you, sir, here you are!" And the seigneur returned home with the whip and as he arrived, he said to himself, "Now I'm going to chop down all the trees on my land and I'll get lots of money." And he sold all the wood on his land.

One Saturday evening, the cook said to him, "Sir, I haven't any wood left, or even any bundles of twigs, so how am I supposed to cook the dinner?"

"I know exactly what to do, cook. Don't you worry about it."

The following morning, which was Sunday, the seigneur said to his staff, his valets and servants, to go off to High Mass, with the exception of Little John,* his head valet, who would stay back at the house with him.

"And who's going to get the dinner ready?" asked the cook.

"Don't worry about it and off you go, like I told you."

So, they all went off to the town. Then the seigneur told Little John to carry the large cooking pot into the middle of the courtyard and to fill it with water. Then he added the fat, the salt beef, the cabbage, the turnips, salt and pepper—well, everything that is needed to make a good stock. Then he took off his jacket, took the miller's whip, and began to whip the pot. But no matter how hard he whipped, the water remained cold.

"What are you doing, sir?" asked Little John, astonished.

"Shut up, you fool, you'll see soon enough."

And so, he continued to whip as best he could. From time to time, he dipped his finger into the pot, but the water was always cold. At last, when he had had enough, he stopped and said, "Indeed, I'm afraid the miller has been making a fool of me."

"Yes, he's certainly made a fool of you, sir," replied Little John.

"Ah well, no matter. He will pay for this with his life."

"I think a good whipping would be sufficient, sir."

"No, no, death! Making a fool of me! Come on, quickly, off to the mill! And bring a sack so we can put him in it and throw it into the pond to drown him."

Little John slung an empty sack over his shoulder and they both went off to the mill. The poor miller was bundled into the sack, then loaded onto his own horse to be taken down to the pond, which was some distance away. On the way, they saw coming toward them

---

* In French, "Grand-Jean," or "Big John." Here I have used the traditional ironic moniker of "Little" to denote someone of inordinately large stature.

on the road a merchant on his way to the fair at Guingamp with three horses all loaded up with goods. The seigneur was frightened.

"Let's go and hide on the other side of the ditch," he said, "until the merchant has gone by." So, they crossed over the ditch into the field. The miller, in his sack, was dumped into the ditch by the side of the road. When he heard the sound of the merchant's horses as they passed by, he cried out, "I won't have her! I won't have her!"

The merchant, astonished, went up to the sack. "Hang on!" he said, "What was that?"

The miller carried on shouting, "No, I won't have her! I won't have her!"

"Whom won't you have?" asked the merchant.

"The only daughter of a very rich seigneur, who had a child and now he wants me to marry her."

"And is she really very rich?"

"Yes, richer than anyone in the whole land."

"Well, then I'd be happy to have her."

"Well, quickly then. You get inside the sack and I'll get out."

The merchant got into the sack and the miller secured him inside, then took his whip and went off toward Guingamp with the three horses, fully laden with goods. After he had gone, the seigneur and Little John returned for their sack.

"I'll have her! I'll have her!" cried the merchant from inside.

"Whom will you have?" asked the seigneur.

"Your daughter, sir."

"Ah, son of a b . . . go and look for her then in the bottom of the pond!" And they threw him into the pond and he was never seen again.

The following day, the seigneur and Little John, his valet, went to the fair at Guingamp. As they walked around all the beautiful stalls, they were completely astounded to find the miller there too, in charge of a beautiful stall selling silverware.

"How is it that you're here, miller?" the seigneur said to him.

"Now surely, sir, you're going to buy something from me?"

"What? Shouldn't you still be in the pond?"

"As you can see, sir, I didn't like it in there, but I must thank you because that is where I found all the beautiful things that you see here."

"Really?"

"Just as I said, sir. My only regret is that you didn't throw me a bit farther in. Then I would have landed among all the gold items."

"Really?"

"As true as my word, sir."

"And it's all still there?"

"As far as I know. But you should hurry if you want to go and have a look."

And the seigneur went back home with his servant and ran to the pond. The seigneur threw Little John into the water and, as he was very tall, his hand was still sticking out of the water, calling for help, as he couldn't swim.

"I see!" said the seigneur. "He's signaling to me with his hand to jump in a bit further. Obviously he's not far enough in for the gold." And he took a run up and jumped in as far as he could.

And not a word has been heard of them ever since.

And that is the story of the miller and his seigneur.

■ 16. Jean and His Rod of Iron

No record of the storyteller; Plouaret, 1873

Jean was three years in his mother's womb and when he came into the world, he was the strongest child that had ever been seen.

When he was fourteen years old, he had made for him a rod of iron that weighed five hundred pounds and he took it with him on his travels.

In a wood, he met an old woman with long, sharp teeth.

"What long teeth you have, grandmother!"

"And sharp ones too, my son," replied the old woman.

"Show me by biting into my rod." And he lifted the end of his rod up to the old woman's mouth. She bit into it and bit off a piece. Jean, upset to see his rod damaged, hit her over the head with it.

"It appears to be hailing," said the old woman, without flinching.

Jean hit her for a second time, then a third. Then he killed her and broke three of her teeth. The first tooth turned into a hollow golden ball and the other two each into solid golden balls. Jean continued on his way.

He arrived at an old castle surrounded by trees, in which another old woman lived. She said to him, "You have killed my sister, but now you'll have to deal with me."

Jean replied simply by dealing her a big blow on the head with his rod and killing her as well. Then he threw her into a large cauldron full of boiling water that was sitting on the fire.

Then he climbed on top of the fireplace, pulling up with him a sack full of stones. A moment later, the old woman's son, who was a giant, arrived home and said, "I'm hungry, Mother, I'm so hungry. . . . Where are you?"

"I'm here," said the old woman, "in the cauldron of boiling water."

"Where?"

"In the cauldron of boiling water."

The giant bent down to look inside the cauldron and Jean hit him so violently on the back of the neck with a stone that he too fell in headfirst.

Shortly afterward, a second giant came in. He also went to look inside the cauldron and Jean dealt with him in a similar fashion.

Then along came a third giant, who, seeing nobody around, called out, "Where are you, Mother?"

"Here I am, my son, on top of the fireplace."

"Then come down quickly and get me something to eat because I'm starving!"

And Jean came down and devoured the giant.

Immediately, three beautiful princesses, three sisters, came into the house and said, "Thank you, Jean, you have saved us! But what have you done with the old woman and her sons?"

"The old woman and two of her sons are cooking away in the cauldron of boiling water over there."

"And the third son?"

"I've eaten him up!"

"Well, you'll have to bring him back up again, and when you've brought him back up, he will try to swallow you whole instead. But this is what you must do to avoid being eaten. When you go to the one place that a servant *can't* go on behalf of his master, bring back a bale of straw, and when you vomit up the giant, immediately cover him with straw, then set fire to it and he will die."

Jean did exactly as instructed and so destroyed the giant he had swallowed.

"But there's still a fourth giant," said the princesses, "and he is far more terrible than the others. This one is a great wizard. He lives in an underground room beneath the castle. He has a bell on his head and when the bell rings, nothing is able to resist him. But each of us will give you a talisman and with them you'll be able to finish him off too."

"Take this gold ring," said the eldest of the three princesses, "and when you place it on your finger, you will become invisible."

"Take this cross," said the second, "and whosoever looks at it, apart from you, will immediately become blind."

"Take this sword," said the third, "which will cut through iron and steel."

"With these three things," said Jean, "I'll polish that wizard off all right and I'd go after him even if he were the Devil himself." He went down into the basement by a staircase that the princesses showed him and he knocked on the wizard's door.

"Who's there?" he asked.

"It's your brother who's come to see you," replied Jean, making his voice sound louder and deeper. The wizard opened the door. Jean was wearing the ring on his finger and was invisible. He held the cross in front of the eyes of the giant, who immediately became blind. Then, with his sword, Jean first cut off his head and then all his limbs, which he dispatched to different sides of the room to stop them re-forming. Then he went back upstairs.

The three princesses were impatiently waiting for him and when they saw him, they cried out, overcome with joy.

"Now we are truly saved! And now you must choose which of us you would prefer to be your wife!"

Jean chose the eldest, but the middle sister killed her out of jealousy and so he married her instead. The youngest then killed the middle sister. But Jean didn't want to marry her. He left the castle to go and do penitence underneath a large rock in the middle of a forest and there he lived the life, and died the death, of a saint.

.

Fourth Veillée

■ 17. The Night Crier

Told by Fanch Ar Manac'h, a servant from Keramborgne, and
Françoise Le Digarher, a farmer's wife from Keramborgne,
but formerly from Kevarhant in Plounévez-Moëdec,
30 November 1891

"In my youth," said Fanch Ar Manac'h, a servant at Keramborgne,
"I was mad for cards and I would walk for miles, every evening after
supper, no matter how tired I was, to find people to play with.
Today I don't do that at all and I won't even go as far as the bottom
of the garden.

"One night, I was at a get-together at Little Kevarhant. I lived
at Great Kevarhant and to get back to the house I had to go across
a field and then through a small oak and pine wood called Wailer's
Wood. The field was quite big, about the same as the large meadow
at Keramborgne. The game finished around ten or half past, so not
really that late.

"As I entered the wood, I heard a shriek a short distance away.
I thought little of it and continued on my way, but as I came out
of the wood and into the meadow, there was another shriek, louder
and a little closer to me. I'm not really a timid fellow, but even so,
I would have preferred to have been home in my bed. I carried on
walking and as I reached the middle of the meadow, there was a
third shriek, but much louder and closer so that I thought that
whatever it was, was right on my heels. I turned around but saw
nothing. But the shrieks now came at more than once a minute and
each time they became louder and louder.

"Now I was gripped with fear and I started to run. The shrieks
followed me and each time they were closer and more piercing so
that they went right through me. At last, I reached the door of the

stable, where my bed was, and just as I got inside, the crier, who I felt was on my heels, let forth a final shriek, louder than all the others, so that I thought that all the buildings around the farmyard were shaking and might even come tumbling down. I slammed the door shut, drew the bolt across, and hid in my bed, more dead than alive.

"I had often heard the crier before, if I got up in the night to check on the horses, but because it had never chased me before and because it had stayed within the wood, I hardly paid any attention to it.

"My brother Yves was also chased by it one night when he returned late from a party (a sausage festival, I think it was). He started to run until he was out of breath and, as he couldn't find an open door, he flung himself, as he passed a cowshed, headlong into a bale of straw that was blocking up a small, low window and he fell into the stable where he hid beneath the belly of a cow. It very nearly drove him out of his wits.

"My brother and I still often hear the night crier, but it doesn't chase us anymore. I should say, though, that we avoid going through the woods once night has fallen and we'd rather go the long way round."

"Oh," said Françoise Le Digarher, a farmer's wife who had lived in Kevarhant in Plounévez-Moëdec, "when I was at Kevarhant I often heard the same thing in the wood. On lovely summer's nights, I would also leave the bedroom window open and I clearly heard it, and other things too, because astonishing things are always being seen and heard in these big old houses."

"What else did you hear then, Françoise?" asked the weaver Fanch Ar Moal.[*]

---

[*] Fanch Ar Moal (François the Bald) was one of the pseudonyms used by Luzel, most notably for publishing poetry.

"Well, I used to hear the spinning wheels and the bobbins turning so quickly that they whistled. It also sounded as if somebody was throwing the furniture and crockery from one end of the kitchen to the other and it was a terrible racket. Then I would hear somebody walking barefoot softly across the floorboards. When I went to bed, I would blow out my candle and place the candlestick on the bedside table. But right away it was as if somebody threw it violently against the wall at the other end of the room."

"How could you stay sleeping there?" asked Fanch Ar Moal.

"I just got used to it. And I'm not a fearful person. I would pray because I thought it was the souls of the people who used to live in the house and that they had come back to make all this noise so that we would pray for their deliverance from purgatory. Then I would sleep peacefully and, in the morning, I would get up and find everything back in its place, as if nothing had moved. Everybody who slept in the house heard the same noises and they sometimes asked me, 'Didn't you hear the noise during the night, Françoise?' and I would reply, 'No, I never heard a thing.' I didn't want to frighten them.

"One night, though, I was afraid. I was woken up in the middle of the night by the sound of footsteps, this time as if somebody was walking around my room in hob-nailed boots. I looked around and didn't see anything at first. Then I saw a very large man coming toward me. He climbed onto the bench at the foot of the bed. I shrank back in fear, closed my eyes and hid my face beneath the sheets, and cowered against the wall.

"The following night, as I went to my room, I was anxious. I didn't tell anybody what I had seen, but I secretly took a barley loaf and a crêpe up with me. I put them on the table next to my bed and I said loudly, before turning in, 'I don't know who you are, whether you're an evil spirit or a tortured soul, but if you are hungry, here's some bread and a crêpe. Eat them up and leave me in peace.' That night, I neither heard nor saw a thing."

"And were the bread and the crêpe eaten?" asked Laouic, the young shepherd.

"No, I found them the following morning, just as I'd left them on the table. They hadn't been touched. The following night, the racket started up again, but I was used to it and paid no attention."

■ 18. The Burning Whip

Told by Marguérite Philippe, September 1889

A greedy and quarrelsome woman took one of her tenant farmers to court because he had cut down a tree on the farm without her permission. The farmer lost the case and because he had no money to pay the fine, he sold all his furniture, as it was all he possessed, and so was reduced to begging.

The owner of the farm attended the sale and bought almost everything at a bargain price. There was nothing left to sell when she noticed a whip hanging from a nail on the stable wall and she said, "Look, there's still a whip. It must be sold as well." It was knocked down to her for three sous.

The woman died shortly afterward, but after her funeral, she was seen every night, lumbering around the outside of the house and the farm's stables, a burning whip at her neck, as she cried out, "Take this whip away! Take this whip away!"

It was terrifying and nobody dared go near her and take away the burning whip that tormented her, so that a priest had to be sent for to exorcise her and throw it into a neighboring mill pond— after which nobody ever saw her again.

■ 19. The Midnight Washerwoman (Soëzic)

Told in Breton by François Thépault, Plouaret, 20 February 1890

A young girl called Soëzic Ar Floc'h, whom I knew well, had been busy with delivering milk to the farm at Loguellou in the commune of Botsorhel, the day before the *pardon* of some saint or other, the patron saint of the local friary or the region where the farm was. It was in April and she was returning alone about nine o'clock in the evening when, as she passed by a meadow, where there was a pond that served as the communal laundry, she heard somebody call out her name, very clearly, "Soëzic!"

She stopped for a moment, looked about her, and seeing nobody, she continued on her way until she came to a little copse that you had to go through to reach the pond. No sooner had she entered the copse than she heard the same voice calling her, but louder and clearer. "Soëzic!" And she still could see nobody.

"That's odd," she thought. "Who can be calling out my name like this, where I can't see a soul anywhere?"

She started to feel afraid and quickened her pace. As she got near the pond, she jumped over the little brook that flowed from it, but at that moment, she heard a paddle being banged on the laundry stones three times, so violently that it echoed down the valley in the distance. She remembered being told that many countryfolk had seen midnight washerwomen at this pond and, stricken with fear, she started to run, as if the Devil himself were at her heels. She quickly went up to the first house that she came to and, out of breath, collapsed lifelessly as she stepped over the threshold. She became seriously ill as a result and very nearly died.

■ 20. The Midnight Washerwoman (The Spinner)

Told in Breton by François Thépault, Plouaret, 19 February 1890

A woman by the name of Marianna Kerbenès very much liked to spin and would spend all her time at the spinning wheel. Even at nighttime, when her husband and her children were in bed, she continued spinning, all by herself, until midnight and often until daybreak, never tiring of it. On Sunday as well, after she returned from mass, she would go back to her spinning wheel. Every Saturday, she would go to the market in Morlaix to sell her yarn and would bring the money back home without wasting a single penny.

One Sunday evening, as she sat up late spinning, as was her wont, she ran out of flax and went outside to look for some more in the shed in the yard. The moon shone brightly and she saw, coming toward her, a woman she did not know and who spoke to her thus:

"I was passing by your home and I saw the lights were on and, as I don't know what the time is exactly, although I think it must be nearly midnight, I was going to come in and ask the time."

They went into the house together, looked at the clock, and saw that it was half past eleven.

"Why are you not in bed at this hour?" the stranger asked Marianna. "Are you not frightened to stay up on your own so late at night? Are you all alone here?"

"No, I have my husband and my children with me, but they have gone to bed. Myself, I don't turn in so early and I normally stay here spinning after they have gone to bed."

"Do you like spinning then—and are you good at it? Me too and, if you wish, I shall stay here with you until daybreak and we can spin together and you shall see how hard-working I am."

"Nothing would please me more," replied Marianna. And she gave the stranger a spinning wheel and a spindle and they set to their spinning, each one trying to outdo the other. But the stranger was an odd spinner. She spun and spun and spun with the speed of a steam engine and Marianna had not finished her first spindle by the time her companion was on her twelfth. She thought this was extraordinary and she watched her companion carefully and saw that she was old—very old—with an unusual face that immediately made Marianna shiver. But as she was tiring from the hard work, she said nothing. As they worked away, the pile of flax had soon run out and been transformed into beautiful bobbins of fine yarn.

"What shall we do now?" the stranger then asked.

"Well," replied Marianna, who was keen to make use of the generosity of such a skillful worker, "if you want, we can now wash our yarn and steam it with hot water to bleach it."

"I would like that very much," replied the other. "Let us wash our yarn and steam it with hot water."

And as the moon was shining brightly, they went to the communal laundry with their yarn, washed it, beat it vigorously to get rid of the water, making a noise that echoed through the whole valley, then carried it back to the house to begin the steaming. They built a large fire by the doorway, put a large pot on top, then, each taking an earthenware jug, they went to fetch water from the well to fill it up.

Meanwhile, Marianna's husband was woken up by all the commotion and he saw the stranger emptying her jug into the pot. Then she went over to his bed and looked at him with eyes that were like burning coals. He was so frightened that he hid his head beneath the sheets and didn't dare say a thing. The stranger returned to the well with her jug. Just as she left, Marianna returned and her husband, recognizing her voice, came out from under the sheets and, seeing his wife was alone in the house, jumped out of bed, ran up to her, and said, "You fool! Don't you see that you have invited a midnight washerwoman into our house? This woman is sent not by God, but by the Devil. First we must shut the door so that she can't come back in, and then we must displace or turn upside down everything she has touched."

And they threw the spinning wheel and the spindle that the midnight washerwoman had been using to the far end of the house and turned the pot upside down, pouring water onto the fire as they did so.

The midnight washerwoman soon returned and, finding the door locked, knocked and cried out, "Let me in, my friend. I have a jug full of water. Why have you shut the door?"

"Don't say anything," the husband said to Marianna. "Not a word!"

And the midnight washerwoman said again, a little louder, "Let me in then, my friend!" And when she still got no answer, she said, "Let me in, oh spinning wheel on which I spun."

"I cannot," replied the spinning wheel. "I have been turned upside down and thrown to the back of the house."

"Let me in, oh spindle with which I spun." (She was also a witch, you see.)

"I cannot," replied the spindle. "I am lying on the floor next to the spinning wheel."

"Let me in," said the witch, "oh pot that I placed on the fire and filled with water."

"I cannot," replied the pot. "I have been turned upside down and thrown into the back of the house."

"Let me in, oh water that I poured into the pot."

"I cannot," replied the water. "I have been poured over the fire."

"Let me in, oh kindling that I lit in the hearth."

"We cannot," replied the kindling. "We have had water poured over us from the pot and have been put out."

Then the witch let out a terrible cry and said, "You have had the good fortune to find someone wiser than yourself to advise you, because otherwise by morning you would have been found cooked in your pot with your yarn!"

And off she went.

And from that day forth, Marianna Kerbenès did not stay up late into the night spinning and went to bed at a decent time, as one ought to.

■ 21. Jean the Strong and the Three Giants

Told to Marguérite Philippe by Vincent Le Bail of Coatascorn (Côtes-du-Nord), 1872

There was a young shepherd on a farm in Lower Brittany. His name was Jean and he was thought to be a simple-minded fellow. Every day at sunrise, he would set out with his sheep and didn't return until the sun had set.

One summer's day, one of the maids brought some crêpes and buttermilk out to the fields for his lunch and spilled a few drops of the milk onto his clothes. A number of flies came to settle there, as it was a hot day. With a single smack of his hand, he killed eighteen of them.

"Eighteen!" he exclaimed to himself, after he had counted them. "Eighteen with a single blow! What a fine fellow I am! I'm clearly too good to stay around here looking after the cows and the sheep like some idiotic half-wit. To hell with the cows and sheep! I'm going traveling to see if I can find anyone who's a match for me. Eighteen with a single blow!"

And he set off, leaving his flock where it was. In the next village, he had written in large golden letters on a ribbon, which he used as a hatband, "I killed eighteen of them with a single blow!"

Then he set off and went to Paris. He went straight to the door of the king's palace and knocked.

"What do you want, boy?" the porter asked him.

"Is the king in need of a good servant who can do absolutely anything, like no other?"

"There was a stable lad who left yesterday and he'll need to be replaced."

"Very well! Then take me and I'll show you what sort of man I am."

He was put in charge of one of the palace stables. The horses were all skinny and in a sorry state as a result of the poor care they had received from the stable lad who had just left. In next to no time, Jean had turned them into the best and most handsome in all the royal stables. The king noticed this and complimented him on it and even developed a great affection for him. This well-deserved recognition nonetheless provoked the jealousy of the other stable lads and they plotted his downfall.

One day, one of them went to see the king and said, "Sire, Jean the stable boy said he was the man to rid you of the three giants."

In a neighboring castle, in the middle of a large forest, there were three giants who caused as much trouble and strife to the king as was possible. They destroyed his crops, stole his cattle, sheep, and horses, and lived at his expense. Many a time, he had sent his armies out against them, but the men were always defeated and came back in the most piteous state. And so, these giants had driven the king to the end of his tether. He immediately called for Jean to be brought to him and said, "Is it true that you have said that you can rid me of these three giants?"

"I have never said anything of the sort, Your Highness," replied Jean, astonished by such a question.

"You did say it and you must keep your word, or you will be put to death!"

"And what will you give me if I do rid you of these three giants?"

"If you rid me of the three giants, I will give you my daughter's hand in marriage."

"Very well," said Jean. "I have killed eighteen with a single blow and I am not a man to be scared of three now, no matter who they are!" And on this note, off he went.

Each day, the three giants came to drink at a large and beautiful spring in the forest. Jean climbed up a large oak tree, whose branches extended down over the spring, and waited silently with a sack full of stones.

The giants came, as usual, to drink. Never before had Jean seen such terribly ugly monsters. Well, the eldest stretched himself out on his belly and started to drink from the spring. Jean threw a stone and hit him on the back of the neck. The giant turned around and said, "Which one of you threw that stone at me?"

"Nobody laid a finger on you," the other two replied.

"Well, don't do it again or you'll be sorry." And he bent down once again at the spring and started to drink.

Jean threw a second stone at him, much harder than the first. The giant got up, furious, rushed over to the brother the stone was lying nearest to, and killed him, just like that! Then he calmly went back to having a drink. Jean threw a third stone at him. The giant rushed over to his other brother and killed him, just like the first.

"I'll teach you to throw stones at me while I'm drinking!" he said.

And he went back to his drinking. Jean threw the stones at him, this time showering him with them like hailstones. Furious and not knowing who to turn to anymore, the giant stamped his feet, gnashed his teeth, and cried out so ferociously that all the animals of the forest trembled and ran away. Finally, he noticed Jean up in the tree and shouted at him.

"So, it was you, you scoundrel! You're to blame for my killing my brothers like that! Come down from there this minute and I'll eat you up!"

"Yes, of course. Right away," Jean replied. "And don't think I'm afraid of you, you great ugly brute! You'll soon see what I'm made of!" And he climbed down from the tree. The giant was bearing down on Jean, with his mouth wide open, ready to eat him up, when he noticed the words written on Jean's hatband: "I killed eighteen of them with a single blow!" And the giant pulled up short, his mouth still wide open.

"Is it true what it says on your hat?" he asked, having suddenly calmed down.

"Of course it's true and you'll find out soon enough who it is you're dealing with."

"What a fine fellow you are! Well, let's be friends and together we'll have no equals anywhere in the world. Come with me to my castle. I'll introduce you to my mother and we'll drink and hang out together."

"I'd like that," said Jean, "but you'd better not play any tricks on me or you'll be sorry." And they went off together to the castle.

"Where are your two brothers?" the giant's mother asked her eldest son when she saw him returning without the other two.

"I've killed them."

"What?! You great ugly brute! You've killed your two brothers?!"

"I've killed them, Mother, but this little man here that I've brought home is worth more than my two brothers put together."

"What do you mean, you fool?"

"See what is written on his hat: 'I killed eighteen of them with a single blow.'"

"And is that true?"

"Absolutely true, Mother, and if it weren't, you know full well that he wouldn't still be alive."

The old woman, like her son, was full of admiration for such a man and suddenly calmed down and was happy enough.

"Well now, you two can go and fetch me some water from the spring so that I can get your dinner ready."

"Let's go and fetch the water for my mother so that she can get our dinner ready," said the giant to Jean.

At the back of the kitchen, there were two barrels, each the equivalent of five hogsheads, which were used by the giants to store the water from the house. When Jean saw them, he said to the giant, "What? Do you use these nutshells for fetching the water for the house?"

"Do you not think they are big enough?" asked the giant.

"They are nothing more than nutshells, I tell you. Get me my pick and shovel, put them in a wheelbarrow, and then we'll be off."

"Why a pick, a shovel, and a wheelbarrow?"

"Why? You fool! In order to bring the spring here, of course, and then we won't have the bother of going all the way there every day."

"No! No! You can't go messing about with the spring!" It's such a beautiful spring. I'd rather go and get the water myself!"

"Off you go then, you fool, but don't expect me to help you!"

The giant went by himself to fetch the water from the spring and when he returned, he said to his mother, "If only you knew, Mother, just how strong this little man is."

"Is he stronger than you?" said the old woman.

"Oh yes. Just imagine, he wanted to tear up the spring from where it is in the forest and bring it here to the castle yard!"

"I don't want him to do that! He's not to lay a finger on my spring!"

"Well, I didn't let him do it and I went to fetch the water by myself."

"Very well, then. Now, off you both go and fetch me some wood so that I can make you some crêpes."

"Let's go and fetch some wood for my mother, so that she can make us some crêpes," the giant said to Jean. And the two of them went off to the forest. The giant set about pulling up the trees, one by one, by their roots, as if they were parsnips in the field.

Jean watched him as he did it, astonished. "How much are you wanting to take back?" he asked him.

"A dozen, at least," replied the giant.

"Is that all? Is there not some good strong rope back at the castle?"

"What for?"

"What for? You fool! So that I can take back a good load, a quarter of the forest, for example, so that we don't have to keep coming back so often."

"Oh, in that case, you'd better let me do this by myself because my mother wouldn't be at all happy if anyone destroyed the forest."

"As you wish, but then I'll leave you to do it all by yourself." And the giant carried back, all by himself to his mother, just enough wood for what they needed.

When they got back to the castle, the giant said to Jean, "Let's go and have a game of boules in the large driveway while we wait for the crêpes to be ready."

"Yes, let's have a game of boules while we wait for the crêpes to be ready," replied Jean. There, in the middle of an extremely long driveway, was a round pebble that weighed seven hundred pounds.

"Let's see," said the giant, pointing it out to Jean, "who can throw this pebble the farthest. Go to the other end of the driveway. I'll throw it to you first and then you can throw it back to me."

"That's it," said Jean. "Let's see who can throw the pebble farthest." And he went right to the far end of the driveway. The giant picked up the stone, threw it, and it landed right at Jean's feet.

"Not bad," he said. "Now it's my turn, so look out! Watch carefully. I'm going to throw it so high that you'll lose sight of it and it will land in the place where I come from, five leagues from here."

"No, no, please, don't do that, Jean, because I'd be so sad to lose my pebble! Such a beautiful pebble!"

"I'll leave it alone for you then, especially as I'd have no use back home for what is only a child's marble. Let's go back to the house and see if the old woman has got the crêpes ready." So, they returned to the castle. The crêpes were ready and there was an enormous pile of them on the table.

"I love crêpes with milk," said Jean.

"Me too," said the giant. "Let's see who can eat the most."

"You're on!" said Jean.

And so, the crêpes began to disappear into the giant's mouth, one at a time, then two at a time, as if into an abyss. Jean held his own and didn't fall behind by a single crêpe. The giant ate them properly, while Jean let them slip down between his chest and his shirt, which he had unbuttoned, so he said, in order to be able to eat more. At the one hundredth crêpe, the giant stopped and looked at Jean.

"So, can't you manage any more?" Jean asked him.

"I've eaten a hundred," replied the giant.

"So what? A hundred of these crêpes. That's nothing!"

And the giant went back to eating and gobbled up another fifty.

"I've eaten a hundred and fifty of them," he said, unable to manage any more.

"Exactly the same as me!" said Jean. "Very well then, if you've had enough for one go, then we can leave it there for today, if you like."

"Yes, let's leave it there for today," said the giant, whose belly was enormous and stretched to bursting. And as for Jean's belly, it didn't look much better.

"Now let's go hunting in the forest," he said to the giant.

"I'd rather have a little nap," he replied.

"A nap? Come on! If you don't want to come with me, then you'll have to admit defeat."

"No, no, let's go hunting."

Jean leaped over the ditches and thickets easily enough, in spite of his load, whereas the giant, by contrast, kept falling over onto the ground and was panting like a dog. When Jean saw this, he pretended also to have no energy left and collapsed onto the ground, saying, "We've eaten too many crêpes!"

"Yes," replied the giant.

"There's only one thing to do!"

"What's that then? What do we have to do?"

"Rid ourselves of what we've had too much of."

"But how are we to rid ourselves of what we've had too much of?"

"Nothing could be easier. You get flummoxed by the slightest thing! Look, just watch me."

And taking his knife, he pretended to open up his belly, whereas all he opened up were his waistcoat and his shirt, freeing up the crêpes, which fell out in a great pile all around him. The giant was completely amazed.

"Now you do the same," Jean told him, "and you'll soon feel better like me."

The giant took the knife, which was as big as a saber, and he opened up the whole of his belly and his guts. A torrent of crêpes and blood flooded out. But soon he himself fell on his back, never to get up again. He was dead.

Then Jean set off on his way back to the king's palace. He arrived quite out of breath and said to the old king, "There we are, sire! So, is your daughter now mine?"

"What? My daughter yours, you rascal?"

"Yes, did you not promise her to me if I rid you of the three giants?"

"And . . . ?"

"And . . . I have rid you of the three giants, because they are now dead. And if you don't believe me, then come with me to the forest and I'll prove to you what I've just said."

The king went with him to the forest and was assured that he really was rid of his worst enemies. He was so happy that he kissed Jean and said to him, "My daughter is yours, along with my crown!"

The marriage was celebrated right away and for fifteen days there was wonderful partying and great feasting to which everyone was invited, rich and poor alike. So it was that every evening you would come across people sleeping drunkenly in the ditches by the side of the road. My grandfather's grandmother, who was from there, was also invited and that is how the story came to me and how I am able to tell you about these things in exactly the way they happened.

■ 22. The Fisherman's Two Sons

Told by Marguérite Philippe, from the commune of Pluzunet, before 1870

There was a time, there will be a time
When all the stories will be told.*

---

* Une fois il y avait, une fois il y aura / Pour donner carrier à tous les contes (Ur wez a oa, ur wez a vo / Ewit rei roll d'ann holl gaozo)

There was once an old fisherman whose wife was pregnant. One evening he returned home not having caught a thing. But his wife had a craving for fish and she made him return to the shore right away. He cast his nets and caught a very beautiful fish. He was very happy about it.

"At least now," he said to himself, "my wife will give me a little peace."

But then, just as he was about to take hold of the fish, it began to speak to him and it said, "When I am dead, give your wife my flesh to eat, to your mare give my heart, along with the water in which you will have rinsed me, and give my lungs and my entrails to your dog."

The old fisherman was astonished to hear the fish speak like a human being. He had never seen such a thing before. He replied, "I will do as you ask." Then he returned home.

When he arrived, he said to his wife, "I've gone and caught a beautiful fish! Come here, wife, and see what a beauty and a whopper it is!"

"It certainly is. I'd better get cooking it!"

"Guess what it said to me!"

"Who? The fish?"

"Yes, the fish."

"And what did it say to you then?"

"That you should have its flesh to eat, that its heart, served in the water in which it was rinsed, should go to our mare, and its entrails and its lungs to our dog."

"In that case we must do as it said."

The fish was cooked and the fisherman's wife ate its flesh, the mare ate its heart, and the dog its entrails.

Soon afterward, the fisherman's wife went into labor and gave birth to twins, two wonderful boys. They were so alike that a ribbon had to be tied around the arm of one, so that they could be told apart from each other. The same day, the mare gave birth to two foals that were absolutely identical, and the dog likewise had two pups that it was impossible to distinguish between.

"A miracle!" said the fisherman. "A foal and a dog for each of our children."

The two children thrived. When they reached the ages of fifteen or sixteen, one of them said to his parents that he was bored with staying at home and he wanted to go traveling. His father, his mother, and his brother each tried in vain to persuade him to stay, but they had to let him go. Before he left, he asked of his brother that each morning, after he got up, he would stick his knife into the trunk of the bay tree that grew in the garden. If it bled, he would be dead, but until then he should not be worried about his leaving.

He left, accompanied by his horse and his dog. He walked and walked until one day he arrived at a long avenue of oak trees. He followed this avenue until at the very end he found himself standing before a beautiful castle. He knocked at the door. It opened and he asked the doorkeeper if there were any jobs to be had at the castle. He was taken on as a stable boy. As he was hard-working, skillful, and also a handsome youth, he pleased the seigneur. And his horse and his dog pleased him too. But if he pleased the seigneur, he pleased his daughter, a young lady of great beauty, even more so. Eventually, he pleased her so much that they were married by the end of the year.

The newlyweds lived happily, going for walks every day in the gardens and the woods that surrounded the castle. One day, the fisherman's son noticed that the windows and the doors on one side of the castle were always closed. He asked his wife why this was the case.

"It is," she replied, "because on this side of the castle there is a courtyard that is full of poisonous animals, snakes, toads, lizards, and other reptiles."

From this point on, he could not stop thinking about the court-yard and he felt a great urge to go and see if what she had told him was true. One day, he was walking by this particular side of the castle with his horse and his dog (his wife was not with him on this occasion) and, passing in front of the gate, he said to himself, "I just *have* to go and see what is in there."

He knocked at the gate and it was opened by a little old woman who spoke to him thus:

"Good day, my son, so you have come to see me at last?"

"Good day, grandmother."

"Come in quickly and come and see the beautiful things that I have here. And here are two chains for you to tether your horse and your dog."

And she plucked two hairs from her head and handed them to him. And immediately they became two chains, which he used to tie up his horse and his dog to the stone posts that stood at each side of the gate. On seeing what was happening, the horse and the dog began to get agitated and struggled to prevent their being teth-ered and started to whinny and bark. But it was all in vain as they were tied up and had to remain there.

"Now, follow me, my son, so that I can show you my castle," said the old woman. "Come and see all the beautiful things that I have there, the likes of which you have never seen before. First of all, come and see the mill of razors."

When they stood before the large wheel, all decorated with ra-zors, she said, "Look, my son, isn't it marvelous?! Just bend down a little . . . a little lower . . . and you will have a better view."

As he bent over the edge of the abyss, without suspecting a thing, the old witch gave him a push and he fell onto the blades and was hacked into tiny pieces and ground like sawdust.

His brother, who had stayed at home, went every morning, after getting up, to stab the trunk of the bay tree in the garden with his knife and, as he drew no blood, he did not worry and said to himself, "God be praised! My dear brother is still alive!"

But, alas, on this particular morning, when he stabbed the trunk with his knife, as he always did, blood gushed forth down the trunk of the bay tree. "Oh no! My poor brother is dead!" he immediately exclaimed. And he went off to find his father and, with tears in his eyes, said to him, "Alas, Father, my poor brother is dead!"

"How can you know that?"

"Before he left, he told me that each day, after getting up, I should go and stab the bay tree in our garden with a knife and he told me that if blood appeared, then he would be dead. Alas! This morning, the blood gushed out of the tree trunk. My poor brother is dead! But I wish to go and look for him and I will not rest, day or night, until I have found him."

His father and his mother tried pleading with him, weeping that he should not abandon them in their old age, but he would not listen to them and he left, taking with him his horse and his dog, just as his brother had done. He kept walking, night and day, without stopping, until he arrived at the same avenue of oak trees as his brother had. He likewise knocked at the door of the castle and it was opened right away. His brother's wife, on seeing him enter the courtyard, took him for her own husband and came down the stairs at full speed and threw herself into his arms, crying out, "There you are, my poor husband! My God, you have caused me so much grief! I was afraid that you had ventured into the courtyard behind the castle, because nobody ever returns from there!"

He realized that he had been mistaken for his brother and he said, "I got lost in the wood. I don't know how, but I came to no harm." And, in the midst of his great sadness, he was overcome with joy to find himself in the castle.

At dinner they ate together and then they went upstairs to the bedroom together. Before getting into bed, the young man placed his drawn sword between himself and his brother's wife. "What are you doing that for?" the young woman asked, astonished.

The fisherman's son, who was afraid of being found out, said that he was overcome with tiredness and he wanted to sleep. But the young woman continued to question him, asking him how he had spent his time while he had been away, and lots of other things too. He became very uncomfortable, as you can imagine, and didn't know how to answer most of the time. He also asked why all the doors and windows were closed on one side of the castle.

"But I already told you. Don't you remember?"

"No, I've completely forgotten."

"Ah well, I'll tell you again then. To the side of the castle there is a courtyard that is full of poisonous reptiles and fierce animals too and whoever enters there will never return."

He realized right away that that was where his brother had gone.

The following morning, after breakfast, he went for a walk around the side of the castle with his horse and his dog. "My brother must be here," he said to himself, "and whatever might happen, I shall go and have a look."

So, he knocked at the gate. The old woman came to let him in. He entered and immediately recognized his brother's horse and dog, even though they had become so thin that they looked as if they were about to die of starvation.

"Good morning, my son," the old woman said to him. "I see that you have also come to visit me. Come along quickly now so that I can show you all the beautiful things that I have here. But first of all, take these two chains so that you can tether your horse and your dog over there by the gate, until you return."

And she pulled two hairs from her head and gave them to him. But he blew them out of her hand and they fell to the ground, where they immediately turned into two vipers.

"Ah!" said the old woman when she saw what had happened. "If you don't want to tether your horse and your dog, leave them to run free in the courtyard and come with me to look at my castle."

And he followed her. When they arrived at the mill of razors, she said, "Look, my son, put your head through this gap here and you will see something wonderful."

"Show me what you mean, grandmother."

"Oh, see, like this, my son."

And she put her head through the gap. Immediately, the fisherman's son took her by the feet and threw her onto the wheel of razors and she instantly fell down, hacked into tiny pieces and ground like sawdust.

Then he walked through the castle to see if he could find his brother. He met a vixen, who said to him, "How did you manage to find your way here?"

"You can speak?" he replied, astonished.

"As you can see."

"Well, I've just finished off the old woman, I have!"

"How did you do that?"

"How? I threw her headfirst onto the wheel of razors and she was hacked into pieces and ground like sawdust."

"Oh, how I wish that were true!"

"But it is true, believe me."

"Then you have saved me."

And immediately the vixen was changed into a most beautiful princess!

"For five hundred years," she said, "I have been held here under a spell by that evil witch."

"And what about my poor brother? Can you tell me what has happened to him?"

"Your brother was thrown by her onto the wheel of razors and he was hacked into pieces and ground like sawdust. But do not worry, I collected everything up, his flesh, his bones, his blood, and with the water of life that is kept in a vial in the old witch's bedroom, we will bring him back to life."

They placed his flesh, blood, and bones into a pile and sprinkled a small bottle of the water of life over it and immediately the body reassembled itself and the fisherman's son stood up, as right as rain, and said, "How well I've slept!"

"Yes, my poor brother, and without me and this beautiful princess, you wouldn't have gotten up for a little while yet!"

The two brothers threw their arms around one another and wept with joy to be reunited. Then, accompanied by the beautiful princess, whom they had saved, they returned to the castle and the young woman was certainly astonished to see two husbands instead of one, and she was unable to tell which was the real one, they were so alike! They told her everything and so she understood why the second brother had placed his drawn sword between her and himself during the night that he had spent with her.

So, the unmarried brother married the beautiful princess who had been in the form of a vixen and whom he had saved.

A beautiful coach was sent to collect the old fisherman and his wife and for a whole month there were sports, dances, and festivities like you have never seen.

My great-great-grandmother's grandmother was distantly related to the old fisherman and she too was invited to the wedding. And that's why around here we know all about this famous wedding.

■ 23. The Cat and the Two Witches

Told by Marguérite Philippe, Plouaret, March 1869

Once upon a time there was a well-behaved and pretty young girl who had a stepmother who wished her no good. Her name was Annaïc. Her father loved her, but his wife did all she could to make him hate her as well. One day, the stepmother went to visit her sister, who was a witch, and asked her to help her get rid of Annaïc.

"Tell her father," replied the witch, "that she is behaving scandalously and he will turn her out."

But the father would not believe anything bad that was said about his daughter and the stepmother went back to speak again with her sister, the witch.

"Very well," the witch said to her. "Here is a cake that I made myself and that you must give to the young girl. As soon as she's eaten it, her belly will swell up as if she were pregnant and her father will have to believe what's said about his daughter's bad behavior."

The wicked woman took the witch's cake home and said to Annaïc, as she handed it to her, "Here you are, my child. Eat up this honey cake that I made especially for you."

Annaïc took the cake and happily ate it without suspecting a thing, believing that it was a sign of affection at last from her stepmother. But shortly afterward, her belly swelled up in such a way that all who saw her thought that she was with child and the poor girl was ashamed and did not know what to think.

"Didn't I tell you," said the stepmother triumphantly to the father, "that your daughter was behaving badly? Look at the state she's in."

So, the father put Annaïc into a barrel, threw it into the sea, and left her to the mercy of God. The barrel was smashed against some rocks and Annaïc climbed out, unharmed, and found herself on a

desert island that she thought was uninhabited. She went into a cave dug out of the cliff and was astonished to find a little bedroom, completely furnished with a bed, some clay pots, and a fire burning in the hearth. She thought that someone must live there, but after waiting for a long time without anybody showing up, she lay down on the bed and slept peacefully.

The following morning, when she woke up, she found that she was still all alone. She got up and went looking for shellfish among the rocks for her breakfast. Then she spent the whole day walking around the island but she found neither another dwelling nor another human being. When evening came, she returned to the cave and slept peacefully again. And so it was for the days that followed.

When her time came, she gave birth to . . . a little cat. Great was her sadness when she saw what she had brought into the world, but she accepted it, saying, "Such is the will of God." And she brought up and cared for the little cat, just as she would have done had he been a child.

One day, as she was bemoaning her fate and weeping, she was astonished to hear the cat speak in a human voice.

"Cheer up, Mother. It is now my turn to take care of you and I won't let you go without a thing." And the cat picked up a sack from the corner of the cave, put it over his shoulder, and went out. He walked all over the island, found a castle, and went in. The inhabitants of the castle were quite astonished to see a cat walking upright on his two hind legs and carrying a sack over his shoulder, like a man. He asked for some bread, some meat, and some wine, and nobody dared refuse, so strange did it all seem. His sack was filled and he went on his way. He went back to the castle every other day and each time he returned with his sack full so that his mother wanted for nothing in the cave.

One day, the son of the castle got into a fight at a *pardon*, lost his papers, and was thrown into prison. Everybody at the castle was distraught and when the cat turned up as usual, he asked why everyone appeared so sad and miserable. They told him all about it. Then he filled his sack as usual and went home. When he got back to the cave, he said to his mother, "Sadness and desolation reign at the castle."

"Why? What has happened?"

"The young seigneur has had a fight during a *pardon*. He's lost his papers and been thrown into prison. But tomorrow I shall visit him in prison and tell him that if he will marry my mother, then I will find his papers and bring them to him."

"What makes you think that he will ever agree to taking me as his wife, my child?"

"We'll see, Mother. Leave it to me."

So, the following day the cat went to the prison and asked to speak to the young seigneur. But the jailer tried to chase him away with his broom. The cat jumped on his face and scratched out one of his eyes, then clambered up the wall, got in through the window, and said to the prisoner, "My dear sire, you have fed my mother and me ever since we arrived on your island and in return for this favor, I will get you out of prison and find your papers, if you promise to marry my mother."

"What's this, you poor animal, can you speak as well?" asked the young seigneur, astonished.

"Yes, I can speak as well and I am not what you think I am. But tell me, will you marry my mother?"

"Marry a cat? Me, a Christian? How could you suggest such a thing?"

"Marry my mother and, I tell you, you won't regret it. I will give you until tomorrow to think about it. I will return tomorrow." And he went on his way.

The next day, he returned, armed with the young seigneur's papers. He showed them to him and said, "Here are your papers. Promise me that you will marry my mother and I will give you them back and, what's more, I will make sure you are set free immediately." The prisoner gave his word and he was set free.

The cat's mother had a fairy godmother who knew all that was going on. She came to visit her while the cat was away and said to her, "The young seigneur has got his papers back and has promised to marry you. When the cat comes back, take a knife and slice open his belly without hesitation and he will turn into a handsome prince and you will turn into a princess of extraordinary beauty. Then you will marry the young seigneur and I will give you fifty fine horsemen for your wedding procession."

When the cat came back, the mother sliced open his belly. Immediately, a beautiful prince, magnificently dressed, climbed out of the skin and the mother turned into a princess of extraordinary beauty. The fifty horsemen arrived as well and a beautiful golden carriage came down from the sky. The prince and the princess climbed in and went to the castle, accompanied by the fifty horsemen.

The young seigneur, who was looking out of the window, was completely astonished to see such a group of strangers. He hurried down to welcome them. The prince stepped forward, holding the princess by the hand, and introduced her.

"Here is my mother, whom you have promised to marry. What do you think?"

The young seigneur was so overwhelmed by everything he saw and heard that he lost the power of speech and could only gabble. "My God, what a beautiful princess! Yes, of course. . . . What? . . . It would be such an honor!"

They were married without delay. During the wedding celebrations, which were superb, there was such entrancing music, the like of which is only heard in Heaven, yet nothing was to be seen. The bride's fairy godmother had sent invisible musicians. She had also sent her the beautiful golden carriage and said to her, "You need only say 'giddy-up' and my magic horses will carry you up into the air and take you to wherever you want to go. But if you go to your father's house, take care not to kiss your stepmother. As far as your father is concerned, do as you wish."

Right away, they got into the carriage, which flew up above the clouds and carried them straight to Annaïc's father's house. He recognized his daughter at once and was very happy to see her again, kissing her tenderly. The stepmother was furious. Nevertheless, the evil woman put on an act and went to kiss her as well. But the prince cried out to her, "Hey! Don't you kiss my mother! You'll get your just desserts!"

They lit a great bonfire and threw the stepmother and her daughter, along with the witch, onto it. Then, for eight whole days, there was a great celebration with games of all sorts, music, dancing and banqueting, all day long.

Fifth Veillée

■ 24. The Night Dancers

Told by Jean Le Laouénan, Plouaret, n.d.

There was once a rich lady who lived in a beautiful castle and had a daughter and a stepdaughter. Her daughter was called Catho and she was ugly, dirty, and badly behaved. Her stepdaughter, who was called Jeanne, was pretty, gracious, well behaved, and kind.

The woman loved only her daughter Catho and gave her everything she desired—beautiful clothes and jewelry—and she hated Jeanne, who was made to dress like a servant and was treated like one too.

In the forest that surrounded the castle there was an old chapel, where every night, so it was said, a long-deceased priest would return to attempt to perform mass, but he was never able to do so for lack of a respondent. Many people also claimed to have witnessed lights in the chapel at the midnight hour and seen and heard terrifying ghosts.

To get to the chapel, it was necessary to pass over a crossroads where, it was said, the night dancers would regularly frolic. And nobody would want to encounter those creatures after sunset.

The wicked stepmother was trying to find a way of getting rid of Jeanne so that her daughter Catho would inherit all her first husband's wealth.

So, late one Sunday evening in December, as she sat by the fire listening to the servants singing their *gwerziou*, their laments, and telling their wonderful stories, just as they were saying their evening prayers together before going to bed, she called out, "Well, I never! I've left my prayer book at the chapel! Quickly, Jeanne, go and fetch it for me."

"Yes, Mother," the poor child replied. But she was frightened and
she said to one of the servants, "Come with me, Marguérite."

"No, no! You will go alone," said the stepmother. "Surely you're
not frightened? At your age? Off you go now!" Jeanne dipped her

finger into the stoup, made the sign of the cross, and left. Her little dog, Fidèle, who accompanied her everywhere, got ready to follow her. But Catho ran after him, gave him a kick, and closed the door to stop him from getting out. The dog jumped through the window, breaking the glass, and rejoined his mistress. Having him there reassured her a little and she stroked him and told him not to leave her side.

It was a beautiful moonlit night. When she came to the crossroads, she saw seven dwarves in large hats singing and dancing in a circle. She stopped, not daring to take another step. But all the dancers, except one, came and gathered around her, shouting out, "Dance with us, young lady! Dance with us! Dance with us!"

"With pleasure, gentlemen," said Jeanne graciously, "if you so wish." And she joined the circle to dance and the singing continued with added gusto. Then the dwarf who was holding Jeanne's right hand said, "Oh, what an adorable and gracious young girl!"

"Then let her be yet half as adorable and gracious again!" replied the one who was holding her left hand.

"Oh, what a well-behaved young girl," said a third.

"Then let her be yet half as well behaved again!" said a fourth.

"Oh, what a beautiful young girl!" said the fifth.

"Then let her be yet half as beautiful again!" said the sixth.

"As beautiful as the stars!" added the seventh, who had not danced with the others. Then each of the dwarves, except for the seventh, kissed the young girl and they all at once disappeared.

So, Jeanne went on her way to the chapel. She saw nothing there, nor heard anything frightening or out of the ordinary. She found her stepmother's prayer book on her seat and took it home to her.

If she had been beautiful before, she was now even more beautiful and her beauty lit up the path, like the sun in May, as she walked along. "Here is your book, Mother," she said, handing the prayer book to her stepmother, who was so dazzled by her beauty that she was struck dumb with astonishment and her mouth fell open.

When at last she was able to speak, she asked, "What on earth has happened to you?"

"Nothing has happened to me, Mother," replied Jeanne. She didn't realize that she was so beautiful.

"Did you not see the night dancers at the crossroads?"

"Why certainly, Mother, I saw them and I even danced with them."

"And they did you no harm?"

"No, they were actually very nice to me."

"Really? And what about the chapel? Did you see anything?"

"I saw nothing unusual, Mother."

"Really? Very well, off to bed now!" All night long, the stepmother kept thinking about what Jeanne had said.

"It must be the night dancers who have transformed her like this," she said to herself. "Tomorrow afternoon, I'll go to the chapel and, as I'm walking around, I'll leave my prayer book there again and in the evening I'll send my daughter to look for it and we'll see what happens."

The next day, she told Catho that she would become as beautiful as Jeanne, if not more so, if she too went out at night to look for her prayer book in the old chapel in the wood. Catho was not exactly over the moon about it, because she was afraid and a coward. Still, she agreed to go, as her mother had promised her that she would become as beautiful as Jeanne, if not more so.

When eleven o'clock struck, her mother said to her, "It's time to go, my girl. Be on your way and don't be afraid. Nothing bad will happen to you." Catho was frightened but, on the other hand, she wanted to be beautiful.

"Fidèle will also come with me," she said and she called for Jeanne's little dog. But he ran off to Jeanne, so Catho gave him a kick and said, "Very well. I don't need a stupid dog like you anyway." And off she went.

When she arrived at the crossroads, she saw the dwarves dancing in a circle and singing. She stopped to watch them and they went up to her and said, "Would you like to dance with us, young lady?"

"Horse dung!" she replied. "I'm not dancing with dirty creatures like you! What a nerve!"

"Oh, what an ugly girl!" said one of the dwarves.

"Then let her be yet half as ugly again!" said a second.

"What a stupid girl!" said a third.

"Then let her be yet half as stupid again!" said a fourth.

"What an unpleasant girl!" said the fifth.

"Then let her be yet half as unpleasant again!" said the sixth.

"And let her vomit horse dung every time she speaks," said the seventh.

And off they went. And Catho also went home, without going to the chapel.

When the old woman saw her daughter, she cried out, "My God! What has happened to you, my poor girl? Have you not brought my prayer book?"

"Certainly not. Go and get it yourself, if you want." And she vomited up a pile of horse dung.

"What's going on? Did you not see the night dancers?"

"Yes, I saw them well enough, the foul beasts." And she vomited up another pile of horse dung. She stank and her face looked like a poisonous old toad. If she had been stupid before, she was now much more so and as nasty as a rabid bitch. Her mother locked her in the bedroom, where nobody could see her, and decided to take revenge on Jeanne.

The news of Jeanne's beauty and kindness spread quickly throughout the land and from all directions the rich and powerful came to see her and ask for her hand in marriage. But the stepmother turned all of them away.

One day, there came a young prince, who was so enchanted by the beauty and the virtues of the young girl that he immediately asked for her hand in marriage. But that witch of a stepmother planned to play a trick on him. She decided to substitute Catho for Jeanne and said to the prince that it would be a great honor for her to have such a son-in-law and that she had no hesitation in agreeing to it and neither did her daughter. The engagement was swiftly announced and the wedding date set. The prince sent his fiancée rings, diamonds, and precious jewelry.

On the day of the wedding, he arrived with a cortege of numerous princes and fine men and women. Catho was covered in jewels and finery that had been sent by the prince and poor Jeanne was imprisoned under lock and key in a large chest so that nobody saw her.

The prince had arrived in a superb, gilded coach. The mother climbed in to ride to the church with her daughter, whose face was concealed by a veil, and when the doors were closed on the three of them, they found themselves in darkness. The prince was told not to speak to his fiancée until they were on their way back from the ceremony, because she was very shy.

The coach set off and the little dog, Fidèle, ran behind barking, "Yappety-yap!" which means "That's not her! That's not her!"

"What's all that about?" asked the prince, astonished.

"Nothing at all, my son," replied the mother. "Pay no attention to that nasty little runt's yapping. He just wants to get inside the coach as well, but he would only get us all dirty."

As they were passing through the forest that surrounded the castle, a little bird came and sat on the roof of the coach and said:

Alas, alas, do not forget
The gentle, charming, sweet Jeanette
All alone at home, as well
Inside a chest, her prison cell.
The evil one meanwhile is found
To have her place and wears her crown
And thinks that now she rules the skies.
Oh prince, oh prince, open your eyes!

"What is that bird singing?" the prince asked, astonished.

"Nothing, my son," replied Catho's mother. "Just ignore it."

"Oh, but this is something very odd and I must know what it is."

The bird repeated its song and the prince made the coach stop and he got out. He opened the doors of the coach, lifted the veil of his bride-to-be, and when he saw the ugly monstrosity that he had been about to marry, he cried out in horror, "Get out, you vile beasts! Snakes and toads! Get out now and I never want to see you again!"

The prince and his retinue then set off at a gallop, abandoning Catho and her mother by the side of the road. And when he arrived back at the castle, he went from room to room, shouting out, "Jeanne, my darling, where are you?!"

"Here!" said Jeanne from inside the chest. The prince took a hatchet, broke open the chest, and helped Jeanne climb out. Then he led her to his beautiful gilded coach, without her first having had the chance to freshen up, but just as she was, and he took her to the church and married her to everyone's great astonishment. And the little dog, Fidèle, who had never left his mistress's side, also went with her, all the way to the altar.

When the cortege passed by, Catho and her mother were still by the side of the road, weeping with anger and floundering about in the mud.

There was much celebrating and feasting and the couple lived happily together and had lots of children.

■ 25. The Cooking-Pot Man

Told by Barba Tassel, Plouaret, December 1868

There was once a fellow who had three daughters. They worked a small farm and they lived poorly from it. Every day, the daughters would go to work in the fields and their father, who had become too old, would stay home and look after the animals. But each day, he would go and see his daughters out in the fields every now and then. One day, he was on his way back from seeing them when he met a fine, well-dressed gentleman. There was only one problem: stuck to his backside, he had a cooking pot.

"Good day, my friend," the gentleman said to the old man.

"And the same to you, sire," replied the peasant.

"Would you give me one of your daughters in marriage?"

"Why certainly, if they agree to it."

"Very well! Go and ask them to come and speak to me."

And the fellow went off to the field and called out to his three daughters, "Marie, Jeanne, Marguérite, come quickly!"

The young girls came running and asked, "What on earth is the matter, Father?"

"Over there, on the road, is a fine gentleman and he wants to marry one of you!" And the young girls all hurried off eagerly to get there first. But when they saw the stranger with his backside in the cooking pot, they said, "Look at that! Who would want a husband like that?"

"Not me, that's for sure!" said the eldest.

"Me neither," said the second, "even if his cooking pot were made of gold!"

"One of you must agree to have me," said the gentleman, "or your father will not return home alive."

"I will have you, sire," said the youngest, who had not spoken up until now, "for I do not want anything bad to befall my father."

And the wedding day was fixed without delay.

When the day itself arrived, many guests turned up. The happy couple traveled to the church in a beautiful coach. When the young bride stepped down from the coach, she was so beautiful in all her finery that her relations didn't recognize her. She was covered in gold and pearls. The groom also stepped down from the coach, but he still had his backside in the cooking pot.

They entered the church and as they passed the choristers' stalls, the groom got his feet outside of the cooking pot, but his backside was still inside.

The wedding celebrations were magnificent with festivities every day and there were games and dances, which continued for eight days. At the end of this time, the groom asked his father-in-law if he had ever met the local seigneur.

"No, not at all. I've never met him," he replied. "Every year at Michaelmas I go and pay his bailiff at Guingamp. But as for him, I've never seen him."

"Well, I am in fact your seigneur. I will give your farm to you and your two remaining daughters and do not worry about the one

I am taking away, because she will want for nothing." Then he got into his golden carriage and he and his wife drove away.

If the old farmer had previously been in financial difficulties, all was now well. And neither were his daughters short of suitors when it came to high days and holidays. One of them soon got married.

"One of your sisters has just become engaged," the cooking-pot man said to his wife one day. You should go to the wedding alone. People will ask after me, but be careful not to say that at nighttime I become free of my cooking pot, because if you say that, no good of it will come for either me or you. And even though I shan't be there, I shall know immediately if you say anything. You will travel in my golden coach, which will be drawn by a mare who breathes fire from her nostrils and with a back like the blade of a knife, and you will have to make the return journey riding on the back of the mare, if you ever reveal my secret."

The young woman promised to be extremely discreet and then she got into the golden coach and went off to her sister's wedding. She was so beautiful in all her finery that there was no other woman who could compare and they were all jealous of her.

When the meal was finished, an old aunt, who had drunk a little too much, came up to her and said, "Well, niece, how beautiful and pretty you are! Sit yourself down next to me. We'll have a glass of vintage wine and you can tell me all your news. And what about your husband? How is he getting on?"

"He's getting on just fine, thank you, Aunt."

"And why has he not come to the wedding? I would have liked to have seen him again and chatted with him. Tell me, my child, does he ever leave his cooking pot?"

"No, Aunt, never."

"Oh, my poor child, you have my sympathy in spite of everything else. It's certainly not pleasant to have a husband who always has his backside in a cooking pot. But what about at nighttime? Does he go to bed, as well, with his cooking pot?"

"Oh no, as soon as he goes to bed, he leaves it." And right away the old aunt went to tell everybody.

The following morning, the cooking-pot man's manservant arrived and told the young woman that she must return home immediately on the orders of her husband. And she was seized with fear and said to herself, "I have done something terrible."

She followed the manservant. When she came to the farmyard gate, she fainted as she saw that there was no coach to take her home, but only the skinny mare with a back like the blade of a knife.

"Get on the mare," the manservant said to her.

"No, I would prefer to walk," she replied, but the manservant forced her onto the back of the mare. Then they left at a gallop. When she arrived at her husband's house, she received a frosty welcome from everyone.

"There you are, you stinking carcass! Whore of the Devil!" the servants all said to her. "When you go into labor (she was with child), you will be put to death like a dog!" The seigneur was also furious.

"You wretched woman, you have the tongue of the Devil," he said to her. "You have forsaken me and now you yourself are also forsaken. I had only one more year of staying in my cooking pot and now I will have to stay there for another six hundred years!"

The poor woman was devastated and she wept and wailed. "Take me back to my father!"

"If your regret is genuine," said her husband, "and you do exactly as I tell you, you may yet be able to save me."

"Oh, ask of me whatever you want. There is nothing in the world I would not be prepared to do for you."

"Then listen carefully. What you must do is to go completely naked and kneel on the steps of the crucifix at the crossroads. You will have hardly been there when it will start to rain, the wind will blow, and it will thunder in a terrifying manner. But don't be frightened, and stay there, on your knees on the steps of the crucifix, no matter what happens. Then a white horse will arrive at a furious gallop, whinnying and making a great noise. Don't be afraid. He will stop for a moment beside you. Pat his head with your hand and say, "Will you be my husband?" Then he will leave and a bull will arrive next, bellowing and making such a racket that the earth will shake with it. However, don't be afraid. Pat him gently on the head and say, "Will you be my brother?" He will leave immediately as well and be replaced by a black cow, who will make more noise and a greater racket than the white horse and the bull put together. But still don't be afraid. She will stop next to you for a moment, like the others, and you must pat her gently on the head and say, "Will you be my mother?" If you have the courage to do all of that, you will still manage to save me and save yourself."

"I will do it!" replied the young woman. And so, she became completely naked and went to kneel on the steps of the crucifix at the crossroads and just at that moment the rain, the wind, and the thunder let loose in a great fury. It was terrifying!

Soon a white horse arrived at a triple gallop and whinnying. It stopped in front of the crucifix. The young woman patted him gently on the head and said, "Will you be my husband?" And the horse left.

Next a bull arrived, making a terrible noise. He also stopped in front of the crucifix and the young woman patted him on the head and said, "Will you be my brother?" and he left right away.

The rain, the wind, the thunder, and the lightning continued to grow all the time. Then the black cow arrived, bellowing and making such a racket that the earth shook. "Will you be my mother?" said the young woman, patting her gently on the head. And she also left, just as the white horse and the bull had done.

Then the rain, the wind, and the thunder stopped and the sky became clear and calm. A golden coach came down from the sky and landed next to the young woman. Her husband got out and gave her some clothes so that she could get dressed and they threw their arms around each other, weeping with joy.

"You have saved us—myself, my brother, and my mother," the cooking-pot man cried out. "The white horse was me, the bull was my brother, and the black cow was my mother. All three of us have been under a spell for a long time, but our troubles are now over and I shall wear my cooking pot no longer. My brother owns a golden castle and he will give it to you to thank you for what you have done for us and we will live there happily together and in peace."

And there was a banquet so beautiful you could hardly believe it! If I could have gotten there myself, I think I would have dined better than I do at home, where I usually feast on fried spuds with potatoes.

■ **26. The Toad-Man**

Told by Barba Tassel, Plouaret, 1869

There was once a widower who lived with his three daughters. One day, one of his daughters said to him, "Father, would you fetch me a jug of water from the well? There isn't a drop in the house and I need some for cooking."

"Very well, my dear," said the old man. And he picked up a jug and went off to the well. But just as he leaned over to fill up the jug, a toad leaped onto his face and stuck there so firmly that all his efforts to remove it proved useless.

"You will not be able to remove me," the toad said to him, "until you have promised to give me one of your daughters in marriage." The old man left his jug by the well and ran back to the house.

"Good Lord! What has happened to you, Father?" exclaimed his daughters when they saw the state of him.

"Alas, my poor children, this creature jumped onto my face just as I was drawing water from the well and said that he will only let go if one of you consents to marry him."

"Good Lord! What are you saying, Father?" replied the eldest daughter. "That I should marry a toad? What a terrible thought!" And she turned her head away and went out. The middle daughter did the same.

"Oh, my poor father," the youngest then said, "I will consent to marry him, as it is more than my heart can bear to see you like this!" Immediately, the toad fell to the ground.

The wedding was arranged for the following day. When the bride entered the church, accompanied by her toad, the priest was quite astounded and said he would never marry a Christian woman to a toad. Nevertheless, in the end he joined them together, when the father of the bride had told him the whole story and promised to give him lots of money.

So, the toad took his wife back to his castle—you see, he had a beautiful castle. When the time came for them to go to bed, he led her to his bedroom and there he took off his toad skin and became a beautiful young prince! As long as the sun was in the sky, he was a toad, and at night he was a prince.

The two sisters of the young bride sometimes came to visit her and they were quite astonished to find her so happy. She was continually smiling and singing.

"There's something going on here," they said to themselves. "We'll have to keep an eye on things so we can find out." One night, they came very quietly to the castle and watched through the keyhole and were completely astounded to see a beautiful young prince instead of a toad!

"Well, I never! A beautiful prince! If only I had known!" they said.

Then they heard the prince say these words to his wife: "Tomorrow I have to go away and I will leave my toad skin at home. Take great care that nothing happens to it, because I must remain like this for another year and a day."

"Aha!" said the two sisters to each other, as they listened at the door. The following morning, the prince left, just as he had said, and his two sisters-in-law went to pay his wife a visit.

"My word, what beautiful things you have! You must be very happy with your toad!" they said to her.

"Why certainly, dear sisters, I am happy with him."

"Where is he now?"

"He has gone traveling."

"If you like, little sister, I will comb your beautiful hair for you."

"I would like that very much, dear sister."

The bride fell asleep as she was having her hair combed with a golden comb and then her sisters took her keys from her pocket, took the toad skin from out of the wardrobe where it had been locked away, and threw it into the fire.

When the young woman awoke, she was surprised to find herself all alone. Her husband arrived home a moment later, burning with rage. "Ah! You foolish woman!" he cried. "You have caused both of us great unhappiness by doing the one thing I expressly forbade. You have burned my toad skin! Now I am leaving and you will never see me again."

The poor woman started to cry and said, "I will follow you, wherever you may go."

"No, do not follow me. Stay here." And he left, running. And she set off, running after him.

"I told you to stay here."

"I will not stay. I will follow you." And he continued to run, but no matter how fast he ran, she was always at his heels. Then he threw a golden ball behind him. His wife picked it up, put it in her pocket, and carried on running.

"Go home! Go home!" he continued to shout at her.

"I will never return without you!" He threw down a second golden ball. She picked it up, like the first, and put it into her pocket. Then a third ball. But seeing as she was always at his heels, he became angry and thumped her full in the face with his fist. Immediately, the blood began to flow and his shirt was splashed with three drops of blood, which left three stains there.

Then the poor woman soon started to lag behind and before long she had lost sight of the fugitive. But she shouted after him. "Let those three blood stains never go away until I, myself, come to remove them."

And despite everything, she continued in her pursuit. She came to a large forest. A little later, following a path through the trees, she came upon two enormous lions, sitting on their backsides, one on each side of the path. She was terrified.

"Oh no!" she said to herself. "I am going to die, as these two lions will surely eat me up! Well, whatever! Into the arms of God!"

And on she went. When she came close to the lions, she was amazed to see them lie down at her feet and lick her hands. So, she started to stroke them, passing her hand over their heads and backs. Then she continued on her way.

Farther on, she saw a hare, sitting on its backside by the side of the path, and when she passed alongside it, the hare said to her, "Climb onto my back and I will carry you out of the wood." So, she sat on the hare's back and, after a little while, it had carried her out of the wood.

"Now," the hare said to her before going on its way, "you are close to the castle where you will find the one you are looking for."

"Thank you for your kindness, you dear creature," the young woman said to the hare. And so, before long, she found herself at a long avenue of old oak trees and, a little farther on, she saw some washerwomen doing the laundry by the side of a pond.

She approached them and heard one of them say, "There you are! This shirt must be bewitched! For two years now, every wash-day, I have tried to get rid of these three blood stains on it, but it's no use, I'll never manage it."

On hearing these words, the young woman went up to the washerwoman who had spoken and said to her, "Please, let me have the shirt for a minute. I think I may be able to get rid of the three blood stains." She was handed the shirt. She spat on the three blood stains, soaked them in water, scrubbed them a little, and immediately the three stains disappeared.

"Many thanks!" the washerwoman said to her. "Our master is about to get married and he will be pleased to see that the three blood stains have gone, because this is his best shirt."

"I would like to get a job working for your master."

"The shepherdess left a few days ago and she hasn't been replaced yet. Come with me and I'll put in a word for you."

So, the young woman was taken on as a shepherdess. Every day, she would take her flock out into a large wood that encircled the castle and often she would see her husband out walking with the young princess who was to become his wife. Her heart would pound strongly whenever she saw him, but she did not dare speak.

She always carried with her the three golden balls and often, to pass the time, she would amuse herself with a game of boules. One day, the young princess noticed the golden balls and she said to her maid, "Look! Look at the beautiful golden balls that girl has. Go and ask her to sell me one."

The maid went to find the shepherdess and said to her, "What beautiful golden balls you have there, shepherdess! Would you like to sell one to my mistress, the princess?"

"I will not sell my balls. Being all alone, I have no other way of passing the time."

"Bah! You are being unreasonable. Look, your clothes are in a terrible state. Sell one of your balls to my mistress and she will pay you well and you will be able to wear clean clothes."

"I want neither gold nor silver."

"What do you want then?"

"To sleep with your master for one night!"

"What? You bad girl! How dare you say such things?"

"I will not give up one of my golden balls for anything else." So, the lady's maid returned to find her mistress.

"Well, what did the shepherdess say?"

"What did she say? I daren't repeat it to you!"

"Tell me quickly!"

"That bad girl said she would only give up one of her balls if she could sleep with your husband for one night."

"Well, I never! No matter! I have to have one of those balls, whatever the cost. I shall put a drug in my husband's wine at dinner and he will be none the wiser. Go and tell her that I accept and bring me back a golden ball."

That evening, as he got up from the table, the prince was overcome by a great need to sleep and he had to go straight to bed. A little later, the shepherdess was shown into his bedroom. She called him the most loving names, kissed him, and shook him violently, but it was all in vain and nothing would make him stir.

"Alas!" cried the poor woman in tears. "Has all my effort been a waste of time? After everything I have gone through! I married you anyway when you were a toad and nobody wanted anything to do with you. And for two long years, in the stifling heat, in the cruelest cold, through rain and snow, through storms, I have searched everywhere for you, without giving up. And now that I have found you, you won't listen to me and instead you sleep like a log! Oh! Woe is me!" And she wept and sobbed, but, alas, he did not hear her.

The following morning, she went back into the woods with her sheep, sad and thoughtful. In the afternoon, as the day before, the princess came walking along with her maid. The shepherdess, seeing her approach, started to play with her two remaining golden balls. The princess wanted to have a second ball, to make the pair, and again said to her maid, "Go and buy a second ball from the shepherdess for me." The maid did as she was told and, to cut a long story short, the business was concluded at the same price as on the previous day: to spend a second night with the master of the castle in his bedroom.

The master, whose wine the princess had once again drugged during dinner, just as on the previous day, went straight to bed after leaving the table and slept like a log. Sometime later, the shepherdess was once more shown into his bedroom, where she started up all over again with her weeping and wailing. A servant, who happened to be passing by the door, heard the noise and stopped to have a listen. He was astonished by what he heard and the following morning he went to see his master and said to him, "Master, there are things that go on in this castle of which you are ignorant, but which you should know about."

"Such as? Tell me quickly!"

"A poor woman, wretched and in great distress, arrived at the castle a few days ago and, out of pity, she was taken on to replace the shepherdess, who had just left. One day, the princess, as she was walking through the woods with her maid, saw the woman playing a game of boules with some golden balls. The princess immediately wanted to have the balls and sent the maid off to buy them from the shepherdess at whatever price she named. The shepherdess asked for neither silver nor gold, but to spend one night with you in your bedchamber for each of her balls. She has already sold two balls and she has spent two nights with you in your bedchamber without your knowing anything about it. It is pitiful to hear her weeping and wailing. I think she must be unhinged, because she says the strangest things, such as, for example, that she was your wife when you were a toad and that she has walked for two whole years looking for you . . ."

"Is all this really true?"

"Yes, master, it is all true. And the reason you know nothing about it is that during dinner the princess administers a drug to your wine, so that when you leave the table, you have to go straight to bed and you sleep soundly until the following morning."

"That's enough now! I'll have to keep on my guard and soon you'll see some changes around here!"

The poor shepherdess was looked on badly and detested by the castle servants. They knew that she spent her nights in the master's bedroom and the cook gave her nothing more than barley loaf, the same as the dogs. The following morning, she went to the woods again with her sheep and the princess bought the third golden ball from her, at the same price as the other two—a third night with the master in his bedroom.

This time, the master was on his guard at dinner. As he was chatting to the guest next to him, he saw the princess pour the drug into his glass. He pretended not to have noticed, but instead of drinking the wine, he poured it out under the table without the princess's noticing. As he rose from the table, he pretended to be overcome by sleep, as on the other evenings, and went to his bedroom. The shepherdess also came along a little later. This time, he was not asleep and as soon as he saw her, he threw himself into her arms and they cried with joy and happiness at having found each other again.

"For now, return to your bedroom, my poor wife," he said to her after a little while, "and tomorrow you'll see some changes around here."

The following day, there was to be a great banquet at the castle to arrange the date of the wedding. There were kings and queens and princes and lots of other important people. Toward the end of the meal, the groom-to-be rose and said, "Father-in-law, I would like to ask your advice on a certain matter. I have a pretty little casket with a pretty little golden key. I lost the key to my casket and had another one made. But a little time later, I found my first key again, so that now I have two instead of one. Which do you think I should use, Father-in-law?"

"Always respect old age," replied his future father-in-law.

And so, the prince went into a side room and came straight back out again, holding the hand of the shepherdess, now dressed in simple but clean clothes and he said, as he presented her to the assembled guests, "Well, here is my first key, that is to say, my first wife, whom I have found again. This is my wife and I will love her always and I want no other but her!"

And they returned to their country, where they lived happily together to the end of their days.

And that is the story of "The Toad-Man." What do you think of it?

■ 27. The Enchanted Princess

Told by Louis Le Braz, weaver, Prat, November 1873

One day in the month of June, a servant at the manor house of Lestrézec, by the river Jaudy in the commune of Runan, saw a grass snake, warming itself in the sun among the ruins of an old derelict tower. He grabbed a stone and got ready to smack it over the head when, to his great astonishment, the grass snake spoke to him thus:

"Don't kill me, Joll (the servant's name was Joll Gariou), but set me free instead and I will make you a king!"

"And what will I have to do?" asked Joll.

"A small matter: just give me three kisses. I am an enchanted princess, entrapped in this form for three hundred years by a powerful wizard. Give me three kisses and the spell will be broken. I will marry you and you will become king of a great kingdom."

Well, our hero was rather embarrassed and not at all sure about it. He found the thought of kissing a grass snake particularly disgusting and, anyway, perhaps it was actually an adder that might bite him and give him a very painful death. But on the other hand, if what it said was true, then he would marry a beautiful princess and become a king. And why wouldn't it tell the truth? He had often heard these tales told, at winter gatherings around the hearth, of the wonderful adventures of poor people, like himself, who became kings in just this kind of way! Why shouldn't he have a bit of good luck as well?

Eventually, he gathered up his courage and gave the grass snake a single kiss, but he could go no further.

"Come back tomorrow at the same time," it said to him, "and you will find me in the same place, but in another form, and you must start the test all over again." And having said these words, the grass snake disappeared beneath the ruins. Joll went back to the manor

house and told no one of his adventure. But he dreamed about it all night and already he could imagine himself sitting on a huge golden throne, glittering with precious stones, with a beautiful princess at his side.

The next day, he arrived at the place at exactly the right time and there he found an enormous lizard with yellow and greenish spots and glistening all over with poison, or so he thought. And the lizard spoke to him, just as the grass snake had the day before:

"Give me three kisses at once and you will become a king."

He kissed it once, then twice, by gathering all his courage, but he could go no further. The horrible creature, which swelled and grew with each kiss, made his stomach turn.

"Come back tomorrow at the same time," the lizard said to him, "and bring all your courage with you, as this will be your last chance." It disappeared beneath the ruins and Joll went back to the manor house, annoyed with himself.

On the third day, he found, in the place where the grass snake and the lizard had been on the previous two days, an enormous toad, who said to him:

"Give me three kisses and you will be king!"

Joll was determined this time to see this through to the end. He kissed the toad . . . once . . . twice . . . he could feel his courage failing him . . . he closed his eyes and gave the third kiss.

When he opened his eyes again, he saw in front him no longer a hideous reptile but a young princess, as beautiful as the day was long, and who spoke to him thus:

"Thank you, Joll Gariou! You have set me free and now I am yours. Come and receive your reward." And taking him by the hand, she took him down below the ground through a door that opened before them and she led him to a beautiful palace full of all kinds of treasure. This was the palace of the wizard who had held her captive for three hundred years. The wizard was not at home. The princess went straight to the stable where there were many horses and a dromedary. She led out the dromedary and said to Joll, "Quick, climb up and I'll sit behind you and we'll be off. There's no time to lose. The wizard will soon find out about our escape and he'll return immediately and set off after us. But I have read his books of magic and I know as much as he does, and we will escape from him." And they were off!

But they had not gone far when they noticed that the sky had suddenly become dark and a black cloud was quickly approaching them.

"It's the wizard," cried the princess. "Let our dromedary be changed into a pond and we will become two frogs under the water. Immediately, that is exactly what happened. The wizard, arriving at the pond, came down from his cloud and stopped to admire it, astonished that he had never noticed it before, and then he went back to his palace to refer to his books. The princess, Joll, and the dromedary immediately returned to their natural forms and carried on their way.

The wizard came after them again, in a variety of disguises, but each time the princess outwitted him by changing them into different things and finally they reached the outer limits of the wizard's realm. From this moment on, they were safe!

The princess led Joll Gariou to her father's kingdom and there she married him. The old king died shortly afterward and Joll Gariou succeeded him onto the throne and lived happily with his queen for the rest of his days.

It even seems that his descendants are still living there, in a distant land, far away, near to where the sun rises, if we are to believe the sailors of Paimpol and of Saint-Malo, who swear that they have seen them.

■ 28. The Devil's Wife

Told by Barba Tassel, Plouaret, September 1887

A young girl by the name of Soëzic Kerbily was one day busy doing the laundry down by the stream that ran alongside the little thatched cottage where she lived with her father and her mother. A distinguished stranger was passing by and asked if she would not mind washing his handkerchief for him.

"I wouldn't mind at all," she replied. "Give it here." The stranger gave her his handkerchief and she washed it in the clear water and stretched it out on a bush to dry in the sun. While he waited for his handkerchief to dry, the stranger struck up a conversation with the young girl and he was so taken by her beauty and her innocence that he ended up asking if she would like to marry him.

"I would like that," she replied, smiling, but without attaching any importance to it.

"Right away?"

"Ah. No. That's not how one gets married around here."

"When then?"

"In two years and a day, as long as you have my parents' permission and you give me lots of money, because I am poor."

"That's a long time, but nevertheless I accept your terms and after two years I will return to keep you to your promise. As for the money, you will have as much as you want."

The stranger went on his way and Soëzic went back home once she had finished the laundry. She lifted the latch and pushed at the door. But although she pushed hard, the door would not give way, which astonished her and she cried out, "Mother, open the door for me."

"I cannot, my child."

"Why ever not?"

"Because there is a large heap of gold coins piled up against it and I don't know how they got there."

"Stop making fun of me. Please let me in!"

"Come in through the window and you'll see that I'm telling the truth."

Soëzic climbed in through the window and she could not have been more astonished to see the pile of brand new shiny gold coins that her mother had told her about. For a few moments, she just stood there looking at them, her mouth and her eyes wide open in disbelief. Then the mother and her daughter started to rush about, hiding all the gold in boxes, under their beds, in holes in the ground, or in the walls of the house.

Soëzic's father, who was a weaver by trade, came home before they had finished up and he filled his pockets with gold and went off into town to enjoy himself and did not return for eight or ten days.

Now, our people completely changed their way of life. They bought an old manor house with fields, meadows, and woodland. They had horses, cattle, oxen, and they ate well. In the countryside, nobody talked of anything else and the rumor was that they had found some treasure, or they had sold their souls to the Devil.

Before long, suitors started arriving from all directions to ask for Soëzic's hand in marriage and at the church and at country fairs there was none so sought after as her. She had never taken seriously the promise she had made to the stranger whose handkerchief she had washed in the stream and she didn't worry about it, so that after one year, she married somebody else and there were great celebrations and much rejoicing and parties that lasted for fifteen whole days.

After nine months, they had a child. However, as the date agreed with the stranger approached, the young woman became worried.

She realized now that the mysterious stranger must have been the Devil and that it was he who had filled the house with gold. She became very anxious and she would often look at her child with sadness, hug him, and say, "Alas, my poor child, I am afraid that very soon I shall have to leave you and go to God only knows where!"

One day, her husband questioned her about the reason for her sadness and she confessed everything to him—her promise of marriage to another and the source of her fortune. "What have you done?!" he cried out. "But I'll find a way to get you out of this."

He prepared a great feast and invited the bishop and all his canons to dinner on the very day that Satan was due to call, convinced that he would not dare show himself among such company. As they sat at the table, a strange-looking person, unannounced, came into the dining room, and not one of the guests recognized him, except the mistress of the house. He went straight up to her and said, "The time has come for you to keep your promise. I have no business with your child or with its father, but you—you now belong to me. Follow me!"

The young woman cried out, terrified. "It's the Devil! Do something! Don't let him take me away!"

But in spite of her crying and putting up a fight, in spite of the prayers and pleadings of the bishop and his canons, he led her out of the room. Once in the courtyard, she said to him, "I won't walk another step. You'll have to carry me."

"Climb onto my back," the Devil told her. But she started to struggle and thrash about and, as she was still breast-feeding, her milk began to leak out down the back of her abductor and, as it did so, he doubled up with pain and let out a terrible scream. He put her down on the ground and said to her, "Walk!"

"I won't walk!" she replied and she lay down on the ground. He threw her over his shoulders, but he had to put her back down on the ground again. He then let out a fearful cry and immediately one of the Devil's imps appeared.

"What can I do for you, master?" he asked.

"Put this woman on your back and carry her back to my place." And the Devil's crony threw Soëzic Kerbily onto his back and immediately put her down again, grimacing and crying out in pain. His master made him pick her up again and, after a great deal of difficulty and having had to put her back down on the ground again several times over, he finally got her down to Hell.

Satan showed her into a beautiful bedroom, nice and clean and well furnished, and said to her, "This is your room and I will come and see you every night. During the day, I am busy with other things. I will leave instructions that you should not want of anything. My only demands are that you should not try to leave, you should keep the place clean, and you should sweep the floor every day, but not throw the sweepings away."

Soëzic was not unhappy with the Devil. He was really very attentive toward her, but at the same time she missed her home, her husband, and her child. Every day, she swept the room herself and put the sweepings behind the door. But gradually, the pile got bigger and one day she threw the lot out of the window and the wind carried it away and with it came a strange noise from which she seemed to be able to make out cries of joyful laughter and even the words "Turgarez, Soëzic!" which mean "Thank you, Soëzic!"

When Satan returned that evening and looked behind the door, as he always did, he saw that the sweepings were no longer there.

"Where are the sweepings?" he cried out.

"It wasn't clean, so I threw them all out of the window."

At these words, he became furious and yelled, "You fool! Each grain of dust was one soul and you have freed them all. Get out of here and go home, otherwise you'll soon have emptied the whole of Hell!" And he pushed her outside by the shoulders.

Soëzic hurried back home to her husband, who was happy to see her again and since then, I've not heard a thing about them.

■ 29. N'oun-Doaré

Told by Vincent Coat, tobacco factory worker, Morlaix, April 1874

The marquis of Coat-Squiriou, returning one day from Morlaix accompanied by a servant, noticed, lying in the ditch by the side of the road, fast asleep, a child of four or five years of age. He got down from his horse, woke up the child, and asked him, "What are you doing there, my child?"

"I don't know," he replied.

"Who is your father?"

"I don't know."

"And your mother?"

"I don't know."

"Where are you from?"

"I don't know."

"What is your name?"

"I don't know," he replied, always in the same way.

The marquis told his servant to carry the boy behind him on his horse and they continued on their way toward Coat-Squiriou. The child became known as N'oun-Doaré, which means "I don't know"

in Breton. He was sent to the school in Carhaix and he mastered everything that he was taught.

When he was twenty years old, the marquis said to him, "You have now learned enough and you will come with me to Coat-Squiriou." And he took him back to Coat-Squiriou.

On the fifteenth of October, the marquis and N'oun-Doaré went to the Grand Fair at Morlaix together and stayed in the best hotel in town.

"I am pleased with you and I would like to buy you a fine sword," the marquis said to the young man and they went to an armorer's together. There N'oun-Doaré looked at many fine and beautiful swords, but he was satisfied with none of them and they left without having bought a thing. As they passed a junk shop, N'oun-Doaré stopped, saw a rusty old sword, grabbed it, and shouted out, "I have to have this sword!"

"What?" the marquis said to him. "Have you seen what a state it is in? It's good for nothing."

"Please buy it for me, just as it is, and you'll see soon enough that it is good for something."

The marquis paid for the rusty old sword (it didn't cost him very much) and N'oun-Doaré took it away, very happy with his acquisition. Then they returned to Coat-Squiriou.

The next day, N'oun-Doaré was inspecting his sword when he noticed that beneath the rust were some letters that had been half worn away, but which could still be made out. The letters said, "I am the Invincible One."

"Marvelous!" said N'oun-Doaré to himself. A little while later, the marquis said to him, "I must also buy you a horse." And on the day of the fair, the two of them went off to Morlaix.

So, there they were at the fairground with all these fine horses from Léon, Tréguier, and Cornouaille. But still N'oun-Doaré didn't find a single one to suit him, so that by the evening, after the sun had gone down, they left the fairground without having bought a thing. On the way back, as they walked along the Côte de Saint-Nicolas, they came across a fellow from Cornouaille who was leading, by a length of rope, a worn-out old nag, as bony as the Grim

Reaper's own horse. N'oun-Doaré stopped, looked at it, and exclaimed, "That's the horse for me!"

"What? That old bag of bones? But just look at it!" the marquis said to him.

"Yes, I want her and no other. Buy her for me, please." And the marquis bought the old mare for N'oun-Doaré, while remarking how he had very queer tastes.

The man from Cornouaille whispered in N'oun-Doaré's ear, as he handed over the animal, "You see these knots on the mare's halter?"

"Yes," he replied.

"Well, each time you undo one, the mare will immediately take you fifteen hundred leagues from where you are."

"Wonderful!" he replied.

Then N'oun-Doaré and the marquis continued on their way to Coat-Squiriou with the old mare. While they were on their way, N'oun-Doaré untied one of the knots on the halter and immediately he and the mare were transported through the air fifteen hundred leagues away. They landed in the center of Paris.* Some months later, the marquis of Coat-Squiriou also went to Paris and quite by chance bumped into N'oun-Doaré.

"My word! Have you been here long?" he asked him.

"Of course," he replied.

"But how did you get here?" And N'oun-Doaré told the marquis how he had happened to get to Paris so quickly. They went together to greet the king in his palace. The king knew the marquis of Coat-Squiriou and they received a warm welcome.

One night, by the light of the moon, N'oun-Doaré went for a walk alone with his old mare outside of the town. He noticed some-

* Luzel's note: My storyteller was a little lacking in his sense of distance.

thing shining at the foot of an old stone cross at a crossroads. He went up to it and saw it was a golden crown encrusted with diamonds. "I'll hide it under my coat," he said to himself.

"Don't do this or you will regret it," said a voice that came from he knew not where.

The voice, which was that of his horse, repeated itself three times. He hesitated for a moment and then carried the crown away under his coat.

The king had put him in charge of some of his horses and at night he would light up the stable with the crown whose diamonds shone in the darkness. His horses were well fed and in better shape than those that the other grooms looked after, and because the king often praised him, the others were jealous of him. It was absolutely forbidden to have a light in the stables at night and they always saw that there was one in N'oun-Doaré's stable and so they went to denounce him to the king.

At first, the king didn't believe a word of it, but as the grooms kept repeating their accusation, he asked the marquis of Coat-Squiriou if there was any truth in it.

"I don't know," replied the marquis, "but I shall go and ask him."

"It is my old rusty sword," answered N'oun-Doaré. "It shines in the darkness because it is a fairy sword."

But one night, his enemies, eyes pressed to the keyhole of the stable door, saw that the light came from a beautiful golden crown that hung on the horse's manger and shone a flameless light. They ran off to tell the king and the following night he lay in wait for the light to appear and then went straight into the stable using his own key (he had a key to all the stables) and seized the crown and carried it away under his coat to his bedroom.

The next day, he called together all the learned men and wizards of the city so that they could interpret for him the words engraved on the crown, but none of them could understand it. A seven-year-old child, who just happened to be there, also saw the crown and said that it belonged to the princess of the Golden Ram.

The king sent for N'oun-Doaré at once and said to him, "You must bring the princess of the Golden Ram here to my court to be my wife and if you don't bring her to me, then you will surely die!" So poor N'oun-Doaré didn't know what to do. With tears in his eyes, he went to find his old mare.

"I know what's the matter," the mare said to him, "and why you are sad. Don't you remember my telling you to leave the crown where you found it or that you would regret it one day? Well, that day has come. But don't despair. If you obey me and do exactly as I tell you, we can still get you out of this mess. First of all, go to the king and ask him for oats and money for the journey." The king gave him oats and money and N'oun-Doaré set off on his way with his old mare.

They arrived at the seashore and there they saw a small fish washed up on the sand and about to die.

"Put the fish back in the water," said the mare. N'oun-Doaré obeyed and immediately the little fish lifted its head out of the water and said, "You have saved my life, N'oun-Doaré. I am the king of the fishes and if you ever have need of my help, you need only call for me by the shoreline and I will come right away." And he disappeared beneath the water.

A little farther on, they came across a little bird that had been caught in a snare.

"Rescue this bird," said the mare. And N'oun-Doaré rescued the little bird, who, before flying off, said, "Thank you, N'oun-Doaré, I will repay this kindness. I am the king of the birds and if I or my friends can ever be of any use to you, you only need call for me and I shall be there right away."

They continued on their journey and, as the mare was able to cross rivers, mountains, forests, and oceans without difficulty, they soon found themselves before the walls of the Castle of the Golden Ram. They could hear a terrifying noise coming from inside the castle, so that N'oun-Doaré did not dare go inside. Near to the entrance, he saw a man tied to a tree by an iron chain and he had as many horns on his body as there are days in the year.

"Untie this man and set him free," said the mare.

"I daren't go near him."

"Don't be afraid; he won't harm you."

N'oun-Doaré untied the man, who said to him, "Thank you! I will repay this kindness. If ever you are need of help, call for Griffescornu,* the king of the demons, and I will come right away."

"Now, go into the castle," said the mare to N'oun-Doaré, "and be afraid of nothing. I will stay here in the woods eating grass, where you will find me when you return. The mistress of the castle, the princess of the Golden Ram, will give you a warm welcome and show you many and various wonderful things. You must invite her to accompany you into the woods to see your mare that is beyond compare in the whole world and which knows all the dances of Lower Brittany and other places and you will make it perform right before her very eyes."

N'oun-Doaré set off toward the castle gate and met a servant who was drawing water from the spring in the woods and who asked him what his business was.

"I would like to speak to the princess of the Golden Ram," he replied. So, the servant went to tell her mistress that a stranger had just arrived at the castle and wished to speak to her. The princess came straight down from her room and offered to show

* His name is a combination of *griffe* ("claw") and *cornu* ("horned").

N'oun-Doaré all the wonders of her castle. When he had seen everything, it was his turn to offer to take the princess to see his mare in the woods. She agreed without a moment's hesitation. The mare performed a large variety of dances for her, which she greatly enjoyed.

"Climb on to her back, Your Highness," N'oun-Doaré said to her, "and she will very happily dance with you." The princess, after some hesitation, mounted the mare. Immediately, N'oun-Doaré jumped on behind her and the mare rose into the air and carried them in an instant over and beyond the sea.

"You've tricked me," the princess cried out, "but your troubles are not over yet and you'll weep more than once before I marry the old king of France."

Soon they arrived in Paris and as soon as they got there, N'oun-Doaré introduced the princess to the king and said, "Sire, here is the princess of the Golden Ram." The king was blown away by her beauty. He could not contain his happiness and wanted to marry her there and then. But the princess insisted first that her ring, which she had left in her room in the Castle of the Golden Ram, be brought to her.

Once again, the king gave N'oun-Doaré the task of fetching the princess's ring. With sadness he went to find his mare again.

"Don't you remember," the mare said to him, "that you saved the life of the king of the birds, who promised to repay the favor when needed?"

"I remember," he replied.

"Very well. Then call for his help. Now is the time."

And N'oun-Doaré cried out, "King of the birds! Please come and help me."

Immediately the king of the birds arrived and asked, "What is it you want, N'oun-Doaré?"

He said, "The king wants me, on pain of death, to fetch the ring of the princess of the Golden Ram, which is in her castle in a cupboard to which she has lost the key."

"Do not worry," said the bird. "The ring will be brought to you." And right away, he called for all the birds of the air, each by name. And they all arrived, as their names were called, but, alas, not one of them was small enough to pass through the keyhole of the princess's cupboard. Only the wren had any chance of succeeding and so he was sent to fetch the ring.

After much difficulty and losing almost all his feathers in the process, he managed to get into the cupboard, take the ring, and bring it to Paris. N'oun-Doaré ran and gave it to the princess right away.

"There you are, Your Highness," the king said to her. "Surely there is no reason for delaying my happiness any longer?"

"There is only one more thing I need, but I must have it, or nothing can happen," she replied.

"Just say it, Your Highness, and what you ask will be done."

"Very well. Bring my castle here, so that it stands opposite yours."

"Bring your castle here?! You can't be serious?!"

"As I said, I must have my castle or nothing can happen."

And once more N'oun-Doaré was told to find a way of moving the princess's castle and he set on his way with his mare.

When they arrived at the castle walls, the mare said, "Call for the help of the king of the demons, whom you set free the first time we were here." He called for the king of the demons, who came and asked, "What can I do for you, N'oun-Doaré?"

"Transport the castle of the princess of the Golden Ram to Paris for me so that it can stand opposite the king's and do it right away!"

"Very well. It will be done immediately!" And the king of the demons called his subjects and a whole army of them arrived, uprooted the castle from the rock on which it stood, lifted it into the air, and transported it to Paris. N'oun-Doaré and his mare followed them and arrived at the same time.

In the morning, the Parisians were astonished to find the rising sun shining on the golden turrets of the castle and, thinking that a fire had broken out, cried out from all quarters, "Fire! Fire!" But the princess recognized her castle and hurried over there.

"So, Your Highness," the king said to her, "there only remains for you to fix the wedding day."

"Yes, but there is one more little thing I need first," she replied.

"What is it, Your Highness?"

"They haven't brought me the key to my castle and without it I can't get in."

"I have some very skillful locksmiths here and they will make you a new one."

"No, there's nobody in the world who can make a new key capable of opening the gate to my castle. I must have the old one that is at the bottom of the sea." On their way to Paris, as they were passing over the sea, she had dropped it into the murky depths.

Once more, N'oun-Doaré was told to fetch the princess the key to her castle and he set off with his old mare. As he arrived at the seashore, he called for the help of the king of the fishes, who came right away and asked, "What can I do for you, N'oun-Doaré?"

"I need the key to the castle of the princess of the Golden Ram that she threw into the sea."

"You shall have it," replied the king. And he immediately called for all the fishes, who arrived in a hurry, as their names were called, but not one of them had seen the key to the castle. Only the wrasse had not responded to the calling of his name. He finally appeared, carrying the key, a very precious diamond, in his mouth. The king of the fishes took it from him and gave it to N'oun-Doaré.

N'oun-Doaré and his mare returned immediately to Paris, this time happy and carefree, because they knew it had been their final trial. The princess could no longer put things off and play for time and the wedding day was set.

With great pomp and ceremony, they went to the church and N'oun-Doaré and his mare followed the procession and, to everyone's astonishment and disapproval, they also went into the church. But when the ceremony was over, the mare's skin fell to the ground, revealing a princess of outstanding beauty, who held out her hand to N'oun-Doaré and said, "I am the daughter of the king of Tartary. Come with me to my land, N'oun-Doaré, and we shall be married."

And N'oun-Doaré and the daughter of the king of Tartary went away together, leaving the king and all of society completely dumbfounded. And I've heard no news of them since.

■ About the Tales

Cadiou the Tailor
Contes retrouvés, vol. 2,137–47
"Cadiou le tailleur"

This story, which Luzel described as "like a nightmare" (146), was first published in the *Revue des traditions populaires,* volume 2, in January 1887. It is a composition of several different stories and fragments that are common within the repertoire of Barba Tassel, from whom he collected the tale. A particular example would be the episode where Cadiou tricks the three giants. Similar episodes can be found in "Goulaffre the Giant" and "The Three Hairs from the Devil's Golden Beard" and this may provide us with some insight into the way Barba Tassel improvised her tellings by drawing on a stock repertoire of incidents and formulas that could be modified and inserted into broader narrative structures, as and when appropriate.

Another particular feature of Barba Tassel's telling is the way that she localizes and personalizes the tale. Luzel remarked that this was a common device employed by the Breton storytellers, although Tassel is especially fond of it, often finishing each story with a comment about how one of her ancestors, or even she, knew the characters, thus asserting its authenticity.

Whether she is trying to assert the truth of the story or whether it is a piece of mischievous joking or humorous bare-faced lying is a point for debate, but there is a certain jocular and ribald tone to the telling of many of her stories.

Tassel not only concludes this tale claiming her grandmother as a witness to the events but has also populated the story with characters who really did exist and would have been familiar in the memories of her audience. Luzel himself tells us that "Cadiou really was a tailor in Plouaret and Iouenn (Yves) Thépault a carpenter in the same town and I knew them well in my childhood" (146).

ATU 1829 (Living Person Acts as Image of Saint), combined with ATU 1875 (The Boy on the Bear's [Wolf's] Tail). See also Delarue 1953 for an extensive study of this tale type.

The Priest of Saint Gily
Contes inédites, vol. 2, 33–39
"Le recteur de Saint Gily"
This jocular tale is common throughout Europe and Uther cites numerous versions (2011b, 402). Massignon comments that it "reflects an attitude commonly found among the people of Lower Brittany, for whom a deep attachment to traditional religion does not exclude a critical mockery of the members of the clergy when they are found to be at fault" (1968, 250).
ATU 1735A (The Wrong Song)

The Purveyor of Paradise
Contes retrouvés, vol. 2, 165–68
"Le pourvoyeur du Paradis"
Another jocular tale collected from Barba Tassel and first published in *Mélusine* in 1878. Here Tassel makes the joke at the expense of the social establishment. It is not just a poor widow who is duped by the traveler, but a woman of means; and her son, who sets off in pursuit of the villain, only to be outwitted himself, is notably a priest. Once again, the rich, powerful, and influential are portrayed as gullible and stupid and certainly no match for the crafty peasant, who triumphs through his wits. As Lewis Hyde says in his study of tricksterism:

> Our ideas about property and theft depend on a set of assumptions about how the world is divided up. Trickster's lies and thefts challenge those premises and in so doing reveal their artifice and suggest alternatives. (2008, 72)

ATU 15 40 (The Student from Paradise [Paris])

The Just Man
Contes de Basse Bretagne, 245–51
"L'homme juste"
Luzel collected another version of this story from Barba Tassel and published Corvez's story in *Légendes chrétiennes* along with a long commentary comparing it to other variants of the same tale, in particular the Grimms' version (1992, 160–63).

It is one of several folktales in which Death appears as a natural and benign force (see also Markale 1986) and exposes the injustice of society. Corvez's story is particularly explicit in its social criticism: the poor cannot expect justice even from God (Christianity) or Saint Peter (the Church). Only Death is just, the true friend of the poor, who treats everyone the same.

ATU 332 (Godfather Death)

The Light-Fingered Cow
Contes inédites, vol. 2, 83–86
"La vache voleuse"

This jocular tale, with its barely disguised sexual content, was collected at a relatively early stage by Luzel from Jean-Marie Le Jean, a poet and schoolteacher. The story is redolent of the medieval sexual, scatological, and satirical literary tale, which in France manifested itself in the twelfth- and thirteenth-century fabliaux, the bawdy humor of the *gauloiserie*, and Antoine de Salle's fifteenth-century collection *Les cent nouvelles nouvelles*.[1]

ATU 1545B (The Boy Who Knew Nothing of Women)

Goazic Who Went to the Land of Earthly Delights and Tricked Death for Five Hundred Years
Contes inédites, vol. 1, 39–44
"Goazic qui alla au Paradis Terrestre et trompa la mort pendant cinq cent ans"

Luzel divides this tale into two parts. It is impossible to know whether the division signifies a break in the telling, as it occurred, but it also consists of two principal tale types.

ATU 313 (The Magic Flight) and ATU 501 (The Three Old Spinning Women). See also Delarue and Tenèze 1976, 215–20.

ATU 470B (The Land Where No One Dies). See also Delarue and Tenèze 1976, 167.

The Two Friends (A Ghost Story)
Contes du boulanger, 177–81
"Les deux amis, conte de revenants"
This story, which extols the virtues of loyalty and friendship, is a curious mix of the local ghost story, traditional folktale motifs, and Christian imagery. The two protagonists have Breton names and, although there is no specific mention of location, the setting is clearly that of a rural Breton community. As such, the story is consistent with other tales of the supernatural that were a staple of the repertoire at the veillées. However, it is told neither as a first-person memorate nor as having happened to a person known to the audience. Instead, the story has acquired a more formal structure and is vague in its local detail. The imagery is heavily religious, increasingly so as the story progresses, from Ewen and Primel's shared ordeal in the night-long, freezing, redemptive baptism in the mill pond to the appearance of the angel, Ewen's halo, and the ascension into Heaven. It is interesting that the tale is introduced as a ghost story, although by its end, the ghostly nature of the narrative seems to have been superseded by the focus on unquestioning devotion as a Christian virtue.

ATU 470 (Friends in Life and Death)

The White Lady (A Ghost Story)
Contes du boulanger, 163–66
"La dame blanche, histoire de revenant"
This story was collected by Luzel's sister Perrine and first published in 1893 in the *Bulletin de la Société Archéologique du Finistère* under the simple title "Histoire de revenant." White ladies appear often in the ghost stories that Luzel collected and this story is interesting from several perspectives. Like many of François Thépault's ghost stories, it is given a local and very specific setting and carries a strong moral and practical warning. The protagonist, Raoul, is guilty of two things—staying out late to drink and gamble and scoffing at the folk beliefs of others in the community. In the first part of the story, Raoul is cured of his skepticism about ghost stories, and in the second, his experiences result in his denouncing his dissolute lifestyle—a common outcome in ghost stories collected by Luzel. Luzel

also collected a version of the tale in 1869 from Jean Le Person, a cobbler from Plouaret (1881, 311–34).

ATU 326 (The Youth Who Wanted to Learn What Fear Is)

The Midnight Washerwoman (Plougonven)
Contes inédites, vol. 2, 67–68
"La lavandière de nuit"
Although Luzel does not attribute this story to any particular storyteller, Françoise Morvan suggests that the tale may well have been collected by Luzel's sister Perrine from Marguérite Philippe. Such stories were extremely popular at the veillées and, typically, the story is populated with named characters and takes place at a specific location, suggesting that it was told as true.

It would seem that the three young men had made two serious social transgressions here. The first is that they had stayed out late drinking and carousing long after was deemed reasonable and decent. Second, by approaching the laundry, they had transgressed what was traditionally a strictly guarded, exclusively female space:

> No man would go near the wash-house.... Nothing was more feared, nor felt to be more excluding, than a group of women gathered together at the wash-house ... criticizing, denouncing, insulting, slandering, relating family histories, deepening rivalries ... expressed through a violent and slanderous speech, of which they seemed to have a monopoly. (Segalen 1983, 139)

It could be read as a cautionary tale for young men that drunken, lewd, and violent behavior toward women is likely to be met with a force twice as powerful.

The Devil's Horse
Contes inédites, vol. 2, 59–61
"Le cheval du diable"
Luzel provides us with no information as to where or from whom this story was collected, but the tale very much has the feel of a ghost story told within the context of a veillée. It has specific local geographical references and

identifies the key protagonists by name, and the informality of the language is suggestive of a social context.

The closing paragraph is perhaps particularly worth noting. Up until this point, the story is that of an unexplained and unnerving encounter with a horse in the wee hours. The final paragraph offers a supernatural interpretation, but not directly by the storyteller: it is other people—Fanch, the protagonist who first told the storyteller the tale, and Old Guyona (a character presumably known to the audience)—who have suggested that the mystery horse belonged to the Devil. In doing this, the storyteller places themself in the same position as the audience and, by not personally claiming to be a witness to the events, but claiming proximity to the witness, they actually increase the believability of the story, in very much the same way that contemporary legends accrue credibility with the claim that they happened to "a friend of a friend" (FOAF), rather than personally to the storyteller.

The story is also told with a clear moral. Before the incident, Fanch, along with his brothers, has a reputation for drinking, gambling, and womanizing. The encounter with the Devil's horse is enough to make him mend his ways, but it appears that the story is not a simple condemnation of immoral behavior. The story appears to emphasize the social imperative of growing out of such behavior—Fanch is sent the warning not because he is a wayward youth, but because he refuses to grow out of his waywardness.

The Little Ant Going to Jerusalem and the Snow
Contes retrouvés, vol. 2, 221–24
"La petite fourmi qui allait à Jérusalem et la neige"

This kind of cumulative story is usually considered a nursery tale and the pleasure of its telling lies as much in the rhythm and verbal dexterity displayed by the teller as in the story itself. In Luzel's own commentary on the story, he states:

> This children's game or mnemotechnical exercise was told to me in 1876 by M. G de La Landelle, the maritime novelist, who learned it as a child in Montpellier.
>
> It should be recited quickly and it will be successfully done by putting each thing in its place, in the correct order, with a nimble execution. (1998, 223–24)

The story was first published by Luzel in the journal *Mélusine* in 1878 and Françoise Morvan claims "it indicates Luzel's interest for all types of popular literature" (Luzel 1998, 224).

ATU 2031 (Stronger and Strongest) and ATU 2030 (The Old Woman and Her Pig)

The Three Hairs from the Devil's Golden Beard
Contes populaires de Basse-Bretagne, vol. 1, 86–97
"**Les trois poils de la barbe d'or du diable**"
Luzel collected four further versions of this story, including another from Barba Tassel ("Fleur d'épine") and one from Marguérite Philippe ("La princesse du palais-enchanté").

ATU 461 (Three Hairs from the Devil's Beard) and ATU 930 (The Prophecy). For a full analysis of the tale type, see Delarue and Tenèze 1976, 147–54.

The Three Promises or The Devil Outwitted
Contes retrouvés, vol. 2, 181–83
"**Les trois paroles ou le diable dupé**"
This story was first published by Luzel in 1893 in the *Revue des traditions populaires*. Luzel offers neither the name of the storyteller nor the date of its collection, but Françoise Morvan suggests that the style is similar to the stories collected by Perrine Luzel in 1890 and 1891 from François Thépault, the baker's boy from Botsorhel, and Jean Le Quéré, the valet at the farm at Keramborgne (Luzel 1998, 183).

ATU 360 (Bargain of the Three Brothers with the Devil) and ATU 1697 (We Three; for Money). Uther suggests that the two tale types began as separate tales but later merged into one (2011b, 383).

Goulaffre the Giant
Contes bretons, 21–38
"**Le géant Goulaffre**"
This story is typical of Barba Tassel's repertoire, in that it combines several widespread tale types and ends with an authentication of the story through the claim that she herself was present at the closing wedding feast. Less

usually, although the story is clearly set in Brittany, she does not set it in specifically named villages and towns, nor populate the story with individuals personally known to her and her audience.

The story is divided into two parts. The first part principally sets a comic tone with the antics, both successful and otherwise, of the two young chancers Allanic and Fistilou. The second episode focuses primarily on Allanic and his attempts to best Goulaffre the giant. Consistent with Tassel's storytelling style elsewhere, she seems to use phrases and formulas that appear in other stories, such as the ruse by the giant's wife to pass off the two boys as her nephews.

Luzel, who tells us that the story is popular in the town of Lannion in the northwest of Brittany, compares it to Perrault's "Le Petit Poucet" ("Hop o' My Thumb") owing to the switching caps episode (2009, 151–66), even though the rest of the tale is more redolent of "Hansel and Gretel." Luzel suggests Goulaffre may be a corruption of the giant Angoulaffre, who appears in the thirteenth-century chanson de geste *Huon de Bordeaux*. Luzel also collected another version of the same tale type from Barba Tassel in 1868, titled "Le perroquet sorcier."

ATU 328 (The Boy Steals the Ogre's Treasure) and ATU 1119 (The Ogre Kills His Mother [Wife])

The Miller and His Seigneur
Contes bretons, 91–105
"Le meunier et son seigneur"
Luzel published this story as one of the bilingual texts he included in *Contes bretons*, remarking that his French version was a "literal translation" from the original Breton. He also subtitled the story "an amusing tale," and the humorous outcomes to the various episodes in which the miller gets the better of the seigneur provide the main narrative impetus. Luzel also published the story in the third volume of *Contes populaires de Basse-Bretagne*, along with a group of six other "facetious tales." The story is redolent of the fabliaux tradition.

The humor, of course, derives from the besting of the socially superior, wealthy, but gullible seigneur by the socially inferior, poor, but wily miller. It is interesting that in the Breton context the story becomes a criticism of the much-hated seigneurial system. One further point of interest is how the story is begun by Barba Tassel. Rather than the more usual formulaic opening, this is more informal, as if it is simply a continuation of a previous conversation.

This translation was previously published, alongside an essay on translation (Wilson 2017), in *Book 2.0*, vol. 7, no. 2, 203–8.

ATU 1535 (The Rich and the Poor Farmer)

Jean and His Rod of Iron
***Contes retrouvés*, vol. 2, 97–100**
"Jean au baton de fer"
Luzel collected several stories with this title, although this particular version was not published until ten years after his death in the *Revue des traditions populaires* (vol. 21, no. 12, in December 1905). According to a note by Paul Sébillot, Luzel refrained from publishing this version along with other variants owing to "a particularly graphic passage."

The story was collected in 1873 in Plouaret, but is not attributed to a particular storyteller, although two years later Luzel collected a story of the same title from Barba Tassel in Plouaret and the way that the teller stitches together different episodes into a single story is not unlike other tales that he collected from her. He also collected an extended version from François Thépault at Plouaret in March 1890 (Luzel 1995c, 183–218) and another from Guillaume Garandel titled "Le poirier aux poires d'or" ("The Golden Pear Tree").

The main feature of this story is its explicit sexuality in the first part and the later scatological references. In fact, at times the narrative logic seems to have been sacrificed for the sake of a sexual pun or a grotesque image. There is also in the text a clear sense of the economy of the telling and the quick pace at which the narrative moves. In a way, the story reads a little like a series of short, dirty jokes and the teller's delight in telling the story (no doubt expounded by Luzel's respectable discomfort) is almost tangible at times. It appears to be a story where the narrative is less important than its effect in the moment of performance.

This translation was previously published as part of a longer essay in French (Wilson 2014).

ATU 301 (The Three Stolen Princesses)

The Night Crier
Contes inédites, vol. 2, 51–54
"Le crieur de nuit"

The method of transcription, whereby the story is recorded as a conversation between several named individuals, is typical of the way that both Luzel and his sister Perrine captured the exchanges and the dynamic of a veillée.[2] Luzel himself is recorded as one of the people present, albeit under one of his many pseudonyms.

This is actually two stories told by different storytellers. The stories themselves are typical of the short, personal-experience ghost stories that were often told at these events and Luzel captures the conversational exchange that characterizes the storytelling. One story inevitably leads to another and the audience is permitted to interrupt to comment or ask questions. The way that the storytelling dynamic proceeds will be very familiar to anyone who has sat with friends and family exchanging ghost stories late at night— even in the twenty-first century.

The Burning Whip
Contes inédites, vol. 2, 31
"Le fouet ardent"

This story is noteworthy for its brevity, unlike many of the longer tales told to Luzel by Marguérite Philippe. Although she is not at all specific about the location or the names of the people involved, it is typical of the short, "told-as-true" ghost stories that were very popular at the veillées (see Luzel 1995b and 2002 for fuller descriptions).

The Midnight Washerwoman (Soëzic)
Contes du boulanger, 175–76
"La lavandière de nuit"

This story, the second of François Thépault's midnight washerwoman tales, is told as true and authentication is provided by the storyteller's claiming acquaintance with the young girl in the story. His inability to provide specific details about the *pardon* that was taking place at that time actually contributes toward the believability of the story; tellers of ghost stories often add credibility to their stories in this way, by combining specific details, such as names and locations, with an inability to convey other details that they may not be expected to know. This story is short and is notable for the lack of any real encounter with the midnight washerwoman (all Soëzic hears is her name being called and a laundry paddle being beaten upon a stone) and the fact that Soëzic has not obviously committed any transgression. It seems, therefore, that the purpose of the story is a call to take the existence of midnight washerwomen seriously, underscored by the near-fatal consequences of the events, as described in the closing sentence.

The Midnight Washerwoman (The Spinner)
Contes du boulanger, 167–70
"La lavandière de nuit"
This story was told by François Thépault of Botsorhel in February 1890 to Perrine Luzel and is recorded as having been told at Plouaret, rather than at Morlaix, where the veillées that Perrine had attended the previous month had taken place. We might assume that it had been arranged for Thépault to visit Perrine in Plouaret specifically for the purpose of retelling some of his stories.

This is arguably the most interesting of all the midnight washerwoman stories collected by Perrine Luzel in that it comes closest to adopting the form and structure of a traditional folktale, especially in the formality of the language, the stylization of the opening and closing sentences, and the use of repetition in the later part of the story. There is also the introduction of the magic objects the witch calls to her aid.

Les lavandières (*cannard noz* in Breton) were fabled in Breton folklore to be three female spirits who at night came to wash the shrouds of the recently departed or those destined to die soon. They are closely related to the *bean nighe* (washerwoman) of Scottish folklore, who perform a similar function and are said to be "the ghosts of women who have died in childbirth" (Briggs 1977, 20), and the Irish *bean si* (banshee), who W. B. Yeats described as "one of the sociable fairies grown solitary through the sorrow or the triumph of the moment" (1993, 24). Although it is unclear whether the midnight washerwomen in the stories collected by Luzel are such harbingers of death, they appear to be, like their Scottish and Irish cousins, solitary creatures and they are doubtlessly malign spirits to be avoided and feared, especially by those who have committed some social transgression.

Nancy Locklin's essay (2004) on the role of the washerwomen in Breton folklore not only maps their multiple functions in stories but also persuasively argues that the laundry itself was an exclusively female place, "one of the few places where respectable women could gather without question" (167) to talk, and was therefore considered by men as "dangerous to their authority over their wives and daughters" (169). "It is," she concludes, "tempting, then, to see the legend as the empowering revenge fantasy of the most downtrodden and vulnerable members of society" (170).

In Brittany (and Normandy), each village would have a communal laundry, a constructed pool or pond, usually on the edge of the village and near to a water source, surrounded by stones for sitting and beating the laundry upon while stories and gossip were exchanged. Hélias gives a detailed description of the process of doing the communal laundry, "the big wash," which involved all the women of the village working together for a three-day period (1978, 2–4) and was clearly one of the key tasks of the year. The remains of these laundries are still evident in many places.

Jean the Strong and the Three Giants
Contes inédites, vol. 2, 131–41
"Jean le fort et les trois géants"
Luzel's attribution of this story, collected in 1872, suggests that Marguérite Philippe, his favorite storyteller, collected it from Vincent Le Bail. Equally likely is that Philippe heard the story from Le Bail and then retold it to Luzel shortly afterward. It is certainly a complex, but well-structured tale, incorporating numerous tale types and episodes that can be found in other stories that Luzel collected.

Marguérite Philippe employs the common device of finishing the story by claiming a personal connection to the narrated events, thus providing a claim for authenticity or entertaining her audience with a humorously outrageous boast.

ATU 1640 (The Brave Tailor), ATU 1045 (Pulling the Lake Together), ATU 1053 (Shooting Wild Boars), ATU 1063A (Throwing Contest), and ATU 1088 (Eating/Drinking Contest)

The Fisherman's Two Sons
Contes bretons, 75–89
"Les deux fils du pêcheur"
Luzel collected this story from Marguérite Philippe some time before 1870 and included it among the six stories in *Contes bretons*. No doubt he con-

sidered it to be a particularly fine example from the repertoire of his favorite storyteller; he added a long note praising her abilities as a storyteller and her "prodigious memory," which allowed her to recall stories with great accuracy and precision (1995a, 89). He also commented on the opening formula as one of many that are used to begin a tale and that each storyteller has a preferred way of doing so.

"The Fisherman's Two Sons" is also one of the three stories that appeared in the volume in a bilingual presentation, that is, in both Breton and French. According to a footnote from Luzel, this was so that others could determine the accuracy of his translations and pass judgment on his methodological approach (1995a, 88).

ATU 303 (The Twins or Blood-Brothers). For a full analysis of the tale type, see Delarue 1976, 147–61; and Thompson 1977, 24–33.

The Cat and the Two Witches
Contes populaires de Basse-Bretagne, vol. 3, 126–33
"Le chat et les deux sorcières"
Marguérite Philippe gives a particularly tidy version of this story, which is characterized by a series of fantastical events. It also places at its center the dignity of the mother. Charles Perrault's "Le Maistre chat ou le chat Botté" ("Puss in Boots") makes for an interesting literary comparison (2009, 115–25).

ATU 708 (The Wonder Child)

The Night Dancers
Contes populaires de Basse-Bretagne, vol. 3, 115–25
"Les danseurs de nuit"
Luzel published two versions of this story in the third volume of *Contes populaires de Basse-Bretagne*. The first, which had the full title "Les danseurs du nuit et la femme métamorphosée en cane" ("The Night Dancers and the Woman Who Was Turned into a Duck"), was collected in Plouaret in January 1869 and is unattributed, although it is commonly believed to have been told by Barba Tassel. This version is told by Jean Le Laouénan, a servant and a farmhand from Plouaret. There is no indication of when the story was collected by Luzel, but he also collected stories from the same storyteller in December 1868, so it is possible that this tale was collected on the same

occasion. Luzel also collected a third version in 1873 from J. M. Ollivier, a carpenter from Tonquédec, along with numerous other stories that deal with the appearance of groups of imps, devils, and spirits.

ATU 403 (The Black and White Bride). See Delarue and Tenèze, who call the tale type The Substituted Bride, for an extensive commentary (1976, 47–58).

The Cooking-Pot Man
Contes populaires de Basse-Bretagne, vol. 1, 341–49
"L'homme marmite"
Luzel collected numerous variants of this story; what is particularly interesting about this version from Barba Tassel is that it is characterized not by sentiment (the story commonly exists as a story where love overcomes adversity) but by the scatological comedy of a man with his backside stuck in a cooking pot. Tassel's sense of humor is evident in many of her stories, but none more so than here, where the comedy also has a strong social commentary to it. At the very beginning of the story, the socially superior seigneur is made to look ridiculous by the presence of the cooking pot stuck to his backside, as is the politely mannered and formal exchange between him and the peasant. At the end of the story, Tassel chooses a humorous formula that emphasizes the difference between the grand banquets of the nobility and the potato-rich diet of the Breton peasantry.

ATU 425 (The Search for the Lost Husband)

The Toad-Man
Contes populaires de Basse-Bretagne, vol. 1, 350–63
"L'homme crapaud"
This story, collected by Luzel from Barba Tassel, is, according to Françoise Morvan, "one of the most represented among all the stories he collected" (Luzel 2007,161). Luzel included six versions in the first volume of *Contes populaires de Basse-Bretagne* alone.

Delaurue and Tenèze suggest that the motif of the gift of the precious objects coming from the husband, rather than the animal helpers encountered en route, is particularly common in Breton versions of the story, as is the episode of the washing of the three blood stains from the husband's shirt (1976, 108). The story may also draw influence from Madame d'Aulnoy's "L'oiseau bleu" ("The Blue Bird"), which was widely circulated in the *Bibliothèque bleue* (2008, 91–132).

ATU 425 (The Search for the Lost Husband) and ATU 425B (Son of the Witch)

The Enchanted Princess
Contes retrouvés, vol. 2, 101–4
"La princesse enchantée"
Luzel collected several stories in the village of Prat, particularly from Anna Le Levrien, a servant. This story was collected in 1873 from Louis Le Braz, who also provided Luzel with "Le château de cristal" ("The Crystal Palace"), which he included in the first volume of *Contes populaires de Basse-Bretagne* (40–65).

ATU 400 (The Man on a Quest for His Lost Wife) and ATU 313 (The Magic Flight). See Delarue 1976, 207–34, for a fuller discussion, including a list of 188 different French variants.

The Devil's Wife
Contes retrouvés, vol. 2,109–13
"La femme du Diable"
Luzel collected two variants of this story under the same title in September 1887 from Barba Tassel. Once again, her sense of humor is evident from the telling, most notably at the end. Soëzic does not escape from the Devil through her own ingenuity, but because her behavior has inadvertently released multiple souls from Hell, leaving the Devil exasperated and in fear of even greater losses should she stay with him. The closing sentence is another playful suggestion that the storyteller was personally acquainted with the main characters in the story.

ATU 811A (The Boy Promised [Destined] to Go to the Devil Saves Himself by His Good Conduct) and ATU 310 (The Maiden in the Tower)

N'oun-Doaré

Contes populaires de Basse-Bretagne, vol. I, 143–57

"N'oun-Doaré"

Luzel collected several stories from Vincent Coat on various occasions between 1874 and 1877, many of which were included in the three volumes of *Contes populaires de Basse-Bretagne*, suggesting that Luzel considered the tobacco factory worker from Morlaix to be a particularly gifted storyteller. Two key features of "N'oun-Doaré" are the fluency of the text and the neat economy of the opening and the close. Another variant of this story ("Petit-Louis, fils d'un charbonnier et filleul du roi de France") was told by Garandel as the first story of the evening at the fourth veillée, described by Luzel in *Veillées bretonnes* (2002, 132–55).

ATU 531 (The Clever Horse)

■ Notes

Preface

1. See Bauman 2012, 95–97, for a brief discussion of theatricality and histrionics in folklore performance.

Introduction: François-Marie Luzel, Folklorist of Lower Brittany

1. Translations of Luzel's folktales have occasionally appeared within larger anthologies of French or Breton folktales in English, but the only volume to date dedicated entirely to Luzel's tales in English has been Derek Bryce's *Celtic Folk-tales from Armorica* (1985), which brings together twelve stories from *Contes populaires de Basse-Bretagne* (1887).

2. See Senn (1974) for an appraisal of Van Gennep's career as a folklorist.

3. For a useful brief history of the development of French folklore studies, see Richard Dorson's foreword to Geneviève Massignon's *Folktales of France* (1968).

4. In 1863 Keramborgne was transferred to the neighboring commune of Vieux-Marché.

5. Bogatyrëv and Jakobson argue that folklore is essentially "an expression of collective creativity" (1982, 43) by a community and that sanction or censure of a folklore item determines its survival and any variance within it. "It follows that for a work of folklore to exist, a group must appropriate and sanction it" (37). This is one of the features that distinguishes folklore/oral tradition from literature/literary tradition.

6. See also Alan Dundes's essay "The Symbolic Equivalence of Allomotifs: Towards a Method of Analyzing Folktales" (2007), in which he addresses issues of variation and argues for a combination of comparative, structuralist, and psychoanalytical approaches to interpret meaning. Dundes argues that allomotifs (the variant motifs that may serve the same Proppian function) serve as symbols, and that not only the symbols may vary, even within a single culture, but also their meaning, thereby challenging the mistaken assumption that "a given object always had one, fixed, standard symbolic meaning" (322).

7. Catherine Velay-Vallantin remarks that "1870, the date of the publication of the first volume of François-Marie Luzel's *Contes bretons*, marks the rapid expansion of collections executed in the spirit of science" (1992, 14).

8. Robert Darnton observes: "Roguery runs through the entire corpus of French tales, though it often takes the milder and more agreeable form of tricksterism" (1984, 55). For a fuller consideration of tricksterism, see Hyde 2008. Importantly, for Darnton, the stories also had a practical purpose: "The peasant tellers of tales did not merely find the stories amusing or frightening or functional. They found them 'good to think with'. They reworked them in their own manner, using them to piece together a picture of reality and to show what that picture meant for persons at the bottom of the social order" (64).

9. As Breton cultural politics constantly evolves, it remains to this day in an ongoing and enduring dialogue with its past and its context, especially in relation to the cultural movements in other small nations and regions of the western Celtic fringes of Europe. The exploration of modern Breton identity by writers and poets such as Francis Favereau, Jakeza Le Ley, Yves LeBerre, and Paol Keineg is a discussion in which Luzel, La Villemarqué, their contemporaries, and successors are still a part.

10. For a fuller discussion, see Hervé Le Boterf, *La Bretagne sous le Gouvernement de Vichy* (1982).

11. For an analysis of the way that nationalists have often appropriated the folktale as a means of defining a supposed pure indigenous culture, and of the tensions between and follies of both nationalist and universalist approaches to folktale scholarship, see Haase (1993) and also Dorson (1963, 96–101). See Abrahams (1993) for a discussion of how the relationship between the study of folklore and "the land-based patriotism (that) arose during the nineteenth century" (5) continues to manifest itself in modern nationalist movements.

12. It is interesting to note that Luzel reserves particular praise for two types of storyteller: the locally based artisan or laborer and the itinerant. In his seminal essay of 1936, "The Storyteller," German essayist and critic Walter Benjamin makes exactly the same observation about traditional

storytellers: "'He who travels, will have a story to tell,' as the saying goes, and we imagine the storyteller as one who comes from afar. But we enjoy listening no less to the one who has earned an honest crust, working the land and knowing its stories and traditions. If one wishes to imagine both these groups as traditional types, then one is embodied in the resident tiller of the soil and the other in the trading mariner" (1977, 386).

13. It is not always clear whether Luzel is referring to Yves Garandel or his son Guillaume, whose profession is listed as tailor in Luzel's notes. It is likely that the blind beggarman, and the Garandel referred to as Iouenn in Luzel's description of the Christmas veillée above, is in fact Garandel *père* and that Guillaume the tailor, from whom Luzel also collected many stories, is Garandel *fils* (see Morvan's footnote in Luzel 2002, 131).

14. These "wandering beggars" (*mendiants ambulants*) appear to be exclusively men and distinguished from the women beggars (*mendiantes*), such as Barba Tassel, who were locally resident and unemployed, living from occasional jobs and the charity of their neighbors.

15. This tradition has been discussed extensively by various scholars. For example, see Jack Zipes, *The Great Fairy Tale Tradition: From Straparola and Basile to the Brothers Grimm* (2001), and Marina Warner, *From the Beast to the Blonde: On Fairy Tales and Their Tellers* (1995). Warner also published a short anthology of seventeenth- and eighteenth-century French literary fairy tales in *Wonder Tales: Six Stories of Enchantment* (1996).

16. Like many of his contemporaries, Luzel did not seem to fully recognize the symbiotic relationship between literary and oral traditions.

17. Darnton, though, does make one important distinction between the (French) folktale and the literary fairy tale: "Unlike the tales of Perrault, they do not provide morals. . . . But they show how the world is made and how one can cope with it. The world is made of fools and knaves, they say: better to be a knave than a fool" (1984, 64).

18. Central to Bogatyrëv and Jakobson's argument is the notion of the *function* of stories within the communities in which they are told. Stories that no longer find a purpose within a particular group will no longer be told: "in folklore only those forms will be preserved that prove

functional for a given community. In this process one function of form can of course be replaced by another. But as soon as one form loses its function, it dies out" (1982, 36). By extension, those stories that continue to have a function will be told and retold and continue to be enjoyed and valued by the community, which may explain the retelling of stories well known to the audience at Luzel's veillées and the requests for them to be told.

19. In *Performance and Practice* (1997, 28), I proposed a model for the "Performance Continuum," as a way of mapping different kinds of storytelling performance from the everyday conversations of the general public to the cultural performances of professional storytellers. I argued that the higher the intensity of the performance frame, the more likely the "rules" and conventions of performance as a mode of communication would be applied. My reading of the Luzel veillées is that most of the storytelling is taking place toward the lower end of that continuum.

20. For example, *Contes populaires de la Haute-Bretagne* (1882).

21. Morvan suggests that, besides collecting stories from the veillées, Luzel would also pay certain storytellers to recite their tales to him (Luzel 1995a, 194–95). It seems that this was certainly the case when eliciting stories from individual tellers on his travels, where he was unable to elicit material from people he already knew and who knew him. This potentially raises questions as to the authenticity of some of the stories he collected under these conditions and seems to contradict Luzel's insistence on accuracy and fidelity to the natural context of the storytelling event. It may even explain why he felt the material he collected outside of Trégor was of a lesser quality.

22. The reference here is to the highest point in the range of hills, atop which sits a small chapel dedicated to Saint Michel, rather than to the more famous Mont Saint-Michel that sits just off the coast in the Baie du Mont Saint-Michel in Lower Normandy.

23. For a full consideration of the role of women as tellers of traditional tales, see Warner's definitive study on the subject, *From the Beast to the Blonde*. Italo Calvino, when working on his major collection, *Italian Folktales*, also noted that most of the stories he was collating came from women storytellers.

24. The actual size is a matter of dispute, as nobody collected her repertoire in its entirety. The writer and historian Charles Le Goffic (1863–1932) visited her shortly after Luzel's death when she apparently confirmed that she knew over 250 songs and 150 stories (reported in *L'ame bretonne*, 1908).

25. Luzel described Marguérite Philippe as the "cigale des brumes," or the "grasshopper of the mists," suggesting a certain magical and musical quality to her delivery and echoing the story "La cigale et la fourmi" ("The Grasshopper and the Ant") in La Fontaine's *Fables*.

26. Martine Segalen points out that although 1850–1880 is considered a period of economic growth in France, this was largely due to the doubling of land prices, which merely widened the prosperity gap between landowners and tenants (1991, 169).

The Tales

1. I am also grateful to Pat Ryan for drawing my attention to the similarity between Luzel's description of Breton veillées at the end of the nineteenth century and the descriptions of Northern Irish wakes and ceilidhs of the late twentieth and early twenty-first century provided by Ray Cashman (2011).

2. Some of the elements and ideas of this section emerge from my essay "Le texte vivant: Le traducteur, le conteur et les contes populaires de François-Marie Luzel" (2014). My argument for the treatment of folktales as performance, rather than literary texts, is developed in my essay "Luzel's Ghosts: The Unfinished Business of Translating Folktales for Performance" (2017).

About the Tales

1. Translated into English by Robert B. Douglas as *One Hundred Merrie and Delightsome Stories* (1899).

2. For a comparative description of contemporary Irish storytelling at a ceilidh, see Cashman 2011, 71–93.

■ Bibliography

Abrahams, Roger D. 1993. "Phantoms of Romantic Nationalism in Folkloristics." *Journal of American Folklore* 106:3–37.

Anon. 1895. "Obituary: F M Luzel." *Folklore* 6 (3): 311–12.

Badone, Ellen. 1991. "Ethnography, Fiction, and the Meanings of the Past in Brittany." *American Ethnologist* 18 (3): 518–45.

———. 2017. "Folk Literature and the Invention of Tradition: The Case of the Barzaz Breiz." *Journal of American Folklore* 130 (156): 204–18.

Bauman, Richard. 1984. *Verbal Art as Performance*. Bloomington: Waveland Press.

———. 1986. *Story, Performance, and Event: Contextual Studies of Oral Narrative*. Cambridge: Cambridge University Press.

———. 2004. *A World of Others' Words: Cross-Cultural Perspectives on Intertextuality*. Oxford: Blackwell.

———. 2012. "Performance." In *A Companion to Folklore*, edited by Regina F. Bendix and Galit Hasan-Rokem, 4–118. Chichester: Wiley-Blackwell.

Belcou, Jean. 1997. *Renan: Un celte rationaliste*. Rennes: Presses Universitaires de Rennes.

Benjamin, Walter. 1977. *Illuminationen*. Frankfurt-am-Main: Suhrkamp Verlag.

Blanchard, Nelly. 2006. *Barzaz-Breiz: Une fiction pour s'inventer*. Rennes: Presses Universitaires de Rennes.

Bogatyrëv, Peter, and Roman Jakobson. 1982. "Folklore as a Special Form of Creativity." In *The Prague School: Selected Writings, 1929–46*, edited by Peter Steiner, 32–46. Austin: University of Texas Press.

Briggs, Katherine. 1970. *A Dictionary of British Folk-Tales: Part A, Folk Narratives*. 2 vols. Bloomington: Indiana University Press.

———. 1971. *A Dictionary of British Folk-Tales: Part B, Folk Legends*. 2 vols. Bloomington: Indiana University Press.

———. 1977. *A Dictionary of Fairies*. Harmondsworth: Penguin Books.

Bru, Josiane. 2017. *Le conte populaire français: Contes merveilleux. Supplément au catalogue de Paul Delarue et Marie-Louise Tenèze*. Toulouse: Presses Universitaires du Midi.

Bryce, Derek. 1985. *Celtic Folk-tales from Armorica*. Lampeter: Llanerch Enterprises.

Cabaton, Antoine. 1919. "Emmanuel Cosquin et l'origine des contes populaires." *Revue des traditions populaires* 34 (6): 278–80.

Calvino, Italo. 2009. *Italian Folktales*. Harmondsworth: Penguin Modern Classics.

Cashman, Ray. 2011. *Storytelling on the Northern Irish Border: Characters and Community*. Bloomington: Indiana University Press.

D'Aulnoy, Madame. 2008. *Contes de fées*, edited by Constance Cagnat-Deboeuf. Paris: Gallimard.

Darnton, Robert. 1984. *The Great Cat Massacre and Other Episodes in French Cultural History*. New York: Basic Books.

Davies, Jonathon Ceredig. 1918. "Breton Folklore." *Folklore* 29 (1): 79–82.

De Salle, Antoine. 1899. *One Hundred Merrie and Delightsome Stories Right Pleasaunte to Relate in All Goodly Companie by Way of Joyance and Jollity*, translated by Robert B. Douglas. Paris: Charles Carrington.

Delarue, Paul. 1953. "Le conte de l'enfant à la queue de loup." *Arts et traditions populaires* 1:33–58.

———, ed. 1956. *The Borzoi Book of French Folk Tales*. New York: Alfred A. Knopf.

———. 1976. *Le conte populaire français: Catalogue raisonné des versions de France et des pays de langue française d'outre-mer*. Book 1, *Contes merveilleux*. Paris: Maisonneuve et Larose.

Delarue, Paul, and Marie-Louise Tenèze. 1976. *Le conte populaire français: Catalogue raisonné des versions de France et des pays de langue française d'outre-mer*. Book 2, *Contes merveilleux*. Paris: Maisonneuve et Larose.

Delarue, Paul, and Marie-Louise Tenèze, with the collaboration of Josiane Bru. 2000. *Le conte populaire français: Catalogue raisonné des versions de France et des pays de langue française d'outre-mer*. Book 4, vol. 1, *Contes-nouvelles*. Paris: Comité des Travaux Historiques et Scientifiques.

Dorson, Richard M. 1963. "Current Folklore Theories." *Current Anthropology* 4 (1): 93–112.

———. 1968. Foreword to *Folktales of France*, by Geneviève Massignon, v–xxxvi. Chicago and London: University of Chicago Press/Routledge and Kegan Paul.

————. 1986. *The British Folklorists*. Chicago and London: University of Chicago Press.

Dundes, Alan. 2007. "The Symbolic Equivalence of Allomotifs: Towards a Method of Analyzing Folktales." In *The Meaning of Folklore: The Analytical Essays of Alan Dundes*, edited by Simon J. Bronner, 19–324. Logan: Utah State University Press.

Gemie, Sharif. 2007. *Brittany 1750–1950: The Invisible Nation*. Cardiff: University of Wales Press.

Grimm, Jacob, and Wilhelm Grimm. 1992. *The Complete Fairy Tales of the Brothers Grimm*, translated by Jack Zipes. New York: Bantam Books.

Guilcher, J-M. 1960. "L'Aire Neuve en Basse-Bretagne." *Arts et traditions populaires* 8:158–64.

Haase, Donald. 1993. "Yours, Mine, or Ours? Perrault, the Brothers Grimm, and the Ownership of Fairy Tales." *Merveilles & Contes* 7 (2): 383–402.

Hélias, Pierre-Jakez. 1978. *The Horse of Pride*. New Haven and London: Yale University Press.

Hopkin, David. 2010. "The Ecotype, Or a Modest Proposal to Reconnect Cultural and Social History." In *Exploring Cultural History: Essays in Honour of Peter Burke*, edited by Melissa Calaresu, Filippo de Vivo, and Joan-Pau Rubiés, 1–54. Farnham: Ashgate.

————. 2012. *Voices of the People in Nineteenth-Century France*. Cambridge: Cambridge University Press.

Hyde, Lewis. 2008. *Trickster Makes This World: How Disruptive Imagination Creates Culture*. Edinburgh: Canongate.

Lang, Andrew. 1878. "The Folk-Lore of France." *The Folk-Lore Record* 1:99–117.

Laurent, Donatien. 1989. *Aux sources du Barzaz-Breiz: Le memoire d'un peuple*. Douarnenez: ArMen.

Le Boterf, Hervé. 1982. *La Bretagne sous le Gouvernement de Vichy*. Paris: Éditions France-Empire.

Locklin, Nancy. 2004. "The Washerwomen of the Night: Women's Revenge in Breton Folklore." *Proceedings of the Western Society for French History* 32:159–70.

Luzel, François-Marie. 1881. *Légendes chretiennes*. Vol. 1. Paris: Maisonneuve.

———. 1887. *Contes populaires de Basse-Bretagne*. 3 vols. Paris: Maisonneuve et Charles Leclerc.

———. 1994. *Journal de Route*. Rennes: Presses Universitaires de Rennes, Terre de Brume.

———. 1995a. *Contes bretons*. Rennes: Presses Universitaires de Rennes, Terre de Brume.

———. 1995b. *Nouvelles veillées bretonnes*. Rennes: Presses Universitaires de Rennes, Terre de Brume.

———. 1995c. *Contes du boulanger*. Rennes: Presses Universitaires de Rennes, Terre de Brume.

———. 1995d. *Contes inédites*. Vol. 1. Rennes: Presses Universitaires de Rennes, Terre de Brume.

———. 1995e. *Contes inédites*. Vol. 2. Rennes: Presses Universitaires de Rennes, Terre de Brume.

———. 1995f. *Contes retrouvés*. Vol. 1. Rennes: Presses Universitaires de Rennes, Terre de Brume.

———. 1995g. *François-Marie Luzel/Ernest Renan Correspondance (1858– 1892)*, edited by Françoise Morvan. Rennes: Presses Universitaires de Rennes, Terre de Brume.

———. 1998. *Contes retrouvés*. Vol. 2. Rennes: Presses Universitaires de Rennes, Terre de Brume.

———. 2002. *Veillées bretonnes*. Rennes: Presses Universitaires de Rennes, Terre de Brume.

———. 2007. *Contes de Basse-Bretagne*. Rennes: Éditions Ouest-France.

Markale, Jean. 1986. *Contes de la mort des pays de France*. St. Étienne: Éditions Christian de Bartillat.

———. 2000. *Contes populaires de toutes les Bretagne*. Rennes: Éditions Ouest-France.

Massignon, Geneviève. 1968. *Folktales of France*. Chicago and London: University of Chicago Press/Routledge and Kegan Paul.

Morden, Daniel. 2006. *Dark Tales from the Woods*. Llandysul: Gomer Press.

Morvan, Françoise. 1999. *Luzel, une biographie*. Rennes: Presses Universitaires de Rennes, Terre de Brume.

Nahkola, Aulikki. 2001. *Double Narratives in the Old Testament: The Foundations of Method in Biblical Criticism*. Berlin and New York: Walter de Gruyter.

Perrault, Charles. 2009. *The Complete Fairy Tales*, translated by Christopher Betts. Oxford: Oxford University Press.

Propp, Vladimir. 1968. *Morphology of the Folktale*. Austin: University of Texas Press.

Schöpflin, George. 2000. *Nations, Identity, Power: The New Politics of Europe*. London: Hurst.

Sébillot, Paul. 1882. *Contes populaires de la Haute-Bretagne*. Paris: Charpentier.

Segalen, Martine. 1983. *Love and Power in the Peasant Family: Rural France in the Nineteenth Century*. Oxford: Blackwell.

———. 1991. *Fifteen Generations of Bretons: Kinship and Society in Lower Brittany, 1720–1980*. Cambridge and Paris: Cambridge University Press/ Éditions de la Maison des Sciences de L'Homme.

Senn, H. A. 1974. "Arnold van Gennep: Structuralist and Apologist for the Study of Folklore in France." *Folklore* 85 (4): 229–43.

Senn, Harry. 1981. "Folklore Beginnings in France: The Academie Celtique, 1804–1813." *Journal of the Folklore Institute* 18 (1): 22–33.

Straparola, Giovanni Francesco. n.d. *The Facetious Nights of Straparola*, translated by W. G. Waters. Dodo Press.

Tatar, Maria. 1999. *The Classic Fairy Tales*. New York: W. W. Norton.

Tenèze, Marie-Louise. 1976. *Le conte populaire français: Catalogue raisonné des versions de France et des pays de langue française d'outre-mer*. Book 3, *Contes d'animaux*. Paris: Maisonneuve et Larose.

———. 1985. *Le conte populaire français: Catalogue raisonné des versions de France et des pays de langue française d'outre-mer*. Book 4, vol. 2, *Contes religieux*. Paris: Maisonneuve et Larose.

Thompson, Stith. 1977. *The Folktale*. Berkeley, Los Angeles, London: University of California Press.

Thomson, Peter. 2000. *On Actors and Acting*. Exeter: University of Exeter Press.

Uther, Hans-Jörg. 2011a. *The Types of International Folktales: A Classification and Bibliography*. Part 1, *Animal Tales, Tales of Magic, Religious Tales, and*

Realistic Tales, with an Introduction (second printing). Helsinki: Folklore Fellows Communications.

―――. 2011b. *The Types of International Folktales: A Classification and Bibliography*. Part 2, *Tales of the Stupid Ogre, Anecdotes and Jokes, and Formula Tales* (second printing). Helsinki: Folklore Fellows Communications.

―――. 2011c. *The Types of International Folktales: A Classification and Bibliography*. Part 3, *Appendices* (second printing). Helsinki: Folklore Fellows Communications.

Velay-Vallantin, Catherine. 1992. *L'histoires des contes*. Paris: Librarie Arthème Fayard.

Warner, Marina. 1995. *From the Beast to the Blonde: On Fairy Tales and Their Tellers*. London: Vintage.

―――. 1996. *Wonder Tales: Six Stories of Enchantment*. London: Vintage.

―――. 2000. *No Go the Bogeyman: Scaring, Lulling and Making Mock*. London: Vintage.

―――. 2014. *Once Upon a Time: A Short History of Fairy Tale*. Oxford: Oxford University Press.

Weissman, Lael. 1991. "Herder, Folklore and Modern Humanism." *Folklore Forum* 24 (1): 51–65.

Williamson, Duncan, and Linda Williamson. 1987. *A Thorn in the King's Foot*. Harmondsworth: Penguin Books.

Wilson, Michael. 1997. *Performance and Practice: Oral Narrative Traditions among Teenagers in Britain and Ireland*. Aldershot: Ashgate.

―――. 2006. *Storytelling and Theatre: Contemporary Storytellers and Their Art*. Basingstoke: Palgrave.

―――. 2014. "Le texte vivant: Le traducteur, le conteur et les contes populaires de François-Marie Luzel." In *Le conte D'Hier, Aujourd'hui: Oralité at modernité*, edited by Hanétha Vété-Congolo, 187–201. Louvain-la-neuve: L'Harmattan.

―――. 2017. "Luzel's Ghosts: The Unfinished Business of Translating Folktales for Performance." *Book 2.0* 7 (2): 159–68.

Yeats, W. B. 1993. *Writings on Irish Folklore, Legend and Myth*. Harmondsworth: Penguin Books.

Zipes, Jack. 1992. *Breaking the Magic Spell: Radical Theories of Folk and Fairy Tales*. New York: Routledge.

————. 1993. *The Penguin Book of Western Fairy Tales.* Harmondsworth: Penguin Books.

————. 2001. *The Great Fairy Tale Tradition: From Straparola and Basile to the Brothers Grimm.* New York: W. W. Norton.

Zipes, Jack, and Joseph Russo. 2009a. *The Collected Sicilian Folk and Fairy Tales of Giuseppe Pitrè.* Vol. 1. New York and London: Routledge.

————. 2009b. *The Collected Sicilian Folk and Fairy Tales of Giuseppe Pitrè.* Vol. 2. New York and London: Routledge.